THE VOYAGE

The Voyage

Christopher Nicole

Severn House Large Print
London & New York

This first large print edition published in Great Britain 2005 by
SEVERN HOUSE LARGE PRINT BOOKS LTD of
9-15 High Street, Sutton, Surrey, SM1 1DF.
First world regular print edition published 2003 by
Severn House Publishers, London and New York.
This first large print edition published in the USA 2005 by
SEVERN HOUSE PUBLISHERS INC., of
595 Madison Avenue, New York, NY 10022.

British Library Cataloguing in Publication Data

Nicole, Christopher
   The voyage. - Large print ed.
   1. Jones, Jessica (Fictitious character) - Fiction
   2. Policewomen - England - Fiction
   3. Kidnapping - Fiction
   4. Yachting - Fiction
   5. Suspense fiction
   6. Large type books
   I. Title
   823.9'14 [F]

   ISBN 0-7278-7411-X

Printed and bound in Great Britain by
MPG Books Ltd, Bodmin, Cornwall.

'Love thyself last: cherish those hearts
that hate thee.'

William Shakespeare, King Henry VIII

The Crime

'There's that man again,' Andrea Hutchins said.

Jessica Jones turned her head, as indicated. 'You reckon? It's not the same car.'

'It's the same beard,' Andrea insisted.

The two policewomen had just finished their Saturday afternoon game of tennis, and were pulling on their tracksuits over their whites. Jessica now turned completely round to face the car, which was parked on the far side of the street from the public courts; Andrea was beside her.

They presented a strong contrast, but both were sufficiently attractive to make it difficult to determine which of them the man with the beard was looking at. Andrea was tall and slim, with long legs and auburn hair, presently confined in a ponytail, and classically handsome features. Jessica was much shorter – she stood five feet four inches in her bare feet – and considerably older, being thirty-eight to Andrea's twenty-nine. But her figure, trained to perfection by the requirements of her job, her straight shoulder-length yellow hair and her crisp features made a no less compelling picture. 'You are going to be

7

either an actress or a model,' her mother had often said. Mrs Jones had not hidden her disappointment that her only daughter should have opted for the more exciting but less remunerative job of a policewoman, and disappointment had turned to concern when Jessica's first big case had involved wrestling with a murderer twice her size. That she had done so successfully, and that her evidence had sent Peter Miller away for twenty years and earned herself enormous praise and publicity, had not eased the old lady's nerves.

Jessica wished that her mother could have lived long enough to appreciate her daughter's progress, from plain WPC to Detective-Sergeant, and was now perhaps the most famous female member of the Metropolitan Police Force, even if she was more and more beginning to have doubts as to how long she wished to continue in her profession. Remarks from both colleagues and the clients she was required to protect as to how someone so petite and pretty had got herself into her position she could take with good-humoured patience. Just for starters, she could out-shoot anyone, male or female, in the division, and was capable of tackling, as she had proved, the largest of crooks in unarmed combat. Equally, being ogled was par for the course, and she had no objection when it was done by reasonably attractive men about her own age. But creeps were a nuisance, especially when they went to such extraordinary lengths to disguise themselves

– anyone could see that the beard was false. She walked across the street, swinging her sports bag rather like a weapon, as, in her hands, it was. The man watched her coming with a petrified expression. 'May I help you?' she asked.

The engine was running. Now the man engaged gear and drove away with a screech of tyres. Andrea had followed her friend. 'You sure put the rocks to him,' she remarked. 'Do you think we should run him in? This is the third time. That's harassment. Or stalking.'

'I don't think he'll be coming back,' Jessica said.

Yet she couldn't help wondering if the man *could* be a stalker. Of her? It was far more likely to be Andrea. Nor could he possibly know that they were both members of the Special Branch Protection Unit. Talk about playing with fire!

She was thinking it was rather amusing as she climbed the stairs to the flat she shared with her partner – it was only four blocks away from the municipal courts, and she enjoyed the brief walk. Tom was away at the moment, on assignment, and the flat as always seemed too quiet and gloomy in his absence. Though over the past couple of years she had from time to time seriously consider-ed ending the relationship – mainly because he was at heart a chauvinist and had no desire for children, which she did. She didn't know if she was ever going to do it, though. They had too much in common. They liked the same music and the same movies, they had the same friends, and above all they shared the same job; they were both detective-sergeants in the Special Branch and thus could understand and share each other's professional problems. So, better the devil you know...

She booted her computer. The one e-mail was brief: *Report tomorrow. Manley*. As Superintendent Manley was her boss, that could only mean an assignment. She was glad of that; she was bored. She poured herself a bath, added salts, and sank into the suds with a sigh. She wondered if she should tell Tom about her strange admirer, and grinned. He'd probably do his nut.

'I can't believe that character is for real,' remarked the Drive-Rite clerk to her colleague as she noted the mileage on the tachometer of the hire car. They watched the customer walking down the street towards the railway station. 'I mean,' she said, 'it doesn't make any sense. He just turns up, hires a car for the day, and drives twenty-seven miles, there and back. Twenty-seven miles!'

'He's been into town,' suggested her friend.

'Not quite, I'd say. Twenty-seven miles, there and back, would take him to some place like ... Clapham, maybe. But now he's going to catch the train. Well, why didn't he just take the train into Clapham Junction? And

10

that false beard! Something out of a bad horror movie.'

'What does his card say?'

'He didn't use a card. Paid cash. Now that's very odd, for a start.'

'Think we should mention it to the boss? Or even the police?'

'Shit, no,' the clerk said. 'We don't want to get involved with the bill. So he's acting out some kind of a charade. Or visiting his girl-friend without his wife or her husband finding out. From our point of view, it's all in order. Whatever turns you on, I always say.'

Am I mad? Michael wondered as the train rumbled into the gloom of the autumnal evening. Undoubtedly. And dangerous. And criminal. Oh, unquestionably, in the eyes of the world. The world had never been able to understand his innocence, and that little bitch least of all. But now he *was* going to commit a crime. The die was cast. If he did not go through with it now, after thirteen years of waiting and planning, he would regret it for the rest of his life. Even if that was not going to be for very long.

The train was slowing, and then stopping. Basingstoke. He stepped out, crossed the platform into the gents. When he emerged, ten minutes later, he was a clean-shaven, pleasant-looking man of forty-five. His jacket was reversible, and whereas he had gone into the toilet bare-headed, he now wore the cap he had carried in his pocket and which had been replaced by the beard. No one paid him any attention. But then, why should they?

He caught a bus to the next village on the railway line, and there picked up his car from the station park. Again, no one had any reason to notice him. He drove south, through the night, and a sudden drizzle. It was nine before he reached Lymington. There was just time for a drink. He entered the pub, taking off his cap.

'Mr Lomas!' John always had a welcome for a faithful customer. 'Wondered if you'd come down this weekend. Peter tells me you're just about ready for the off.'

'Just about.' Michael drank, deeply.

'Nervous?' John asked.

Michael grinned. 'Not really. It's been in the pipeline for so long.'

'Mickey, old son.'

Michael sighed: he hated being called Mickey. Come to that, he didn't really like Cooper, anyway. 'Evening, Alistair.'

'Someone I'd like you to meet.' Alistair Cooper was a well-known yachtsman, a big, heavy man who strained the seams of his blazer. 'Margaret! This is Mickey Lomas.'

'Well, hello.' The woman was in her twenties, attractive, with dark hair cut short; she wore a dress, unusual in a bar crowded with yachting people, and thus revealed that she was a trifle overweight – but in all the right places. 'I've heard so much about you.'

'Really?' Michael asked. 'Drink?'

'I have one, thanks.'

'Then I'll have another,' Michael said. John raised his eyebrows. Michael grinned again. 'I'm sleeping on board.'

'Is it true you're leaving any day now to sail single-handed round the world?' Margaret asked. Michael nodded as he sipped his second pint. 'Gosh, that sounds tremendous. It's part of a race or something, is it?'

Michael shook his head. 'It's something I want to do. Always have.'

'Bonkers,' Cooper commented. 'Stark, raving bonkers.'

'It's something I'd love to do,' Margaret said. 'Mind you, I've only ever done a bit of crewing, for Alistair, out there in the Solent. The idea of being alone, at sea, for ... how long?'

'I have no idea,' Michael said. 'I'm not trying to break any records; no one is sealing up my engines. I'm just going for a sail, which may take a year or so.'

'Just like that,' Margaret said admiringly.

'He has a radio,' Cooper pointed out. 'He'll be in touch.'

'It must be a tremendous boat,' Margaret said. 'I'd love to see it.'

'Well, I'm going on board as soon as I finish my drink.'

Margaret glanced at Cooper. 'No way,' Cooper said. 'Not tonight.' He winked. 'We have things to do.'

She needs her head examined, Michael thought, coming down here for the weekend with that lump. Maybe she thought so too, as

13

she made a moue. 'Wander down tomorrow,' he suggested. 'If you can spare the time. I'll show you over.'

'I'll do that,' she promised. This time her glance at Cooper was defiant.

It was still drizzling when Michael parked his car in the marina compound. Peter the dock master came out of his office to identify him, and then to greet him. No one could get on to the pontoons without a key for the lock on the gate, which indicated that he was a boat owner, but it paid to be ultra-careful. 'Okay, Mr Lomas?' he asked.

'Couldn't be better,' Michael said.

'Set a date yet?' Peter was sceptical. An ex-merchant seaman himself, he had never had the money to own an expensive yacht, or the time to sail one. He could understand that for someone who loved the sea, setting off by oneself must be the ultimate pleasure, but there was something unusual about Mr Lomas, not to say odd. Of course Peter was aware of the man's tragic background – Lomas had told him himself – but to his mind that didn't suggest the sort of mental stamina, the self-contained determination, to sail alone for several months on end.

There was also the fact that although Lomas had been preparing for this voyage all summer, he had resolutely refused to set an actual departure date. His reason was cogent enough: he didn't want the publicity which an announced departure date would entail.

14

But as week had succeeded week, Peter could not help beginning to wonder if he was actually going at all, or just indulging in some huge psychological exercise. He returned to his office, watched Lomas fade into the dim lights that let into the pontoons themselves. He was still a lucky man, Peter thought, to be able to look at such a ship and say, this is all mine.

Michael turned on to the finger and looked at his ship. *Maria Anna* was a fifty-foot yawl; that is, in sailing terms, her mizzen-mast was aft of the helm. She was a good sailing vessel, stiff and fast, but she also had the attributes of a motor-sailer, several of which he had added himself since commissioning her and having his idea take shape. Thus, built of steel, she was entirely enclosed, or certainly enclosable. The wheelhouse, just aft of amidships, had only the one sliding door, which he now unlocked. There were large, spacious windows to either side and looking forward and aft, as there were big ports on the cabins below deck, but there were also steel shutters waiting to be slid across all of them to negate any risk of shattering glass in the event of exceptionally heavy weather. Because of all the metal, his biggest problem so far had been swinging the compass.

Everything a navigator could possibly want was in the wheelhouse, from helmsman's chair to satellite navigator and weather fax, together with the radar receiver and the depth finder, the two Sailor radios – one VHF and the other MF – and the controls for the twin diesels situated beneath the wheelhouse deck. Leading into the after deck, above the main sleeping cabin, were the solar panels which would keep his batteries topped up.

He went down the forward companionway into the saloon. Here were his navigation books, and his charts case, his bar, and at the aft end, his galley. Forward again was a head, and a double cabin. Both of these were presently crammed with tinned food, which varied from the immediate protein and carbohydrate of stacks of plum puddings through the balanced-diet necessaries of tinned meat and potatoes and green vegetables; his diet would be supplemented by the fish he would catch. And to support the vegetables and remove any risk of scurvy, the bilges were stowed with plastic containers of concentrated lime juice.

Forward again was what could be called the crew's quarters, where there was a pipe berth as well as sail storage and a chain locker; here additional food supplies were stowed. Thus heavily loaded, *Maria Anna* would be a slow sailer in the early part of her voyage, but he would not be in a hurry. It was the trim that was really important, and pinned to the saloon door was the stowage chart, with every item listed as to its position and the date when it was to be removed and used, and which of the remaining bags and containers needed adjusting in its place.

He went back up the short ladder into the saloon and down the after companionway into a narrow corridor. To either side now were the fuel tanks, two hundred and fifty gallons in each. Beside the companionway was the bulkhead door giving access to the engine room, where he would have to drop to his hands and knees because of the low deck head. Each tank had a sight gauge, presently showing full, but the fuel too would have to be very carefully monitored as regards consumption; one could not motor round the world without filling up very regularly, and he had no intention of doing that. But five hundred gallons allowed him a gallon a day for the generator as a back-up to his solar power, if necessary, in order to keep his radios and navigational gear working, and at the end of a year at sea he would still have sufficient fuel to motor into port, if needed. If the end of the year ever came.

Lastly, the after cabin. This was home. If the rest of the ship was sheer utility, this was a place to savour, with glowing lights, a comfortable double bunk set against the port bulkhead, another bookcase with all of his favourite novels and non-fiction works, a television set – he had an adjustable satellite dish mounted on the mizzen-mast – and a tray of his favourite videos, an en suite bathroom. His clothes were stowed in drawers beneath the bunk; there was no reason to leave room for hers, because she would not have any, save what he had already provided for her, and they were stowed with his own.

He undressed and slid beneath the duvet, switched off the light, and lay in the darkness, listening to the slurping of the water against the hull, inches from his ear. His home, forever and ever and ever. He knew that this was the final moment of decision. There had been others, but here was the crunch. He was going to sail, if not round the world, certainly into oblivion, realizing a lifetime's dream even if it had to end in death. That decision had been made a long time ago.

Now it was simply a matter of starting the engines, dropping his mooring warps, and leaving the harbour. He knew these particular waters as he had once known his prison cell, therefore he could go at any hour of the day or night. In any event, he had his radar, his satellite navigator, and his GPS. As he was prepared to challenge the worst the sea or the wind could throw at him, the actual weather at the moment of departure did not matter in the least. He could leave this very minute. Or he could leave when he was ready. When he had accumulated his chosen companion. When he had committed his crime.

'Tell me about him,' Margaret said as she got into bed. There was no longer any mystique about sleeping with Alistair Cooper; she had done it too often. There was no longer any great pleasure about it, either. She did it because it kept her job warm.

'Who? That idiot, Lomas?'

'Why do you say he's an idiot? For wanting to sail round the world? Then there are a lot of idiots about.'

As Alistair still seemed to find sleeping with *her* exciting, further conversation was impossible for several seconds. But it never took longer than that with Alistair. Then he was lying on his back, puffing. She wondered what he would say, or do, if she ever really made love to him. Probably jump out of bed and run for his life. 'I'll admit he's had a hard time,' he said.

Margaret propped her head on her hand, her elbow dug into the pillow. 'Have you known him long?'

'Not really. He suddenly appeared, oh, about two years ago. He never joined the yacht club. Just took a berth for his then yacht while this one was being built.'

'You mean he's a man of mystery?' She was intrigued.

'Not at all. Apparently he was a bank manager down to a couple of years ago. Seemed to have it all. You know, good job, charming wife, nice house ... Then Maria Anna died. Just like that. Came home one day and announced she had ovarian cancer, and keeled over three months later.'

'You are an unfeeling bastard,' Margaret remarked with feeling.

'Well, no use crying over these things, I say.'

'But Lomas did. Weren't there kids?'

'No. He went round the bend, just about. Resigned his job ... Well, the bank tried to help, offered him extended leave; he declined. Then he sold his house. Must have had some put by as well, I suppose, and I gather there was a policy on the wife. So he had this boat built. They don't come cheap, made to that specification. Seems it's always been a dream of his to sail off into the wide blue yonder.'

'You don't suppose he bumped his wife for the insurance?'

'Who, Mickey Lomas? Not a chance. His idea of committing the most horrendous crime in history is to get a parking ticket. Anyway, the illness was genuine; she died in hospital.'

'He told you all this.'

'Well, of course he did. Why should he lie about something like that?'

Margaret lay on her back. 'Still waters can run very deep.'

'No depths there,' Alistair insisted. 'Sheer escapology. And what happens when he gets back, I ask myself. Pushing fifty, no job, no money, no prospects ... I suppose he could sell the yacht. Still a pretty grim prospect.'

'Hm,' Margaret commented, and switched off the light. Even shallow pools, she thought, can be interesting, especially when you can't actually see the bottom.

'Hi!'

Michael had been greasing the track for the mainsail slides. He looked up with a start. The drizzle had ceased and it was a good October morning, not yet cold, but with the

20

suggestion that winter was hovering. An excellent time to leave England and sail south. 'Well, hello,' he said, stepping from the life-raft on which he had been standing – it was strapped to the saloon roof – on to the deck.

'Remember me?'

'I promised to show you the ship.'

'Well ... will you?' She was a most attractive woman, more attractive in pants and a blazer than she had been in her cocktail dress of last night; there were less sags visible.

'It'll be a pleasure. Do you know boats?'

'Fairly well. Should I take my shoes off?'

'Rubber soles are okay by me.' He held out his hand and she took it to step up from the pontoon over the low rail. 'What's Alistair at?'

'Still in bed. He means to go out later, so I can't stay too long.'

Michael pushed back the wheelhouse door. 'You're his regular crew?'

'I suppose you could say that.'

'And also, whenever possible, spelt with an "s" in front of it? Or am I being damnably rude?'

'You are,' she agreed, stepping down on to the wheelhouse floor. 'But yes is the answer there too. I do like sailing, and am quite prepared to put up with some inconveniences to indulge a hobby.' She looked around. 'Nice gear.' She went down the forward companionway. 'Cosy. How much food do you have in here?'

'Enough for a year.'

21

'Looks like it could be two. Years, I mean. Or were you expecting to pick up a passenger?'

When he made no reply, she turned her head, and frowned at his expression. Then he grinned. 'You never know your luck.'

Margaret went back up the companionway, checked at the top of the after ladder. 'May I?'

'Be my guest.'

She went down the steps. 'Now this *is* cosy.' She sat on the bed. 'Are you seriously looking for a companion?'

'Then it wouldn't be single-handed, would it?'

'Is it that important, to be single-handed? Are you being sponsored?'

She was both embarrassed and eager. He couldn't make up his mind whether she was passionately fond of the sea, or passionately fond of men. Of course, it could be both. In which case she might be a gift from the gods, sent to save him from himself. Except that he didn't want to be saved from himself. He wanted to go out in a blaze of glorious criminality. He was looking for vengeance, and the victim had already been chosen. On the other hand, she so clearly wanted it, so very badly. And he could not help wishing to know if he could.

'No sponsors.' He sat beside her. 'I need to be alone.'

'I know. Alistair told me. May I say how sorry I am?'

'You may, certainly.' He touched her breast through the thick jumper. 'Are you going to scream rape?'

'I didn't come here to scream anything.'

He kissed her mouth while he caressed the sweater. She fell backwards on to the bunk, carrying him with her. Her arms were round him and she was running her fingers up and down his back. He decided that she was more passionately interested in men than in boats. He slid his hands down her sweater and found the belt of her jeans, unbuckled it and released the zip; she did not seem interested in taking off her blazer. She did the same to him, and their hands found each other at the same time. She felt good, but that was surely because it was so long since he had touched a woman's flesh. She might be plump but he could feel her hip bones, and her buttocks were firm. She kissed his mouth again, her fingers busy, but a faint frown gathered between her eyes. 'Do you have a problem?'

He brought his hands up beneath her sweater to hold her breasts. 'Didn't I tell you? I'm impotent. At the moment.'

Her hands emerged from his jeans as if they had caught fire, and she sat up, moving his hands to pull down her shirt and sweater. 'Are you ill?'

'In a manner of speaking, I suppose I am. Psychologically. Happened when Maria Anna died. Well, no. Happened when she told me she was going to die.'

'I'm sorry.' She stood up to zip her jeans

23

and refasten the belt. 'Haven't you tried Viagra?'

'I prefer not to at the moment. I'm sure it'll come back. And is it that much of a turn-off? We could play with each other. I'd enjoy that.'

'That's ... well...' She licked her lips.

'Kids' stuff? Who really knows what kids' stuff is, Margaret?'

'Well,' she said, 'as I said, Alistair is planning to catch the tide, so I simply have to rush. Lovely boat.'

'It's a ship,' he said, dressing himself in turn. Silly cow, he thought, as she clambered over the rail and bounced along the pontoon. But it had been a narrow escape. If, just supposing, he had made it, might he not have settled for her? Sailed away with her into the sunset, and thereby ruined the last year of his life? In any event, it had made the final decision for him.

Michael spent the week on board, working, making sure everything was perfect. 'I'm just going up to town to get some gear,' he told Peter on Friday morning. 'I'll be back down tomorrow night.'

Peter nodded. 'I won't be on tomorrow, Mr Lomas. But I'll tell James. You mean, you're off?'

'Who knows,' Michael said, and winked. 'But you won't mention that to a soul.'

'Mum's the word, Mr Lomas.' Peter watched him go through the gate, wondering if he'd ever really do it.

★ ★ ★

Michael drove first of all to his parole office. 'Good morning, Miller,' Watkins said. He did not approve of paroled wife-murderers, and considered that in Peter Miller's case, life should have meant life. 'I see that you have not yet found a job.'

'Do I have to?'

'No,' Watkins said sourly. 'Not with all that money stashed away. You were just born lucky.'

'You reckon it's good luck to spend ten years in gaol for a crime you didn't commit?'

'Don't start that shit,' Watkins advised. 'You committed a horrible crime. The evidence was irrefutable. That little girl tied you up in knots, quite literally. What was her name?'

'Her name was WPC Jessica Jones,' Michael said.

'I reckoned you'd remember. She caught you red-handed and then duffed you up, her being half your size, and you still claim you were innocent? Get out of here.' He pointed. 'And I don't care how rich you are, Miller. When you come back next week, I want you to have found a job.'

Michael choked down the retort he wanted to make, contented himself with a mental, you'll be lucky, and went to his bank. He withdrew three hundred pounds in cash, then asked to see the manager – a request that was immediately granted to a customer with his balance. 'I'm afraid I'm dropping out of circulation for

25

a month or two,' he explained. 'I'd like the lot placed on deposit at your best rate. Leave five hundred in the current account to cover outstanding cards.'

'Oh, dear, Mr Miller. You're not being sent back?'

Michael gave one of his disarming grins. 'Not right now. It's a new job I'm taking on. The parole people are very happy with it.'

'That's brilliant. Congratulations.' The manager checked his computer. 'One hundred and twenty-seven thousand?'

'Sounds about right.'

'I'll have it transferred right away.' He shook hands, and then gazed at the door for several seconds. Such a pleasant fellow. Hard to believe he could ever have committed such a crime. But he seemed on the straight and narrow now. Although it would have been nice to know on what he had blown more than two-thirds of his capital over the past two years. Probably on a woman. Well, he couldn't be blamed for that, not after ten years in prison. But it was good news that he had found a job and obviously intended to settle down.

Michael spent the night in the flat he rented in a quiet London suburb. Next morning he had a late and leisurely breakfast, then packed up the last of his gear. These were mostly irrelevant items, save for the big sail bag containing the brand new spinnaker; all of his real gear was already on board. Then he carefully inspected the flat. The rent was paid for the next year, and he needed anyone entering to find only the bachelor home from which this widowed ex-convict would have so strangely disappeared. But they wouldn't even know where to begin looking for him.

He carried the gear downstairs to the car, greeted one of his neighbours, drove out of London, chose a different small town from the previous occasion, this one much closer to Basingstoke; the only essential was that it should have a railway station with a car park. He pulled his ticket, and selected a space in the centre of a row of cars well away from the office; it being late morning, there was no one about, and his car, a small white Ford, was as inconspicuous a vehicle as it was possible to find. He bowed his head while he put on his beard, then locked the car and walked out of the park, carrying his briefcase. He wore a dark suit and was clearly a businessman on his way to keep an appointment. The attendant in the office did not look up.

The hire car office was beside the station. 'For the day, is it?' the girl asked. 'We close at six. But if you don't get back by then, just park the car outside and put the keys through the letter box.' She raised her eyes to smile at him, did a double-take at the WG Grace whiskers. 'If the keys aren't there in the morning, we'll have to charge you for another day.' He nodded, and held out a sheaf of notes. 'Oh,' she said. 'Well...' She studied his signature on the hire agreement. 'Mr Smith, don't you have a card?'

'I'm afraid not. What's wrong with money?'

'It's just that it's a bit difficult adjusting it afterwards. Like if you don't return the car on time. And then there's filling up the tank.'

'How about if I pay you for two days? That'll cover everything, won't it?'

'Well...' She looked as if she would have liked some help with the decision. But she was alone in the office, and business had been slack recently. 'I suppose so. But what about your refund?'

'Have lunch on me,' he told her.

She simpered, but handed over the keys. She would remember every word of this conversation, but it didn't matter. The police would in any event trace the hire car back to this office. But they would be able to go no further than that.

It was an hour's drive back up to South London. He stopped on the way to have a light lunch, and afterwards sat in the pub garden enjoying the autumnal sunshine – there was no point in arriving at his destination much before five. He went over every detail of the coming hours in his mind, and then started going over the entire plan from the beginning.

The beginning! Presumably that had been when he had opened the bedroom door, already perturbed because of the scream, and gazed at Mary Ann's body. He had felt shock, outrage, horror, but more importantly, disbelief that this could have happened, even to

28

a woman he had long ceased to love. Incredulously, he had picked up the bloodstained knife that had done the damage, had been holding it when he had heard the woman calling. He had turned, all his earlier emotions suddenly shrouded in fear. 'Hello,' she had said, coming up the stairs. 'Mrs Miller?' He had stood on the landing, looking down at the youngest, prettiest policewoman he could have imagined, who was looking up at him with a half-quizzical, half-embarrassed expression. 'Mr Miller? A neighbour rang about the screams, and the door was open...' Then she had seen the knife, and her expression had changed.

He had lost his head. His sole idea had been to get away. He had thrown the knife at her and followed it down the stairs. It had never occurred to him that so small and dainty a girl would attempt to stop him. But she had tripped him, followed him when he rolled past her, and mastered him with a few karate blows; his principal memory was of her sitting astride his back, skirt pulled to her thighs, holding him helpless with a grip on his twisted right arm while she used her radio. She hadn't even lost her hat.

Her evidence had been conclusive. His story, that he had been in the garden and heard the screams and come running in seconds before the policewoman had arrived – she had apparently been sitting in a patrol car just down the road when she had received the emergency call – and his insistence that the front door could only have been unlocked if someone had gone out of it immediately following the murder, was not believed, simply because there had been no other person seen entering or leaving the house, added to the established fact that he and Mary Ann had not been getting on, crowned by his panic-stricken attempt to escape arrest.

He had gazed at her from the dock, and she had ignored him while she had spoken in a soft, clear voice. Then, for ten years – half of his sentence – he had dreamed of her, and what he would do to her when he got out. In the beginning it had been nothing more than a dream, something to pass the time. But the dream had slowly hardened into a determination every time he was raped – a repeated humiliation which had left him so traumatized he had become unable to get an erection.

His determination became even stronger when he had learned that his uncle had died – of a heart attack brought on by his conviction – and left him three hundred thousand pounds. All of that money for him to enjoy ... and he was in a prison cell. It had been scant solace that it was accumulating interest and had nearly doubled by the time he had been let out.

But when he *had* got out, he had put it to good use. It had taken him all but two years to have his yacht built, two years in which he had collected all the material he could about the now famous Detective-Sergeant Jones.

He almost felt he knew her better than he knew himself. And now he was ready to implement his revenge, and spend a last glorious year doing what he liked best in the company of a woman who was going to pay for everything that he had suffered in those ten years.

It was just on five when he drove slowly past the tennis courts. He had been here so often he knew the area as well as if he lived here. Just as he had monitored Jessica's movements so carefully – most of the time certain that she had no idea she was being watched – that he knew what she did with every moment of her week when not on duty. Last Saturday had been a freak. She had taken him by surprise, as much by the realization that she had, after all, seen him watching her, as by the bold way she had approached him to see him off. She hadn't changed, still projected almost macho confidence. But he was going to change all that, reduce her to what she really had to be: a frightened little woman.

He parked the car on the street away from the tennis courts, walked the rest of the way. Jessica played tennis almost every Saturday afternoon when the weather was fine – and when she was not away on a protection assignment. If it had been raining, or she was by any chance not playing today, well, he would just have to postpone his departure by a week. No one would find anything odd about that, the way he had set things up.

But it was a fine afternoon, and she was there, with her good-looking friend and two others, rushing up and down, laughing and squealing as they played and missed. She was a most evocative sight in her shorts, splendid cheeks promising to slide in and out of the skimpy material, surprisingly full breasts bouncing beneath her shirt, shoulder-length yellow hair secured in a ponytail but still flopping to and fro, and above all, magnificent legs, slender and smooth and golden. All his, in a matter of minutes now.

Her routine, he knew, was to put on a tracksuit, say goodbye to her friends, and walk the four blocks to her apartment. He returned to his car, drove it to a position equidistant between park and house, and stopped on the wrong side so that his driving door opened on to the pavement. He laid his briefcase on his lap, and appeared to be doing some work, a commercial traveller filling in his returns. In reality he was taking off his beard and filling his hypodermic needle.

The hypodermic had been the only really difficult part of the plan. It had taken him weeks of study to determine what was best for his purpose, and then another few weeks to obtain it without arousing suspicion: always disguised, always good-humoured, always pleasant. And now she was here. He saw her in his rear-view mirror, walking along the pavement, wearing her tracksuit, carrying her sports bag. She had released the ponytail but added a retaining band so that her hair was a mass of sweaty wisps, and she was smiling to herself. She must have won.

He inspected the street. It was half past five in the afternoon, and in October dusk was just drawing in. There was a woman walking towards him on the far pavement. She was taking no apparent notice of him, but when asked by the police, she would probably remember something about the car. He lowered his head so that she would not be able to see his face, or indeed anything about him. She drew abreast and continued on her way. In his side mirror he saw Jessica just coming up to him.

He opened the door, and she gave a startled exclamation and side-stepped. 'Ooops!' he said. 'I'm most terribly sorry.'

'My fault,' she said magnanimously. 'I was in a daydream.' Her voice, sharp the previous week, was in repose as attractive as the rest of her – just as he remembered it from thirteen years ago, low and soft.

Michael got out. 'Do you live around here?' The woman was well down the street now. If he handled this right, there would be no reason for her to turn round.

'The next block.' Jessica frowned at him. 'Do I know you?'

He wondered what she saw. A pleasant-looking and well-mannered man in early middle age. If she recognized anything it could only be those parts of his face which had not been disguised by the beard. His nose and forehead, perhaps his ears. Most likely his eyes, but she had only ever been close to him once. And the voice? He needed to hurry. 'Sadly, no,' he said. 'But you can help me, if you would. I'm looking for Wimbledon.'

'Oh. I'm afraid you're about two miles away from it.'

'Can you tell me how to get there?'

'Well...' She looked up and down the now empty street, trying to work out how to start.

'I have a map,' he said. 'Do you think you could show me? That's a lot easier than directions.'

'Well...' Again she hesitated, but she placed her sports bag on the ground.

'I'll get it.' He opened his briefcase, took out the map, and spread it on the driving seat.

Then he stood back, allowing Jessica to lean into the car to study the map. 'It's just...'

Michael gave a quick glance up and down the street. The woman had disappeared, and there was no one else in sight. Even if, by the sheerest bad luck, there was someone looking out of a window in one of the houses, he doubted they would understand what had happened until it was drawn to their attention by the police. But this was still the trickiest part of the operation. He had practised and rehearsed it a dozen times, spent hours in the gym training for it, taking his always powerful body to a maximum of fitness. 'When you're sailing alone around the world,' he had told the instructor, 'you can't be too careful.'

Now he leaned over the woman, apparently seeking to follow her directions, their bodies almost touching, encircled by the car door frame. He had taught himself to use the maximum amount of power in a confined space, and as practised, struck her neatly on the pressure point where her neck joined her shoulder, putting all of his strength into the blow. She gave a little gasp and fell forward. His heart was pounding. There were so many imponderables to be afraid of: that he might have hit her *too* hard, that she might have bruised her face on the hand brake ... but she hadn't. As for the other, he held her round the waist to shift her over into the passenger seat, and could feel her heart beating.

She slumped in the seat, head lolling against the window, retaining band starting to come off. But he knew she would only be out for a couple of seconds. The hypodermic was in his pocket, charged and ready. He gave another glance up and down the empty street before taking the syringe from its plastic holder. He pushed the sleeve of her tracksuit top up to the shoulder, found the vein in her forearm that he wanted, tore the antiseptic pad from its sterile packet and dabbed the flesh – he had also rehearsed this many times – and thrust the needle into the firm golden flesh. She gave a little sigh, as if she had been on the verge of waking up. Then she subsided even more completely than when he had hit her.

He pulled her straight, then released the seat so that she was lying as far back as possible. Anyone looking into the car would assume she was asleep. He pulled the seat belt across her and buckled it. His hand brushed her breast and he had the strongest urge to do more. So much more. But there was a time and a place for everything. He threw her sports bag into the rear seat, started the engine, and drove away, looking in his rear-view mirror. There was no one running on to the street shouting at him to stop. Kidnapping, he decided, was the easiest thing in the world. It was what happened afterwards that mattered.

Soon he was out of the houses and driving down a secondary road. The dose he had given her, according to his calculations, would keep her out for about two hours, which was really ample time to change cars. He would need one more before reaching Lymington, just to be absolutely safe, but he also understood that he should not top her up until the first dose had all but worn off. He glanced at her, lying there, eyes shut, breathing evenly. She was so utterly desirable he felt quite faint when he considered what he had done, what he had accomplished. What lay in the future.

Suddenly he didn't know. He had reached the point of no return, and now he had lost his way. He wanted to avenge himself for those lost years, the lost future, but he didn't want to desecrate that beauty. He wanted to make her feel the despair of knowing there was no way out of her prison, but he also wanted her company for these last months. He wanted to make her weep, but he also wanted to see her smile. And he wanted to have sex with her – even if he did not know if that would be possible.

He wondered what would happen when she woke up. He doubted that someone like the famous Jessica Jones would go in for screaming hysterics. And he needed always to remember her skill and power in unarmed combat. But he was bigger, stronger and himself more skilful than the last time they had met head-to-head. All he needed was to be careful, and if necessary, ruthless.

It was getting dark now. Michael kept to country roads. This took longer, but was safer. He had to pass through the occasional town or village, and there were traffic lights, but she continued to lie there, face perfectly relaxed, looking to anyone glancing into the car like a wife obviously exhausted after a hard day and bored with the drive home.

By now her partner would be wondering why she had not come in from tennis. Would he have raised the alarm? Not yet: people, even policemen when off duty, never supposed it was going to happen to one of theirs. Besides, from his observation of the couple, they lived parallel rather than interlocked lives, except for the rare occasions when they were both off duty and actually doing something together. Even if Lawson was not on assignment, it would be another couple of hours before he'd begin to worry. Then he'd call her friends, like the girl Andrea, to see if she might have gone to her place. Yet Michael was still afraid that something might go wrong, that she might wake up early. She would have to have an extra shot, if only for his peace of mind.

By the time he pulled off into a lay-by it was six thirty, and utterly dark. He leaned over to look at her in the gloom, could not stop himself from kissing her on the lips. She stirred slightly. It was time. He pushed up her sleeve, applied another antiseptic pad. She sighed, and passed out again. Michael put on his false beard.

Half an hour later Michael was in the town where he had hired the car. He drove into the car park, stopping to take a ticket. The bored attendant ignored him. There were scattered lights in the park, but he had chosen his earlier spot with care, directly beneath a tree. There were more cars now, and he had to park the hire car some distance from his own, and wait for several minutes as people moved to and fro; a train had just come in. But after a quarter of an hour it was quiet again, and no one had taken any notice of either him or his car – or its contents. He got out, went to his own car, unlocked it. Then he returned to the hire car, and lifted Jessica out. Holding her against him so that if anyone was looking she would appear to be drunk, he carried her the fifty feet and laid her on his back seat, then covered her with a blanket. Leaving her there, he returned to the hire car to fetch her sports bag. This he laid on the floor beside her. Then he got behind the wheel and started the engine. The man in the box was, as before, too disinterested to look into the car and notice the blanket spread over something on the rear seat. Michael drove out of town slowly and carefully. Then he was on the road to Lymington. He took off the false beard. There was only one major hurdle ahead.

The buzz of the mobile made him jump: as he didn't own one, it had to be hers, and as she wasn't wearing one, it had to be in her sports bag – it hadn't occurred to him to check that. He braked, reached into the back to lift the bag on to the seat beside him, and unzipped it. The phone was buzzing repeatedly. It was a great temptation to find out who was calling, but the risk was too great. He switched it off instead.

But the call had disturbed him, and as he was stopped anyway and it was a lonely road, he decided to give Jessica one last shot before reaching the marina; he couldn't risk any accidents now. He used this opportunity to insert her into the sail bag. He put her inside the spinnaker, which gathered around her, largely disguising such things as elbows and knees and feet, but left the neck open. The bag had several air holes in it, but he wanted her to breathe as freely as possible up to the last moment. Then he drove into the town and down the steeply sloping streets to swing along the front. The pub was crowded. But that was part of his plan, too.

The berth-holders' car park was almost full, but Michael found a slot, parked, and walked to the gate, where there were always several large wooden handcarts waiting for the transportation of gear and sails on to the pontoons; it was starting to drizzle, which was ideal. He wheeled the cart to the car, checked that there was no one around, then pulled the sail bag over Jessica's head and tied the cord. Then he lifted the bag into the cart, again covering her with the blanket. To the mound he added the other items he had picked up from his flat, as well as his briefcase and the sports bag, then pushed the cart to the gate and unlocked it. As he wheeled it through, James emerged. 'Evening, Mr Lomas. Want a hand?'

'No, thank you, James. I can manage.'

The dock master continued to approach. 'Peter said you might be thinking of taking off this weekend.'

'I am thinking of it, yes.' Michael pushed the cart towards the sloping ramp leading down to his pontoon.

'But he said you didn't want anyone to know.'

'I don't.'

'Nasty weather about,' James commented.

The drizzle was settling on both of them, and on the mound of gear in the cart. If it was to penetrate the sail bag and perhaps wake her up...

Michael kept his cool. 'If this is the worst I'm going to experience, James, then I'm laughing,' he said. 'I'll check with you before the off, but I was thinking, when I get this gear aboard, I might just go up to the boozer for a last pint.'

'You do that, Mr Lomas,' James said, and retired to the shelter of his office. Dutch courage, he thought.

Michael wheeled the cart down the pontoon and on to the finger. He unlocked the wheelhouse door, checking again to make sure he was alone. The dock master's office overlooked all the pontoons, but the finger, and therefore the wheelhouse door, was on the side of the yacht away from the office, and even if James was watching through binoculars – which he had no reason to do – and could see clearly in the drizzle, all he would be able to tell was that Mr Lomas was lugging a large sail bag on board, almost certainly containing a spinnaker.

Michael seized the bag by the neck, and exerting all his strength, lifted it over the rail and down the short ladder to lay it on the wheelhouse deck. Then he fetched the rest of the gear, closing and locking the door before lifting the sail bag down the after companion into the master cabin and untying it. For a moment he knew real fear that something might have gone wrong, but when he put his hand on Jessica's neck, it was warm and pulsing. It's done, he thought.

'Andie?' Tom Lawson asked into the phone. 'Let me speak to JJ.'

'What makes you think she's here?' Andrea asked.

'She was playing tennis with you, wasn't she?'

'Sure. We finished three hours ago.'

'Then where is she? We were supposed to be going to the pub this evening.'

'Have you called her?'

'Ten minutes ago. And here's a funny thing. It rang several times, and was then switched off.'

'Ah. Well, I'm sure she'll be home soon.' Andrea was well aware that all was not entirely well between Tom and Jessica; obviously, whatever Jessica was doing, she didn't want to be interrupted.

'Silly bitch,' Tom growled as he hung up.

The Prisoner

Carefully Michael lifted Jessica out of the sail bag; she was quite dry, having been protected from the drizzle by both the bag and sail as well as the blanket.

He laid her on the bed. Her face remained peaceful, her breathing even and gentle. He reckoned she would be out for at least another hour, but he couldn't take any risks, as he had to leave her for most of that hour to maintain the pattern of absolutely normality that was his safeguard from suspicion.

He had the two pairs of handcuffs he had purchased long ago as well as various lengths of cord already prepared. She was lying on her back. He extended her arms and legs, handcuffed one wrist above her head to the upright for the bookcase and the other to the grab-rail by the door, on the other side of the bed. Then he tied her right ankle to the other upright for the bookcase and her left ankle to the mizzen-mast which rose out of the centre of the cabin; to do this he had to extend the cord for several feet, but when he was finish-ed she was spread-eagled and could not move any of her limbs more than an inch or so. Then he cut a length of adhesive tape and affixed it over her mouth. This was a risk, in that if she awoke she might panic sufficiently to choke, but it was a risk that had to be taken. Anyway, he was sure she wasn't the panicking kind.

He arranged a pillow under her head, straightened her tracksuit top, looked down at her, and felt quite weak. He had never wanted anyone, or any thing, so badly in his life, and the realization that he had her absolutely in his power was frightening. Now for one last display of acting.

Michael's own suit was wet through. He changed into blazer and jeans, put on an oilskin top, and left the yacht. He switched off all the lights, although there was no way anyone could see into the after cabin anyway; the glass in the ports was tinted.

He gave James a wave as he went through the gate, then walked up the hill to the pub. 'Hello, Mr Lomas,' John said. 'What'll it be?'

'One for the road,' Michael said.

'Named the day yet?'

'Monday morning, crack of dawn,' Michael said, and winked. 'That's official.'

John winked back. 'You mean...?'

'That's official,' Michael said again, and watched Cooper and Margaret coming towards him. He wondered if she had confessed his failure of that morning last week to her current lover, and decided that she had not, both because Cooper looked the same as usual and because for Margaret to have told

44

him would have entailed her confessing that she had been on board *Maria Anna* looking for sex. 'Had a good sail today?' he asked.

'Bloody awful,' Cooper remarked. 'Hardly any wind, and that fucking drizzle.'

'We drifted,' Margaret said. 'And got soaked.'

'There's wind about, so they say,' Michael commented.

'Well, we're up to town in the morning. The wife's coming back from her mother's.' Michael looked at Margaret, who made a face and waggled her eyebrows, as if to say, I might change my mind about crewing for you. If she only knew. 'So when's the great day?' Cooper asked. 'When this lot of weather clears?'

'Maybe. Maybe while this lot of weather is still around.'

'Bonkers,' Cooper commented.

'Makes sense,' Michael argued. 'If you leave port in bad weather, you can be certain that it's going to improve.'

'And you stand a chance of losing some gear.'

'If a gale in the English Channel causes damage,' Michael pointed out, 'then the gear isn't capable of taking me round the world anyway, so I put back and have a general overhaul.' Cooper snorted.

'Last orders, ladies and gentlemen,' John said.

'I think I can stand one for the walk down the hill,' Michael said.

45

When he left the pub fifteen minutes later, he was well satisfied. He had been the most normal person in the bar.

The yacht was as he had left her, moving gently to her warps as the tide came in and the wind freshened. Michael locked the wheelhouse door behind him, went down the after companionway, opened the cabin door and switched on the light.

Jessica also lay exactly as he had left her, spread-eagled on her back. He sat beside her, pulled the tape from across her mouth. Her lips immediately parted as even unconscious she sought the extra air. He continued to sit beside her, gazing at her, at the rhythmical movement up and down of the tracksuit top. God, he wanted her. But he could not take her until they were at sea. Well, then, the sooner he put to sea the better.

He went forward, made himself a sandwich, and returned to the cabin to look at her as he ate. She wouldn't have eaten since lunchtime; when she woke up she would be ravenous.

He simply had to touch her. But he didn't want to risk undressing her yet, in case he couldn't stop himself. All of that lay in the future, again and again and again. He found himself having an almost full erection as he thought of it. Was she really going to be the answer to his dream? And his problem? He pulled off the retaining band to free her hair entirely, rippling the strands through his fingers; they felt like silk. He stroked her

46

breasts through the tracksuit top; they were bigger than he had any right to expect in so small a woman. He hoped she had big nipples. Something else to look forward to, to discover.

He pulled off her trainers, and then her socks. She had splendid feet. He already knew she had splendid legs. How he wanted to explore her. He touched the waistband of her tracksuit, and she gave a little stir. Suddenly he was afraid. He could not contemplate facing her here and now. That had to be done the first time when she was far away from any possibility of succour. When he was in complete control.

He fetched his hypodermic, pushed up her sleeve, and gave her a fourth injection. She would be so full of pethidine it would take her hours to come round fully. That was all to the good. For the time being, temptation had to be resisted.

Michael stowed the sports bag forward, but removed the mobile and placed it on the console; that had to be got rid of at the first opportunity, but in deep water. Then he slept on one of the saloon berths. He did not need an alarm; he knew he would wake the moment the tide turned.

In fact he was awake when it was still full, sitting up with a start. The drizzle had stopped, and the wind was getting stronger; the anemometer in the wheelhouse showed a steady twenty knots, gusting thirty. It was going to be a wild Sunday, but the wind direction was ideal, from the north-east. And the weather fax indicated that if right now it was deteriorating, he would be moving towards better conditions out in the Atlantic.

He felt a tremendous sense of exhilaration. He dressed in seagoing clothes, went aft. Jessica continued to lie absolutely still, breathing slowly and evenly. She would be coming to the end of her drugged state, but he calculated she had another hour to go, and he was sure she would remain drowsy and uncertain for some time after that. In an hour, he would be beyond reach. He pulled on an oilskin, climbed down on to the pontoon, and unplugged the electricity shore supply. Then he went up to the office. 'Got an account for me, James?'

'You're not pulling out now, Mr Lomas?'

'I reckon. I've told everyone Monday morning. If I leave now I can avoid the publicity.'

'Weather's not too good.'

'Ideal conditions, James. North-easterly wind, tide about to turn. Couldn't be better.'

'They're forecasting a gale come morning.'

'So? I'll be clear of the Needles by dawn.'

James nodded; so the man really meant it after all. He punched up his computer, then the printer, and the sheet reeled out. 'There you go.'

'I've cut the shore supply,' Michael said, and handed over his credit card; this was issued in the name of Michael Lomas and would be paid by direct debit on the account in that name he had opened in another bank, and into which he had, over the past two years, surreptitiously transferred funds from his Peter Miller account. 'You can fill in the amount when you've read the meter.'

'What'll I do with the receipt?'

Michael grinned. 'Keep it. I'll be back.'

'What about your car?'

Shit!! What a silly mistake! He forced a smile. 'Do you know, I'm so used to just parking it there, getting on board, and going for a sail, I forgot all about it. I don't suppose you could have it stored for me?'

James considered. 'I should think I can. You'd better let me have the log book.'

'Ah! That's in my safe at home. In London.' The car was, of course, registered in the name of Peter Miller. James was starting to look uncertain, so he said, 'I really would like to get away now. I've told so many people I'm off, I'll look a complete fool if I'm here tomorrow.'

James hesitated a last time, then nodded. 'Okay, Mr Lomas. Just give me a note saying I have your permission to drive it and store it.'

'Thanks a million.' Michael wrote the note, then felt in his pocket and handed over five ten-pound notes.

'You don't have to do that, Mr Lomas,' James protested.

'For your expenses.' Michael gave him the keys.

James hung them on one of the hooks

49

behind him. 'Well,' he said, 'I have to say something to you, Mr Lomas, and I hope you won't take it badly, but ... there were times I wasn't sure you'd do it.'

'You know something, James,' Michael said, 'there were times I didn't think I'd do it, myself.'

They shook hands. 'And may the winds always be fair,' James said.

Michael walked back down the pontoon. The adrenalin was still flooding through his arteries. This was it, in a bigger way than James could even imagine. And now there could be no turning back. But there had been no turning back from the moment he had opened the car door into Jessica's path.

The yacht, with all of the other boats around her, was lifting to the swell of the tide, warps making the pontoons creak. With the wind north-east, getting off the berth would be no problem; he just needed to be sure he wasn't driven into the next row before he got the ship under full control. He checked the aft cabin; Jessica was beginning to stir, making restless little movements, always restrained by the handcuffs and the cords binding her. Her eyes remained shut.

He went on deck, took off the sail covers, set the mainsail on the mooring in order to take two reefs; it filled and sent the yacht moving to and fro until he lowered it again, securing it on the boom with just two ties. Then he went into the wheelhouse and started the engines. Once they were running smoothly, he stepped on to the pontoon to release the after warp, and *Maria Anna*'s stern floated away from the dock and towards the adjacent boat. Michael stepped back on board, released the bow warp, and threw it on to the pontoon. *Maria Anna* was already drifting astern, quite quickly. Michael darted aft and in the wheelhouse door, and grasped the throttles. A touch astern on the starboard engine, and she slid neatly round to port, bow clearing the pontoon with inches to spare. Now she was broadside to the next pontoon, with its complement of boats, but a touch ahead on the port throttle checked her reverse movement, and as Michael eased up the starboard throttle to bring both engines into line at slow ahead, the yacht moved steadily through the water. She was still carrying leeway, but a touch of the starboard throttle brought her bows up, and another on the port took her round in a neat turn into the channel between the pontoons and the ferry dock.

James, watching from the office through binoculars, sat down again. He didn't really like Michael Lomas, and he knew Peter felt the same way. There was something about the man that was slightly sinister. And he was undoubtedly as nervous as hell – fancy forgetting about his car? But he certainly could handle a boat. James fully expected to see him gliding into his berth in a year or so, stepping ashore and collecting his gear, with

51

as little fuss as he had made over his departure.

Michael continued to experience the exhilaration he had always known when putting to sea as he helmed *Maria Anna* down the narrow, twisting channel to the Solent. There was no problem navigating. Not only had he made this passage a hundred times before, but the various beacons were lighted and easily identifiable, even in a rising wind.

In the channel the sea remained calm, but as soon as he passed the outer beacon there was movement, slight as yet in the sheltered waters and with the wind off the land. Michael checked his position with the various lights, made sure he was well clear of any shallows, then brought the yacht up into the wind, holding her there on autopilot while he went on deck to release the ties before returning to the wheelhouse to set the reefed mainsail; all his sails, save the mizzen, could be handled from inside the cabin. Then he unfurled the roller jib, just enough, and closed down the autopilot – he had two: the one aft worked off the wind and was therefore free, but the one in the wheelhouse consumed battery power. He had calculated that he should have ample electricity because of the bank of solar panels, but he wasn't certain how efficient those were going to be until he reached more tropical climes. Then he stopped the engines as well.

Now *Maria Anna* was drawing clear of the

land and was picking up the wind. Michael eased the sheets on both sails – he had not yet bothered to set the mizzen – and the yacht surged forward into the still short seas of the Solent as she raced towards Hurst Point and the passage between the mainland and the Needles. Wind and tide were running in the same direction, and for the moment the yacht was reacting smoothly. But the waves would be bigger out in the Channel.

Michael switched on the VHF radio, listened to the odd traffic, and hummed a little tune. A glance at the radar established his position with regard to the land on either side. Half an hour later he was past the Needles and out into the broad waters of the Channel. The woman should be waking up about now. He re-engaged the autopilot to enable him to check, but first opened the wheelhouse door and threw the mobile into the sea. He felt fully up to it now.

Consciousness was a miasmic haze, shrouded with pain, and some discomfort. Jessica was totally disoriented. Her head hurt, as did her neck, her brain seemed to be swimming in fog, and her wrists and ankles felt sore. Meanwhile her whole body was somehow distended. Nor could she believe what she saw when her eyes opened – or heard, for that matter.

She was in a very small room, because even in the gloom she could see that the ceiling was only a few feet above her head. It was a

53

room that was moving, regularly up and down, but also, it seemed, forwards and backwards, with the occasional tremble from side to side. The only noise was the wailing of the wind, until a rattle of spray lashed across the ports. She was in a cabin, on a boat! In a storm!

She tried to draw up her legs and found that she could not. Neither could she move her arms, and they in particular were heavy with a lack of circulation. She was tied, on her back, on a bed, in a boat. Oh Lord! She hated boats, because she was always seasick. On the only extended sea voyage she had ever made, returning from South America the previous autumn on a British destroyer, she had been unable to leave her bunk.

How had it happened? She felt as if she had been hit on the head with a sandbag. Her brain was dull. Even memory was difficult. She had been playing tennis, and then walking home. She had been almost there, lost in a pleasant daydream, when a rather nice, vaguely familiar man had got out of his car, almost knocking her over, and asked for some directions. Then ... nothing.

A rather nice man! And she, Jessica Jones, who had survived several attempts on her life, had felt no suspicion! It really was time for her to retire – supposing she lived long enough to make that decision. Men who kidnapped senior policewomen rarely wished merely to discuss the political situation.

But of course he couldn't possibly know

who she was. Nor could he be allowed to find out, until she was free of her binds, and free too of both the dizziness she was experiencing, presumably caused by the blow she had received, and the seasick nausea she could feel lurking...

She had to find out who he was working for. She also needed to discover how many of them there were. Only one man had actually attacked her, but she had to assume it would take more than one man to sail this boat.

Until those matters were resolved she had to be just a frightened woman, unable to understand what had happened to her. Jessica opened her mouth, with some difficulty; her jaws seemed glued together, and her entire throat and mouth were parched. She had to lick her lips several times before she could make a sound. Then she shouted, 'Is anybody there?'

There was no response; she did not suppose her voice would have carried very far in the wind. She considered. She was at sea, but how far at sea? How long was it since she had been snatched? Judging by the darkness beyond the cabin ports it was now night, but the last thing she remembered – the man getting out of the car – had been about half past five in the afternoon. That had to have been at least three hours ago, but both her instincts and the emptiness in her stomach suggested it might be much longer than that. And now she was in a cabin, on a ship at sea. Had she been placed on board this boat in the Thames, or driven to the coast? Either way, she could have been at sea for several hours.

Don't panic, she told herself. That would be fatal. So, you were stupidly careless and knocked out with almost certainly a karate chop, and taken somewhere, and put on a boat, and now you are at sea. Going where? And what had happened between being hit and now? Almost certainly she had been given some kind of drug: she would never have stayed unconscious for several hours from one blow. And her left arm did feel sore.

She raised her head, looked down at herself. Her eyes were becoming accustomed to the gloom by now, and she could see her feet. They were bare. But she was still wearing her tracksuit, and she could feel her tennis clothes underneath. Of course they could have been taken off and put back on again, but surely if her captor had raped her she would know about it. She would feel at least sore. Instead she felt only a full bladder. My God, she thought. Suppose there is nobody else on board and I just have to lie here...

The movement of the ship perceptibly increased; now it surged more violently, and rolled more violently too, while every so often there was a heavy crash, which seemed to check it for a moment before it resumed sailing.

Jessica did not know enough about the sea. Utterly fearless, because of her skills and experience, when confronted with a living

56

adversary, she had a horror of drowning. At any moment one of those waves she could hear battering on the hull might come storming into the cabin to submerge her. Keep calm, she told herself. Something must be going to happen.

And suddenly it did. The light was switched on, and she stared at the man who had got out of the car, and who she now understood had hit her and drugged her and kidnapped her. A man whose face was again vaguely familiar. 'Don't be frightened,' he said, voice loud above the noise of the gale. 'This won't last long. But this is a busy stretch of water, you understand. There's nothing on the radar at the moment, save for land, but I can't stay too long. Thirsty?'

He was speaking in an entirely matter-of-fact manner, as if having women tied up in his cabin was something that happened every day of the week. Maybe it was, in his world. Although she did get the impression that he was nervous. Equally, he didn't look either vicious or depraved. Jessica licked her lips. 'I need to go to the toilet.'

'Ah. Forgot about that. Can you hold on a moment?' He disappeared.

Jessica tried to think, to force her still fogged brain to formulate some kind of a plan. He was going to untie her, so...

Then he was back again. 'Still all clear. But we have to be quick.' He freed her ankles, and her knees seemed to come up against her stomach of their own accord. Then he released her right wrist. Jessica drew a deep breath, and as he freed her left wrist, the one nearest to him, she struck at his neck, right hand held rigid. If she could just land one blow...

But her arm and hand were still numbed from lack of circulation, and he had expected some such reaction and caught her wrist; he was still holding her other one. Jessica tried to kick him, but he evaded her feet easily enough and sat beside her, pushing her flat on to the bed again, pinning her wrists to the mattress; whatever her combat skills, she could not overcome someone twice her strength in a straightforward wrestling match.

His face was only inches away. 'Too predictable,' he said. 'Your secret has always been surprise, hasn't it, JJ? The fact that so few people know what you are capable of. But I do, you see. I hope you don't mind me calling you JJ? That is your nickname in the force, isn't it? And we are going to get to know each other so well, so intimately.'

My God, she thought. He knows who I am! 'Who are *you*?' she gasped.

'Time enough for that. But you'd better go to the head. Remember now, I don't have too much time, so if you are stupid, I am going to have to hit you.'

Still panting, Jessica sat up when he released her. He got off the bed and opened the head door for her. 'In there. Don't worry about flushing. I'll do that later. It's a little complicated until you get to know it.' Jessica stood up, and the yacht lurched. Her knees in any event did not feel as if they really belonged to her, and she would have fallen if he had not caught her round the waist. 'Takes time,' he acknowledged. 'Can you manage?'

Jessica grabbed the handrail by the door, and half fell into the confined space beyond. Now her head was spinning and so was her stomach, while her mouth filled with saliva and she knew she was going to be sick. Michael gave her an encouraging smile as she pulled the door to. He could hear her scrabbling for a bolt, but there was none: he had made sure that none of the doors on the ship had locks. Besides, he knew she would be in a hurry.

He left her to it, went into the wheelhouse, and studied the radar. There was a ship about fifteen miles away to the south-west, the blip coming and going in the swell. But a moment's calculation of her course and speed convinced him she was no danger. He was staying north of the big ship lane, within about five miles of the shore, and his only real concern was coasters. But there was nothing else to trouble him at the moment.

He went forward to pick up a plastic bowl, then back down into the cabin. The bathroom door was still shut. He opened it, and found her kneeling beside the toilet, vomiting. 'Takes time,' he said again, and held her armpits to lift her up.

'Leave me alone, for God's sake,' she muttered.

59

'You'll feel better lying down,' he assured her, dragging her across the cabin and laying her on the bunk.

'God,' she muttered, as she retched again.

'Grab this.' He put the bowl into her hands, and left her to it while he flushed the toilet. As he had anticipated, lying down she was less violently sick. He took the bowl away, flushed the contents and wiped it clean, then covered her with the duvet. 'Mustn't get chilled,' he said.

Back in the wheelhouse, he checked the radar again, then went down to the galley, fetched a box of salt biscuits and took them into the cabin. Jessica lay on her back under the duvet, breathing stertorously. Every so often her eyes drooped shut. 'Have a salt biscuit,' he said. 'It'll do you good.' She ignored him, her brain again dulled by the drugs in her system. He did not think she was going to be any trouble for a while.

Jessica came to slowly, and with a very disjointed memory; that she had woken up and been very sick seemed part of a general nightmare, but from the ache in her stomach muscles and the bitter taste in her mouth she knew that it had been real. She felt she was dying of thirst.

She was not tied up in any way, but lying in relative comfort beneath a duvet. There was something else different, too; it was daylight outside, and the motion of the yacht was quite unlike the last thing she remembered. It still moved, but in a rhythmic fashion. Because it wasn't driving through the water. She looked at her watch: seven fifteen. But if the yacht had stopped...

Jessica pushed back the duvet, swung her feet to the floor, sat up, and lay down again as the cabin once more revolved round her head. But she wasn't going to be sick. Not if there was a chance...

She heard an engine. Quite close. But not on this boat. There was another vessel, just out there. A voice shouted. 'Ahoy, *Maria Anna*!'

Jessica forced herself back to her feet, held on to the nearest grab-rail, made herself move towards the door – just as it opened. 'Not a sound,' Michael said. Jessica opened her mouth, and he caught her throat and forced her across the bed. She wriggled and tried to fight him, but was still too weak from the drug, and before she could figure out how best to tackle him, she had been rolled on her face and her wrists handcuffed behind her back. Then he rolled her on to her back again, and slapped a strip of sticking plaster across her mouth. The engine was very close now, so close she felt the other boat had to be virtually alongside. 'Ahoy, *Maria Anna*! Anyone aboard?'

Michael brought Jessica's ankles together and secured them also, this time with a length of cord, then decided there wasn't time to cut away the tape he had put across her mouth, and left the roll hanging from her face. He dumped her in the centre of the bed and left the cabin, closing the door behind him. 'Woke me up,' he shouted.

'You all right?' the voice asked. 'You're a bit exposed here. If the wind were to shift...'

'Just having a kip,' Michael explained. 'And waiting for the tide to turn. I'll be on my way before the wind comes onshore.'

Jessica started moving to and fro, the roll of tape slapping her cheeks. She had to fall off the bed, with as much noise as possible.

'Where are you from?' asked the voice.

'Lymington.'

'And bound?'

'Well,' Michael said. 'You could say, Lymington. I'm off around the world.'

'You're kidding,' the voice said. 'Mind if we come alongside?'

Around the world? He had to be mad! Jessica rolled over and reached the side of the bed.

'I'm afraid I do, old man,' Michael said. 'It would break the rules, see, for anyone to come on board until the voyage is over.'

'Ah,' the man said. 'Never thought of that. Well, the best of luck.'

Jessica fell off the bed.

The thump reverberated through the yacht, but the noise was lost as the other boat gunned its engine and moved away. Shit, shit, shit, she thought. The cabin door opened. 'That was a near one,' Michael said. 'Thought I could at least have a nap in peace.'

She had expected him to be angry, but he merely lifted her from the deck and laid her back on the bed. 'You're not being very co-operative,' he said. 'Now, I am going to cook some breakfast before we leave. I'll bet you'd like some breakfast.' He pulled the sticking plaster from her mouth. The pain was sharp, and she could not have immediately spoken if she had intended to. But the mention of food had made her realize how hungry she was. 'Thought you would,' he said as she licked her lips. 'However, you are going to have to behave yourself. Got me?'

She stared at him; he couldn't possibly expect a reply to that. 'If you don't,' he said, untying her ankles, 'I am going to flog you.' He grinned at her, and rolled her on her face to release her wrists. 'The first thing that you must understand is that you are on a ship, at sea, and I am the captain. You are the crew. And any disobedience by the crew to the captain's command is mutiny. Right? You must have seen *Mutiny on the Bounty*?'

'Suppose I don't want to be your fucking crew,' Jessica muttered, rubbing her hands together.

'Half the crew of the *Bounty* were press-ed men,' he pointed out. 'Now listen: that bloody inquisitive fishing boat is still knocking about. And as I have told him I'm alone on board, if he were to see you he'd probably get interested again. So while I want you to come forward while I cook breakfast, you have to crawl across the wheelhouse floor.

Understood?' Jessica nodded without thinking. 'Right. Come on, now.'

He went along the corridor and up the companion ladder, stopped at the top, waited for her to come up to him. 'Hands and knees,' he said. Jessica dropped to her hands and knees. Suddenly she was so hungry she couldn't think straight. But when she had some food in her...

He walked beside her across the wheelhouse deck. She looked left and right. It was broad daylight outside, and the wind was still whistling, while clouds scudded across a surprisingly blue sky. To the north she could make out green cliffs, but from her position she couldn't see the fishing boat. Yet he had said it was still close. If only it would come back, for some reason.

She reached the top of the steps leading down to the saloon. 'Don't stand up,' Michael said. 'Turn and sit, and come down on your bottom.'

Jessica obeyed; there were only three steps. 'Sit on the starboard bunk,' he told her. 'The right-hand one.' Again she did as she was told, while looking around. Someone sailing alone around the world would surely have a weapon. Somewhere. Any kind of weapon. But she could see nothing, save perhaps the frying pan into which he was now breaking eggs. Any knives were clearly in a drawer. 'I'm Michael,' he said. 'Michael Lomas. *Now.* You may remember me as Peter Miller.'

Jessica blinked at him. The name was

64

certainly familiar.

'Can't remember? I suppose you've arrested so many men since then you can't think of them all. But you once held me in your arms. Briefly.'

Peter Miller! My God! she thought. 'You were—'

'Your first big case. The newspapers were full of it. So I went up for twenty years, thanks to you. I got out after ten, of course. But it was a long ten. So, I sort of reckoned that you owe me a bit back.'

'That case was thirteen years ago. I was—'

'Twenty-five. And as pretty as a picture. But you know, you're even prettier now.'

'If you were paroled after ten...'

'I had things to do, this ship to have built; I suppose you've also forgotten that I came out of prison a rich man. Then there had to be sea trials; she had to be everything I wanted. Then there was you to be watched, plans to be made...'

The man with the beard! My God! Her nostrils dilated to the smell of frying bacon.

'I'm sorry I had to hit you,' he said. 'But things were rather fraught at the time. I mean, if I'd just asked you to come away with me, you would probably have said no. You'd probably have hit me with one of your karate chops. So I decided to hit you first. Have some orange juice.'

He gave her a plastic cup, and she drank greedily; nothing had ever tasted so good. 'What do you want from me?' she muttered.

65

'There's a question. I want so many things from you, JJ. So many things of which I was deprived for so many years, maybe forever. But let's begin at the beginning. Right now I want you to be my crew.'

He was definitely a maniac. And very possibly a homicidal one; she knew that he had already committed one brutal murder. Which meant even more that he had to be humoured until the effects of the drug had worn off and she had got over her seasickness – she hoped – and thus be able to deal with him on a level playing field. She licked her lips. 'I don't know anything about boats. I've never been on one before. Not a small one.'

'In most cases, neither were the men who had been pressed. But the navy soon licked them into shape. Breakfast.'

Two steaming plates were placed on the table, and he indicated that she should sit opposite him. There was even a knife and fork. But the knife wasn't very sharp. Anyway, the sight of food drove all other thoughts from her mind.

'You *were* hungry,' he remarked, watching her clean the last of the yolk from her plate with a piece of bread. 'Coffee?'

'Thank you.' Sanity. She had to maintain a state of total, well-mannered sanity.

'Milk? Sugar?'

'Thank you.' She hoped it might hype her up. Her brain remained dull, obsessed with the sense of disbelief. Of course, there was still some of the drug in there as well.

66

He placed the mug in front of her. 'Things will be better when we're out of the Channel. Tomorrow. The Channel is one huge shipping lane, you see. But once out of that, we'll be able to relax.'

She drank the coffee. 'You told that man you were sailing round the world.'

'That's right. Something I've always wanted to do.'

'And you want me to come with you? But ... you kidnapped me, to go with you? Round the world?'

'Well, we're on our way. I don't propose to turn back. I intend to enjoy your company. You're a very lovely woman.'

Instinctively, Jessica drew up her legs beneath the table. But for all her understanding that he had to be treated with kid gloves for the moment, she could not stop herself saying, 'But you know you are going to go back to gaol. My people are looking for you now. They'll never let up till they find you. Find *me*.'

He grinned. 'If you're there to be found. Let's hear what they have to say.' He switched on the radio receiver above his head. 'If anything.'

But after various items of international news, the reader said, 'Police are mounting a massive hunt for missing Detective-Sergeant Jessica Jones. Thirty-eight-year-old Sergeant Jones disappeared yesterday on her way home from playing tennis in a public park, in broad daylight and apparently within a few hundred yards of her home. She is described as being five feet four inches tall, of slim build, with shoulder-length blonde hair, wearing a dark blue tracksuit. Police are anxious to interview the driver of a blue Ford Fiesta, seen in the vicinity of Sergeant Jones' home at about the time of her disappearance. The driver may be a man with a beard.'

'Brilliant,' Michael said. 'As I wasn't wearing a beard, that means they've interviewed your good-looking friend. But they haven't yet traced the car.'

'They will,' Jessica said.

'Of course. To a car park in Steventon, from where it was hired. By a man in a beard. After that, nothing.'

The newsreader was still speaking. 'Detective-Sergeant Jones, one of the Special Branch's best-known operatives, will be remembered for her part in bringing the drugs baron Ramon Cuesta to justice, for foiling the kidnap attempt on the Princess of Kharram, and in destroying the Korman terror network.'

'There,' Michael said, switching off the set. 'Did you know how famous you are? But you'd think they'd mention your first big case: me. The fact is, they've forgotten all about me.'

'But they'll never forget about *me*. That's why they'll be searching for me. They'll be waiting for you when you get home.'

'That is a long way away. Let's talk about that nearer the time.' My God, she thought.

68

He means to kill me. It was time to use her negotiating training – she had never supposed she would have to do that on her own account. He seemed able to read her thoughts. 'I don't mean you any harm, Jessica. Just so long as you behave yourself. But I will have discipline on board my ship. Please remember that. Now tell me, how do you feel?'

'Better,' she conceded. 'Listen. You've made your point. To continue with this lunacy can only end up badly for you. If you turn this boat around and take me back to England, I give you my word that I will not press charges. I'll say that I just came for a short cruise with you.'

'You must take me for an idiot. Get up and wash these dishes, and we'll be under way. The tide turns in half an hour.'

She refused to reveal either her disappointment or her apprehension. She finished her coffee and got up, a little uncertainly. She stood beside him at the sink; the port was above her head, and she couldn't see out. She didn't want to ask him if the fishing boat was still about, but there was surely something she could do. Only she couldn't think of what at the moment: her stomach was beginning to roll again.

'We have to be careful about our hot water,' he said. 'We're getting it off the engine, but starting tomorrow I shall only be running the engine for an hour a day, so we'll have to fit in our dishwashing with that. We can, of course, boil a kettle, but that will burn gas, and we need to be economical with that, too. It's a gas stove, you see, and we only have four cylinders. They're thirty-two pounders, and used carefully should each last about two months. Fortunately, as we go south, hot showers won't be necessary. Talking about showers, you must feel like one.'

'I'll manage,' she muttered.

He took away the dishtowel. 'We'll talk about showers when we're away from land. Now, I am going to get the ship under way. I don't want to have to tie you up again. Do you want to be tied up again?'

'No,' she said.

'Right. You can come into the wheelhouse with me. But on your hands and knees. And when you get there, you sit on the deck, and you don't move until I tell you. Understood?'

Jessica nodded. She went up the steps and sat on the floor, sliding across against the settee berth that ran along the starboard side, forward of the hatch.

'Good girl.' Michael stood at the helm, checking his instruments.

Jessica looked through the window above her head at the sky, across which the clouds were still scudding to the south-west. The idea of going back out into that made her feel sick before she even got there. She could still see land to the north, but the fishing boat remained invisible, and she couldn't hear its engines, either. But he would have to leave the wheelhouse to bring up the anchor, surely. And to set the sails. Then she would at least be able to get up and look out.

To her consternation, he didn't. The sheets controlling both main and jib were fed into the wheelhouse, as was the halyard for the main, and all his winches could be operated from there as well. As she watched, he un-ravelled the jib, which was rolled round the forestay, and sheeted it in. *Maria Anna* im-mediately began dancing to the waves. Then he pressed a button and the anchor came up, and stowed itself automatically. 'Last time we'll be using that for a while,' he said. Once the anchor was out of the ground, the yacht fell away and started sailing. Michael now set the mainsail, again without leaving the wheel-house, and *Maria Anna* gathered speed. 'There we go,' he said. 'Next stop, well ... wherever we wind up.'

Before they were even properly out of the bay the yacht was pitching to the waves, and Jessica immediately began to regret her break-fast. Michael grinned at her. 'You need to lie down. On the settee. You can get up. There's nobody about.' Jessica heaved herself up and fell on to the settee. Michael had been adjust-ing the wind-vane automatic helm. Now, satisfied, he pulled the PVC lee-board into place, secured by cords suspended from the wheelhouse roof, so that even if Jessica rolled she could not fall off the settee. Then he went below and returned with a blanket, which he spread over her. 'Warmth is the key,' he said.

Lying down, the initial nausea began to

pass, but Jessica still felt too dreadful to contemplate moving. She realized that in getting into the bunk she had forgotten to look for the fishing boat. And it was too late now. Michael had been inspecting the shore through binoculars. Now he stowed them, and stood above her. 'You're still full of pethidine,' he said. 'Go to sleep. When you wake up, you'll feel a whole lot better.'

'What are you going to do to me?' she muttered.

He grinned. 'Nothing – until you're feeling better.'

Jessica closed her eyes. She was utterly at his mercy. But only as long as it took to shake off the effects of the pethidine. And get her sea legs.

Jessica awoke suddenly, as if she had never been asleep at all. The yacht still pitched and surged, but less violently; she thought the wind might have eased. And it was still daylight, although the sun was now in front of them, shining on the spray-encrusted wheelhouse windows. And she was both thirsty and needed the toilet. She pushed herself up, and realized that she was alone. Suppose he had been washed overboard? She had no idea how to sail a yacht. But she could call for help.

She didn't know what had happened to her sports bag and her mobile, but she gazed at the huge, green-painted Sailor radio system on the after bulkhead, mounted above the steps leading down to the master cabin. And on the forward bulkhead, above the helm, there was another green-painted Sailor radio, this one much smaller. That would be the VHF, used for short-range calls. She looked out of the window. Land was still visible to the north, not more than ten miles away. It was simply a matter of getting to the set. She threw off the blanket, and released the lee-boards far enough to slide her body out of the bunk. When she stood up, the day again began to rotate around her, but she bit her lip and staggered to the helmsman's chair, holding on to it while she regained some of her balance. She stretched out her hand for the VHF mike, and Michael's hand closed over it. 'I can see you're going to be a troublesome wench,' he said.

Jessica's knees gave way and she sank to the floor, shoulders hunched, fighting waves of nausea. But those could be sheer disappointment. 'I think,' Michael said, 'that the time has come for you and me to have a little chat. About the facts of life.'

'We have a lead, sir,' Detective-Sergeant Tom Lawson said.

Commander Adams raised his head, somewhat wearily. He was a big man, with sharp eyes and a lantern jaw. Normally he looked masterful and decisive; that went with being in charge of the Protection Division of the Special Branch. This afternoon he looked defeated: Jessica Jones was his favourite subordinate. 'What sort of lead?' he inquired.

Tom was also a big man, with heavy shoulders, lank black hair and craggy features. He had also spent a depressed twenty-four hours. As Jessica's partner for the past seven years he still adored her, however often he found her infuriating. But he was looking much happier now. 'The Drive-Rite people in Basingstoke have called. One of their offices rented a blue Ford Fiesta to a man with a beard yesterday morning. The clerk found it odd because he paid in cash.'

Adams did not look pleased. 'Have you any idea how many men there are with beards in England? Or how many of those do not use cards? Or how many blue Ford Fiestas there are? Do the numbers tie up?'

'I'm afraid not. The female witness who reported seeing the car in the street did not make a note of the number.'

'Then we're no further ahead. Has the car been returned?'

'In a sense. The car was rented in Steventon for the day. It was not returned until after the office had closed, but was left in the station car park as arranged. However, the keys, which were to be pushed through the office letter box in case of an out-of-hours return, were left in the ignition.'

'What is suspicious about that?'

'Well, sir, as I say, the car was hired for the day, and was used for the whole day and obviously into the night, yet it had only sixty miles on the clock.'

Adams frowned.

'And I have checked the map,' Tom went on. 'Steventon is just on thirty miles from Clapham.

74

Sixty miles there and back.'

'Circumstantial. Have forensics had a look?'

'Yes, sir. And found nothing. You see, it is company policy with Drive-Rite to have every car completely vacuumed and cleaned the moment it is returned. This includes wiping the steering wheel as well as the door handles. So there were no liftable prints.'

'But whoever did this cleaning would have reported anything like bloodstains, I presume.'

'Yes, sir. But I do not believe that Jessica was killed.'

'It may well be that she was not killed in the car. If that is the car. But there is no other reason for her to be snatched.'

'Well, sir...'

'Oh, quite, Sergeant. She is a very handsome woman. But I cannot believe anyone would dare kidnap JJ for the purpose of rape – or that she would submit to that without breaking every bone in his body. As for this car, is there anything further? Any samples that could be used for DNA analysis? A sighting of the man when he dropped it off?'

'No, sir.'

'As there should have been had he been carrying JJ, or her body. That's a dead end, Lawson. This is a case of revenge. That's the angle we need to work on. One of Cuesta's Bolivian thugs or a remnant of Korman's organization. Believe me, I want to know who is responsible, and I want her back. You take the rest of the week off. But follow those lines of inquiry.'

'Yes, sir,' Tom said dejectedly.

Resistance

Jessica made no effort to resist Michael as he dragged her to her feet and half carried her to the after companionway; her sole idea was to not vomit again, and she felt it was very close. He carried her down the steps, one arm round her waist, and let her fall on to the bunk. He scooped up her legs and rolled her over, and she lay there, gasping. 'Come on,' he said. 'I know you're pretending.'

'I'm not,' she panted. 'Oh, God! The bowl...'

It had remained in the cabin, and he held it for her, then took it away to flush it and wash it. She lay on her back, staring at the cabin ceiling, reaching for breath. 'Waste of a good breakfast,' he remarked, standing above her.

'Go away,' she begged. 'For God's sake, leave me alone.'

To her surprise he did that, although he left the cabin door hooked open, no doubt so that he could hear her if she got up. She guessed he felt the need to look at the radar. As long as they were in the English Channel, with so much shipping about, and with her being seasick, she was inviolate; he had neither the time nor the inclination to touch her. But they would be out of the Channel in another few hours, he had said. And no one could be seasick forever. She rose on her elbow and took a salt biscuit from the box by the bed, chewed it slowly and carefully. And actually felt better.

But her mouth tasted foul. Well, she hadn't cleaned her teeth since yesterday morning. Was it only yesterday morning? But not only her mouth was feeling dreadful; she hadn't bathed since yesterday morning, either. In fact, she hadn't bathed since the night before last. She had been going home from tennis to have a hot tub ... and she had wound up on this bed puking her guts out, at the mercy of a madman. Who wanted only vengeance!

How on earth had she allowed it to happen? Simply by allowing herself to relax. Wasn't she entitled to relax, once in a while? But self-pity was not going to get her out of this mess. Well then, what was? Only, as she had realized from the beginning, patience and cunning. She was one of the most highly trained operatives in the world. He could not possibly match her for any length of time.

She sat up, and to her enormous relief the cabin no longer rotated. But that was not necessarily a good thing. She might be getting over her seasickness, but she knew she was still full of pethidine, and thus operating only at quarter strength. Meanwhile, if he realized that she was recovering, he would probably inject her again, or at least tie her up again, until he was ready to...

After the way he had spoken she had no

desire to consider what he ultimately intended for her, but she had no doubt it would begin with rape. As with any woman, the thought revolted her, but she had been sufficiently well trained not to let the idea dominate her mind. Although she had never *been* raped, in the line of duty she had come close to it more than once. Her business then, and now, was survival until her returning strength enabled her to place this animal under arrest and return him to where he belonged: a prison cell.

The seasickness was definitely in recession, as it were. As for the pethidine, she even felt she could cope with that. So why not find out? If he had a strong sexual attraction for her, as he claimed, then to indulge it might make him lower his guard, give her an opportunity. Even if she knew she was far from fit, she also knew that every mile they sailed away from England would add to the difficulties of getting back.

She left the cabin and went to the companionway, holding on to the various grabrails; the yacht's movement was more regular now, but there was still a lot of it. She climbed the steps, stood at the top. He was making notes in his log. She wondered what he had entered in there so far. She didn't suppose he was recording his kidnapping.

He heard her, and turned his head. 'Feeling better?'

'I did.' Suddenly the nausea was back.

Jessica sat on the step, her head between her knees, feeling utter despair.

'Well, try not to be sick there,' he recommended.

She had to keep going, had to try. She raised her head. 'I'd like to have a shower.'

'Good idea. Hold on a moment and I'll come down.'

'I can manage on my own.'

'No, you can't,' he said. 'You don't know how everything works. Just stay there a moment.'

She pulled herself to her feet, but remained in the wheelhouse, looking out. It was mid-morning now, and very bright; the clouds had entirely gone, save for some fluffy fleeceballs, and the wind had dropped too, although it remained strong enough to have the yacht creaming through the water, with a distinct heel to port. The sea was still a mass of white-caps, but the waves were smaller, and she thought the movement was easing all the while.

To the left she could see two steamships. The sight gave her quite a pang. Just over there were people, no doubt looking at the yacht through their binoculars and making notes in *their* logs. If only they could be contacted. But they were several miles away, rising and falling on the swell.

To the right were low green hills, again several miles off, she reckoned. 'Cornwall,' Michael explained. 'We're making good time. By this evening we'll have rounded the

Scillies, and have the whole Atlantic to play with. But I can't be off the bridge for too long in these waters; go below and strip off. I'll be with you in a few minutes.' Jessica hesitated, chewing her lip. He grinned at her. 'You're going to have to some time, Jessica. You don't want me to do it for you, do you?'

Jessica went down the steps and into the cabin. She had deliberately created this scenario; there was no point in getting cold feet now. She took off her tracksuit, throwing both top and bottom on the deck. Then she added her tennis clothes to the pile, and heard movement behind her. 'Nice,' he said. 'Did anyone ever tell you that you are an incredibly attractive woman?'

Jessica tossed her head. 'Lots.'

'But there's only me to tell you now. Let's see the rest of you.' Jessica drew a deep breath and took off her bra. This too she dropped on the floor; like all her clothes it needed washing after being worn non-stop for forty-eight hours. 'They're just right,' Michael assured her. 'Although some may say they're a bit large. But those tits ... divine.' He was waiting, flushing. With anticipation, or desire? Jessica slid her knickers past her thighs and stepped out of them. 'Oh, that's good,' he said. 'It's not just the ass – although that is perfection. It's the hair. I do like a big bush.'

'Are you trying to tell me you haven't looked at me before? While I was uncon-scious?'

His flush deepened. 'No. I didn't want to.

80

Well, I wanted you to be awake when it happened.'

She had to keep matching his mood. 'I've always thought there was too much of it.'

'Well, maybe one of these days I'll shave you. Would you like that?'

'I don't know,' she said. 'I've never shaved there.'

'You know, all those nights in prison, I dreamed of you. Of having you tied up naked, at my feet, so that I could do anything I liked to you. Squeeze you, beat you, even cut you...'

Jessica took a deep breath. Oh, God, she thought. Here it comes. And she wasn't ready for it: her limbs still felt as if they were filled with water – she wasn't even sure they would respond. She gazed at him, uncertain what was going to happen next. Of course he knew that he had all the time in the world, time to savour her bit by bit, visually. This was just another form of mental sadism.

'Now, looking at you, having you here...' His voice changed; his eyes lost their dreamy look. 'The shower head is adjustable,' he said. 'And it's a mix tap. I'm afraid there isn't very much hot water, so I'd put it full on.'

Jessica turned away from him, not sure what he had meant, muscles still tensed in expectation of at least a touch. 'I bought some things for you,' he said. 'Things I thought you might need. They're in the top right-hand drawer of the locker. You have to press the tit on the handle to open it. That's

81

to stop the drawer from flying open in a seaway, you understand.'

To reach the head door, she had to brush virtually against him. Never had she been so aware of being naked. She drew a quick breath and stepped past him. He didn't moved. She reached the door and found she was holding her breath. A buzzer sounded. 'Damn,' he said. 'That's a warning that something is within radar range. I'll be back as soon as I can.'

He went up the companion ladder, and Jessica let out her breath in a rush. She stepped into the tiny bathroom – what did he call it; the head? – and closed the door. This time she investigated it thoroughly, but where the bolt had once been was now painted over. She used the loo, flushed with some difficulty by following the instructions printed above it – it was a business of opening and shutting valves and pumping in the right order – then opened the drawer he had indicated, with even more difficulty; depressing the little button into the recess in the handle was harder than she had expected – she nearly broke a nail.

In the drawer there were several plastic bottles of spray deodorant, as well as bars of scented soap, and plastic bottles of matching shampoo. It was not a scent she had ever used before, but it was quite pleasant. There was also a stock of toothbrushes, brand new in their cellophane, and tubes of toothpaste. Again, it was not her brand, but she would have settled for anything. There was even a safety razor and a stack of spare blades. She needed it for her legs, but she didn't want to risk using it under her arms until the movement had calmed down.

She cleaned her teeth, and felt better. Each cake of soap had a length of thick string attached, and she removed the wrapping and looped one of these round her neck, hooked a bottle of shampoo over the rail, and stepped into the shower stall, which was simply a small curtain-enclosed area of slatted wood over the plastic deck, in which there was a drain. She turned on the water, having adjusted the mix to 'high' as he had recommended, and was taken aback to discover that the flow was salt! It was quite warm, and extremely pleasant, but she had intended to wash her hair.

Hastily she turned off the water, and gathered her hair into a crown on her head, then realized she had nothing to tie it with. She drew the curtain, but before she could locate anything to use, the door opened. 'It's only me,' Michael remarked, slowly looking her up and down. Standing facing him, with both hands holding her hair in place, she felt even more exposed than before. 'Is there a problem? I heard you turn off the water.'

'I need something to tie my hair,' she said.

Then the boat lurched, and she fell forward. He caught her neatly by the armpits, while she released her hair, which came down in tumbling profusion on to her shoulders. Now she was against him, and he was still holding her, and their faces were only inches apart. And she was still terribly aware of being too weak to do anything about it. He kissed her, very gently, on the lips. 'I'll get you something,' he said, and set her back on her feet. She shuddered, breath coming in short gasps. He left her and went into the cabin, returning a few moments later with a length of blue ribbon. 'Tell-tale,' he said.

'What?'

'When the wind is very light,' he explained, 'too light for the anemometer to be effective, we tie one of these to one of the stays, and its flutter tells us what the wind is doing.'

'Oh.' She took the ribbon, and raised her hair again, but her fingers fumbled as she tied it in place and several strands fell on to her neck.

Michael leaned against the doorjamb. 'I can't make up my mind, whether you are more lovely with your hair up or with it down. You know, in normal circumstances, a woman's hair sets off her beauty. But your face is so classical it's actually improved by having nothing around it.'

He had the knack of leaving her with nothing to say. She turned away. 'I'd like to wash it,' she said. 'But I can't wash it in salt water.'

'Well, I suppose you *can*,' he said. 'But if it'll make you uncomfortable ... How often do you wash it?'

'Every two or three days.'

'Hm. You may have to spread that a bit until we get some decent rain. We will, soon enough. Right now, I think you can use some fresh water. Do you do it before or after your shower?'

'After, as a rule.'

'Okay. Have your shower, and when you're ready, use that faucet on the basin. That's the fresh-water tap.'

'I know. I used it to clean my teeth.'

'Well, fill the basin and wash your hair. I'd be grateful if you'd use as little as possible. As I said, when we get some good rain, I can refill our tanks, but it's better to be safe than sorry. Incidentally, that shampoo is intended for use with salt water; you won't get much of a lather, but it should be sufficient. And don't forget to pump out the water afterwards.'

'Is the drain blocked?'

'Of course it is, silly girl. By a non-return valve. Otherwise we'd sink, wouldn't we? The pump is that switch over there; it's electrically operated. Just press it until the water is all gone. Right? Have a nice bath.'

'Thank you,' she said, and stepped back into the shower. He remained standing there, looking at her, as she drew the curtain. Well, she would have done that even if she had been alone.

As there was not apparently any restriction on the use of salt water, she took a long, slow shower, pleasantly surprised by the amount of lather she did manage to get. But the jet was steadily growing colder, and at last she had to leave it. She was now ankle deep in water, so she pressed the switch as instructed, and it slowly gurgled away. Then she took another deep breath, and drew the curtain, every muscle tensed. But the bathroom was empty.

Jessica gave a sigh of relief, dried herself, and then half-filled the basin with fresh water. The thought crossed her mind to let it run and run and run until the tank was empty, but that would have made life as difficult for her as for him – she didn't see him putting back to England, at least not until he had murdered her first. In any event, it would have been a most difficult task, as the water only came out while she held the faucet down; the moment she released it, it cut out.

She released the ribbon, scooped her hair forward and shampooed, using a minimum of gel. That felt almost as good as the shower. She nearly went off into a daze, slowly scratching her scalp, when she felt his hands on her bottom, one on each cheek. Jessica jerked upright, unable to see him in the mirror because it had steamed up. But he was equally blinded for the moment, as he had received a faceful of wet hair and soap.

He grabbed the towel and wiped himself clean. 'I'm sorry, I didn't mean to startle you. But I couldn't resist touching you. Do you know, you have the most beautiful ass I have ever seen. I want to get between those cheeks. Would you like me to do that?'

Jessica's nerve finally cracked. 'No, I would

not like you to do that,' she shouted. 'You are a kidnapping, raping, bastard of a pervert. If you touch me, I'll ... I'll kill you.' He looked utterly surprised, and then raised his hands, as if he *was* going to touch her again. She swung at his face, fingers bent to use her nails, and at the same time brought up her knee, aiming for his crotch. But he was far too quick for her drug-slowed attack, and far too strong as well. He caught her wrists while at the same time side-stepping her knee. They cannoned into each other and he swung her round so that her back was to him, still holding her wrists in a powerful grip. 'Let me go, you bastard!' she snapped. 'You fucking shit! Let me go!' Those were not words she habitually used, at least to other people. But she had laid a trap and fallen into it herself.

He pushed her forward, out of the head and across the cabin floor. Her knees struck the bed and she fell on to her face, gasping for breath. Oh, God, she thought again, this *is* it. But to her surprise he released her wrists, and instead placed his left hand firmly in the middle of her back, holding her across the bed on her face. She tried to roll away from him and turn over, but before she could he had slapped her naked backside. The blow was very hard, and for a moment robbed her of muscular power. 'Ow!' she bawled, and then screamed as he slapped her again, five times in rapid succession. To her consternation and self-disgust she burst into tears, but they were mainly anger and indignation – she had never been spanked before. Desperately she kicked her legs and tried striking behind herself, but there was nothing she could do; the hand pressing into her back and holding her down on the mattress was simply too powerful.

Then, after six slaps, the pressure was gone. Jessica rolled on to her side, gazed at Michael. He stood by the door, his face flushed. 'You needed that,' he said, and went into the companionway.

Jessica knew nothing but white-hot anger, compounded by the stinging in her buttocks. She leapt off the bed, ran into the head, and grabbed a can of deodorant spray from the drawer, then scrambled up the steps behind him. He had gone directly to the helm and the radar screen, and she hurled herself across the wheelhouse floor to throw one arm round his neck and the other over his shoulder to direct the spray into his face as she pressed the button. 'Bastard,' she said, exerting all the power she could command on his neck with her forearm. 'I am going to throttle you!'

He struck back with his elbows, with a force she had not anticipated; she thought she might have broken a rib as she collapsed to her knees, face falling against his pant leg. 'I should take you apart,' he said, wiping spray from his stinging eyes. 'Maybe I will.'

She lay on the wheelhouse deck, totally winded, while he groped at her, still half-blinded. He dug his fingers into her armpits and lifted her to drag her across the deck and throw her down the steps. She landed in a jumble of arms and legs, again losing her breath. 'Your hair is wet and full of soap,' he shouted at her. 'What are you trying to do, catch cold? That's the last thing I need, a snotty-nosed female hanging around the place.' He came down the steps, got her by the armpits again, and lifted her up. 'Get in there,' he said, 'and rinse yourself.'

Jessica staggered into the bathroom and held on to the basin. Michael followed her.

'Just remember,' he said, his mouth seeming to be situated around the nape of her neck. 'I can dump you overboard now, and no one will ever know, save you and the fishes. Don't suppose you can possibly be connected to me. I'll weight you so that your skeleton will stay down there forever. Until I decide to do that, you're mine, all mine.' He put his arms round her, held her back against him, and cupped her breasts as she gasped. 'All mine,' he said again, and released her.

For several seconds Jessica couldn't move. She had come into contact with sufficient primitive violence in her years on the force – she had occasionally indulged in it herself. But never when both naked and feeling like death, and never without the presence, or at least the knowledge, of a back-up, as when she and Andrea and Chloe had taken on the might of the drugs baron Ramon Cuesta, so confident in their superiority, both with guns and unarmed combat, and almost literally blown him away.

Now she was absolutely alone, unarmed and helpless, at the mercy of a man who, whatever his desire for her, also undoubtedly hated her. And now he had spelled it out. She was his prisoner, and when he had had enough amusement out of her, he was going to kill her. And she had no idea how soon she would regain her strength. Worst of all, in view of his strength and obvious training, she had no idea if she could defeat him, even at her best.

She rinsed the last of the soap from her hair, wrapped her head in the towel, and, clutching the duvet around her, went back up to the wheelhouse. 'There,' he said. 'That feel better? You certainly look better.'

She sat on the settee berth. 'Am I allowed to get dressed?'

'Cold?'

It was actually as warm as toast in the cabin, with the sun shining through the glass. 'I'm just not used to wandering around in the altogether.'

'Then get used to it. You've the figure for it, and I like looking at you.'

'You mean I don't have any other clothes? You'll get bored, looking at me naked all the time.'

'There's a profound thought. You mean you do have a brain? Yes, there are clothes. I bought some for you. If you must, try the locker under the bed.' He grinned. 'I can

90

always take them off again.'

'I don't suppose you would have a hair dryer?'

'I'm afraid not. Never thought of it.'

She returned to the cabin, rubbed her hair some more with the towel, then threw the towel into the bathroom, leaving the yellow strands damp on her shoulders. She opened the locker, frowned. There were no brassieres, but she took out a pair of white panties trimmed with lace. Silk! She had never worn silk next to her skin in her life. There were several pairs. He must have spent a fortune. There were also tee shirts and jeans, a couple of pairs of sandals, one of trainers, and four tracksuits. But no dresses: they weren't going anywhere civilized. She put on a pair of panties and one of the tracksuits, but didn't bother with shoes. Then she sat on the bed and brushed her damp hair, again and again and again. While she did that, she gazed at her own discarded clothing, still lying on the cabin sole.

They should go into a bin, if there was such a thing; judging by what he had said, she would not be able to wash them until they had some rain, and that could be several days off. But ... suppose her clothes went overboard? And were found. A set of female clothing floating about the Channel would surely cause an investigation, and she had no doubt that the police would be able to trace the clothes back to the missing Detective-Sergeant Jones. Then they would be able to trace

91

the ships using this area at the time. Did she dare try it?

She was still shaking from the violence of his assault. Her ribs still felt tender. But what had happened had been only the beginning. She was stuck with it. She kept telling herself she had to accept that, until she was ready. And then she did stupid things like trying to attack him. Her nostrils twitched. The most delicious smell of cooking food was drifting through the ship, attacking her empty stomach with an almost living intensity. But if he was cooking, then he had to be in the saloon, and the wheelhouse would be empty.

She dropped the brush, gathered the clothes into a bundle, tying them together so that they would not drift apart, and went up the steps. She gazed at all the instruments. The ships to port were gone, but on the starboard hand there was a lighthouse, gleaming in the noonday sun. If it was manned, the lighthouse keepers would certainly be watching the yacht making its way down-Channel, tracking her on radar. She didn't think she had the time to work out what wavelength he might be listening on, but if she were to seize the helm and wrench it off autopilot so that the entire ship turned round, and suggested it was in trouble...

That was for after she had thrown her clothes overboard. She crossed the wheelhouse to the sliding door on to the deck.

'That's the Lizard,' Michael said from the forward companionway. 'Means we're nearly

92

out of the Channel. You weren't thinking of playing any more tricks, were you?' Jessica's shoulders slumped. Michael took the bundle of clothes from her arms. 'There's a bin for these. We'll have a washday when we get further south.' He threw them back down the steps. 'I like a girl with spirit,' he said. 'But spirit needs to be properly directed. Like a horse, you know? Every rider wants a spirited horse. But the horse has to be broken first, so that it obeys the rider, and only reveals its spirit when its rider tells it to. I see I am going to have to break you. Drop your pants and bend over.'

Jessica bit her lip. 'No,' she said, hating herself for begging. 'Please. I won't do it again.'

'Promise?'

'Yes,' she said. 'I promise.'

'Well, just remember, if you break your word, I am going to make you suffer, really and truly.'

'You don't think you've already made me suffer?' She could not resist that.

He grinned. 'I haven't even started yet. Now come below and have some lunch.'

He wondered what she was thinking as he sat across the table from her, watching her eat. Right now, only of food. After her seasickness and her long abstinence before that, he reckoned she must be starving. She was probably going to have an attack of indigestion. But after that, she would be normal again. Even the drug would have worn off, he
93

reckoned. Would she then submit? He didn't think so. There was nothing docile about her. He would have to beat her some more. He knew he was going to enjoy that. But he didn't want really to break her spirit. He only wanted to make her accept her situation and stop trying to fight him. 'Would you like a cup of wine?' he asked.

She raised her head, her damp hair resting on her shoulders and half across her face. He reached across the table and pushed it away from her eyes. 'It'll do you good.' He uncorked the bottle, poured them each a cup. 'Do you drink, normally?' he asked.

'Sometimes. I don't want to drink now.'

'But I want you to. It'll make you relax.'

She licked her lips, picked up the cup. He wondered if she was going to throw it at him, but she had clearly had enough fighting for the moment. She sipped, and made a face. 'It'll grow on you,' he assured her. She took another sip. 'That's my girl. Drink it all.'

He wondered what effect the alcohol would have if there was still any of the drug left in her system. She put down the cup, empty. 'It was all right,' she said.

'We'll have some more in a minute. Now we need to get a routine going. Can you cook?'

'Yes.'

'Well, then, it might make a change if you did some of the cooking.'

Jessica got up, a trifle uncertainly. 'Shall I make coffee?'

'I think we'll skip coffee this afternoon.'

94

She tried the tap. 'There's no hot water, so I'll have to boil a kettle.'

'Wash them in cold water. I told you, we don't have any gas to spare.'

She had never washed dishes in cold water before. And now she realized that, as in the shower, the water was salt. 'Isn't there a chance we'll catch something?'

'If we do, we'll go together. Wouldn't you like that?' She made no reply, and started scrubbing plates; every so often her hand brushed the drawer, which he knew she was dying to open, to discover if there were any good-sized knives in there. So much for her promise. But if she wanted to play it tough, he was quite prepared to meet her halfway.

He watched her move as she worked. The tracksuit was loose-fitting and not in itself a turn-on, but just looking at her was. Suddenly she yawned. The alcohol was getting to her. But then the buzzer went. She turned her head to look at him. 'I know you promised to behave, but there's no point in putting temptation in your way, is there? Leave those for a moment and come up with me.' She hesitated, then dried her hands and preceded him up the steps into the wheelhouse, where he checked the radar and then used his binoculars. Jessica had already spotted the ship, inshore and thus quite close. It was a small freighter, as were the others rising and falling on the swell. 'On the floor,' Michael commanded.

Jessica obeyed; she reckoned the ship was

too far off for anyone to see into the yacht wheelhouse, even with binoculars. Her backside still hurt, so she lay on her side. Michael made an adjustment to the course. 'She's out of the Scillies. Once we're round them, we'll give the shipping routes a miss. Should be there by dusk. We're being very lucky with our weather.'

He glanced at her. Her face was expressionless, but he knew she was thinking that *she* wasn't being very lucky with the weather; she would have preferred a storm severe enough to drive them into port. She didn't yet understand that he was prepared to take his chances in a hurricane, with this boat ... and her. He sat beside her on the floor. 'You okay?'

'Yes.'

'But your ass is sore. Let's have a look at it.'

'I haven't broken my promise,' she protested.

'That has nothing to do with my wanting to look at your ass. Lie on your face.'

She obeyed, pillowing her head on her arms. He dug his fingers into the waistband of her tracksuit and pulled it down. He was trembling with a mixture of anticipation and apprehension. There was so much he wanted to do to this woman, do *with* this woman, that he was afraid to touch her, afraid she would disappear and become again just a dream. But she was real. He pulled the tracksuit bottom down to her knees, then eased the silk knickers to join them. 'You ever owned a pair like these before?' he asked.

She didn't reply. Perhaps she had fallen asleep. The softly rounded flesh was still blotched pink from the spanking, and there was a bruise on her thigh. He rubbed it, and she gave a little shudder, the whole length of her body from her neck to her ankles, like a cat. He could feel himself erecting, but as usual only partially. Certainly he could never make an entry with what he possessed. But did he want to make an entry? He had a dreadful feeling that to complete the act would somehow alter their relationship. Did they have a relationship, apart from master and servant, desire on his side and fear and loathing on hers? But maybe that was what he wanted to preserve. He continued to stroke her buttocks for some moments. She wasn't asleep, because she was keeping them tight and closed, and when he tried to slip his hands between the cheeks she gave another little shiver.

He rolled her on to her back. Her legs instinctively came up, knees pressed tightly together, and he gently pushed them flat again. She was staring at him, eyes huge. He stroked her pubes. 'I'm not sure this isn't the best thing about you,' he said. Her stomach rose and fell as he rested his hand on it. He raised his head to look at her and she sat up and struck at him, clapping her hands together, aiming for his ears as she had been taught, and as she had done herself in the past to puncture an assailant's eardrums and leave him in agony. But still she was too slow and he was too quick, and too strong. She gasped in a mixture of frustration and fear as he caught her wrists and forced her flat again, rolling so that he lay on her. 'You're going to have to surrender,' he told her, straddling her so that the crotch of his jeans pressed into her pubes. 'For God's sake, stop fighting me.'

Her body heaved against his. 'I'm going to fight you till I die, you bastard,' she shouted. 'So you may as well kill me now.' She stared at him, eyes bigger than ever, and he realized she had not meant to say that – just in case he took her up on it.

'You think you're a real toughie,' he said. 'But you don't know the meaning of the word.' Still holding her wrists he rose to his knees. 'Well, if that's how you want to play it.' He pulled her to her feet, sat her on the settee berth. 'Move a muscle and I am going to whip you.' He released her, and she sat there, panting, hands pressed into her lap. But he could tell she hadn't surrendered yet; her brain was working. He checked the course and distance off, then turned back to her. 'Okay, pull up your pants and finish those dishes.' He followed her into the saloon. He thought he could do it now. But it would be better to wait. It could only build.

By dusk they were, as Michael had estimated, abeam of the Scillies. 'And so we say farewell to sunny Britain,' he remarked.

Jessica had spent the afternoon lying on the

98

settee berth. For the moment at least she seemed to be passive, a sort of armed truce, he supposed – she was waiting for another assault, while trying to make up her mind what she could do, if anything. Their relationship still had to be sorted out: he didn't want to have to kill her, at least until the voyage was nearly over. That meant they had to accept each other – or she had to accept him, certainly. As for sex...

'In a day or two,' he suggested, 'you'll have your sea legs.' He adjusted the course. 'Now we'll just get as far as possible from any shipping, and we should be able to have a good night's sleep.'

'Shouldn't you call up, or something?' To his surprise her voice was normal; she had come to some decision. 'Tell the coastguard you're clear of land?'

'They can see I'm clear of land. I checked out at Lymington. Now, how'd you like to cook us supper?'

'Oh. Right.' She swung her legs off the bunk, and sat up, hesitating.

'Oh, I'm coming down with you.' He followed her down the steps. 'Although you want to think about this,' he said. 'Not right now, but in a couple of days' time, when we're well out to sea, should anything happen to me, you'll be up shit creek without a paddle.'

'I had thought about that,' she said equably. 'What would you like me to cook?'

'Well, obviously the fresh food needs to go first. There are some lamb chops in the cool box.'

'And potatoes? I see some in the bin.'

'And some carrots.' He opened the drawer, took out a kitchen knife. 'I'll slice them for you.' She gazed into the drawer, where there were two more knives, one of them quite large. He closed the drawer. 'You do remember promising to behave?' She bit her lip, and seasoned the chops.

'It would be much better for both of us if you'd stick to that,' he recommended, slicing the vegetables with great expertise, then washing the knife himself and restoring it to the drawer. To do that he had to stand against her, and when she refused to look at him, he kissed her on the neck. 'You really do something for me. Do I do anything at all for you?'

'No,' she said, and at last turned her head, gazing at him with her mouth open, again as if she hadn't actually meant to be so frank.

'Well,' he said, 'maybe I'll grow on you.' He poured some wine while she cooked; this time she didn't object to drinking any of it. It was already dark outside, and the yacht was sliding along very well, almost upright. 'They said the wind would shift,' he said. 'But it hasn't done so yet. That's good for us.'

'Can you really just go to bed and go to sleep, in the darkness, with ships all around you?' she asked.

'There aren't any ships all around us. Anyway, I'm going to put the radar up to thirty miles – that's its maximum range – before I turn in.'

'Aren't you going to burn your batteries flat?'

'I'm going to keep the generator on for tonight; we can spare a few gallons of fuel. From tomorrow we'll be shutting everything down to give the solar batteries a chance to put in a charge.' He grinned at her. 'Don't panic. The odds on being run down by another ship in the middle of the Atlantic are about ten million to one. Another cup?'

'Why not?'

He poured and she sipped. 'As I'm going to run the generator, how would you like to watch a video?'

'I'd prefer to listen to some music. Do you have any discs?'

'Sure. Do you like The Honeycombs?'

'The who?'

'Not The Who. The Honeycombs.'

'I've never heard of a group called The Honeycombs.'

'They were very big, oh, forty years ago. When I was a kid. It was a male band with a girl drummer. They had a song called *Have I the Right to Love You* that topped the hit parade for weeks.'

'I've never heard of it,' Jessica said again. 'Don't you have any classics? Vivaldi?'

'We'll watch a video,' he decided. 'Something nice and blue, to get us going.'

'If that's what turns you on,' she agreed.

'That is the idea, to turn me on. To turn us on.' He moved round the table to sit beside her. 'I really am happy that you are being

101

sensible. Look at me.' She turned her head, and he kissed her on the mouth. After a couple of seconds her lips parted and he could find her tongue.

While he kissed her he pushed up the track-suit top to hold her breasts. But she remained absolutely passive. 'You need to shave,' she said when he took his mouth away.

He rubbed his chin. 'Okay. I'll shave. One forgets these things, on a boat. Come to bed.'

'I haven't washed up.'

'Put everything in the sink. You can wash up tomorrow morning. Go below and get into bed. Take everything off.'

She went down the after companion. Michael checked the course and the navigation lights, then dropped the main and set the mizzen so that while they would keep under way, any sudden squall would not be dangerous. Then he started the generator. Its growl hid even the whine of the wind and the hissing of the sea, leaving them cocooned in a private world. He studied the radar screen, but did not immediately adjust it as they were still within twenty miles of land.

He went below. Jessica had switched on the light, and was in bed, the duvet pulled to her throat. 'Good girl,' he said. He went into the head and shaved, came back to her, took off his clothes. She watched him, her eyes wide, but with a faint frown on her forehead. 'You do turn me on,' he assured her. 'It'll grow.' It was going to happen. He was sure of it. He selected a film, pushed it into the slot,

102

switched on the set, then got into bed, carrying the handcuffs.

'Do you have to do that?' she asked.

'I think so. How can I relax when I don't know when next you'll attack me? When I feel I can trust you, now...'

She submitted. This time he cuffed her wrists together, then secured them to the grab-rail with a length of cord, leaving it loose enough to allow her to be reasonably comfortable. Then he got beneath the duvet beside her. He slid down the sheet, and their thighs touched. He felt her shudder, and knew she was considering moving away but had realized there was nowhere to go. He thrust his arm under her neck to hold her against him as they watched the movie unfold. 'Enjoying it?' he asked.

'I didn't know they were allowed to film things like that,' she said.

'You mean the hard-on? They can film anything they like, even if you have to buy the video under the counter.' Then he could wait no longer. Because he had one himself, at last. He rolled on top of her, kicking away the duvet. She gave a startled exclamation, but realized she could not resist him. He straddled her, feeling her pubes against his, kissed her, desperately. Her legs were together, but he got one of his in between and separated her knees and then her thighs. Then he was in position ... and fading.

He thrust his hands down to drive them underneath her; he grasped her buttocks and squeezed. She gave a little gasp of pain. But he was still fading. He had to do something. He slid down the bed, rising to his knees, still holding her buttocks to raise her from the bed as well, and began kissing and sucking. 'Oh,' she gasped. 'Oh!'

He kept at her for several minutes, but nothing was happening to either of them. Disgustedly he let her go and rolled on his back. The actors on the screen were still working away, panting and grunting. 'Don't you have any feelings at all?' he asked.

'Not when I'm being handled like a sack of coal,' she said.

He raised himself on his elbow to look down at her; her eyes seemed to gleam in the gloom. She reckoned she had gained a victory. Perhaps she had. He had the strongest desire to hit her, again and again. But to bruise her face, cut her lips and cheeks, would be self-defeating.

He turned off the video, went up to check the radar and the night; there was nothing on the screen at all, save for the fast-dwindling land behind them. He changed the setting to the maximum range, switched off all the lights and went below. Her eyes were open. He got into bed beside her, and she shuddered and turned away from him.

'Well?' Andrea asked, seating herself across the desk from Tom.

His shoulders were hunched. 'Not a sausage. Cuesta's organization has collapsed. So has

Burke's. Nobody wants to know. Korman's group has just disappeared.' He sighed. 'Maybe it was a sex attack after all, and we'll find her body in some bush.'

'JJ? I can't believe that. Anyway, it had to have been planned. JJ isn't some dreamy schoolgirl to be plucked off the street. Whoever did this had it planned down to the last detail. We know he had us under observation for some time, without realizing what he was really after.'

'Maybe,' Tom said. 'But I'm back on duty tomorrow. The case is in the hands of CID.'

'Do you mind if I have a go? I have a couple of days off.'

'Have a go where?'

'I'm certain this is out of JJ's past. I'm going to track down every villain she ever helped to send up, back to her first day in the force.'

'Good luck,' Tom said.

Menace

Jessica did not expect to sleep. Her brain was a total jumble of confusion. Somehow, until now, her ordeal had been just that. And ordeals always ended. The proximity of land, the approach of those ships, even the fights she and Michael had had, but especially the fact that he had been too busy properly to pay attention to her, had been aspects of the ordeal, of an event quite out of her perception or imagination. But that was now over. England was gone, the voyage had actually begun, and she was lying in bed, naked, beside a naked man. Her kidnapper. With whom she had just had sex – of a sort. As if that mattered in the context of the catastrophe that had overtaken her life. Now he was deeply asleep, breathing slowly and evenly beside her, their thighs touching. She gave an abortive tug on the cuffs binding her wrists, but she knew that was hopeless.

So, tomorrow he would no doubt want to do it again. And fly into another fury of desperation? She knew he had come close to beating her: she had seen his eyes blazing. And if she had not expected such self-control from a wife-murderer, as she knew he had snapped at least once in his life, she had to anticipate that it might happen again. But surely his sexual frustration offered a chance of salvation. Up to a point, at least. If she stopped fighting him, actually cooperated, kept him sexually sated, whatever his problem, that would keep him happy – and her alive, until something turned up. Something! She could no longer have any faith in her returning strength, her combat skills. He was at least as good as her, twice as strong, and he was *prepared*.

But if she could just keep him happy, surely, sometime when he felt he was absolutely safe, he would lower his guard: Scheherazade had kept the sultan going for a thousand nights. How many times had she told herself this was the solution to her situation? But how difficult it was to do.

Jessica realized the cabin was light. Tomorrow had arrived. And her wrists had been freed. She had, in fact, been awakened by an attack of pins and needles that had followed the removal of the handcuffs. She sat up, rubbing her hands together.

Michael was in the head, but he came out a moment later, having shaved and cleaned his teeth. 'How'd you sleep?'

She opened her mouth to tell him she had not, and then realized she had, very deeply, and felt much the better for it. 'Very well, thank you.'

'Jolly good. Come up whenever you're ready.'

Last night might never have happened, and he was leaving her alone! Presumably he supposed he had either beaten or seduced her into submission. Or he felt that now that they were out in the ocean she wouldn't dare attempt anything because she didn't know how to manage a boat without him. But there were still the radios. And they couldn't be that far offshore yet.

Jessica showered, grimacing at the sticky feeling. She was no longer feeling either seasick or half-drugged, and she hunted through the bathroom for a weapon, any kind of weapon. But there was nothing she felt would be the least effective. Yet there had to be weapons, or a weapon, somewhere on board. Belaying pins! She had read how people at sea used belaying pins to knock each other out. Her problem was that she wouldn't know a belaying pin if she bumped into one.

She dressed herself in the tracksuit, and joined him in the saloon. It was not such a good day as yesterday. There was a lot of cloud, through which the sun peered fitfully from time to time, but as it was still early in the morning and they were sailing just south of west, it was behind them.

There was neither ship nor land in sight. The wind had veered too, and was southerly, which meant that the yacht was close hauled, the sheets drawn hard to keep the sails taut; Michael had already reset the mainsail. He had also shaken out the reef, as the wind had dropped to just over twenty knots. That was

108

sufficient, however, to make the yacht plunge from time to time, and send a rattle of spray across the wheelhouse roof. 'Much better going downhill,' he remarked. 'But you can't win them all. Now, I need to free the jib before we have breakfast; the roller gear seems to have stuck. So, sit on the settee.' He produced the handcuffs.

'Do I have to be tied up all the time?' she asked.

'I'm afraid so, like I said, until I am sure I can trust you. And that is up to you.'

'I promise I won't do anything.'

He kissed her on the nose while he clipped her wrists together and round the long stanchion that rose from the settee berth to the wheelhouse roof. 'You promised that yesterday, remember? Without any intention of keeping your word.'

'I'm sorry about that. Won't you trust me?'

'I said, not right now. You can sit on the berth; then you won't be too uncomfortable.' Satisfied that she was secure, he went to the forward companion.

'Can't I help you with the sail?'

'You'd go overboard. Look, just sit there. I won't be long.'

'Are you going to use a belaying pin?' she asked as innocently as she could.

'Belaying pin? Those went out with the ark.'

'Oh! What were they used for?'

'Mainly for making lines fast. Belaying them, right? Now we use cleats.' He went down the companionway and out of sight forward. He was going on the foredeck, which was rising and falling vigorously as the yacht plunged into the head seas. He had said she would go overboard up there. Suppose *he* did? With her secured to the stanchion and helpless, unable to reach either radio, and the yacht all alone on the ocean?

She watched the forehatch open and Michael climb through. To her great relief she saw that he was wearing a harness, which he proceeded to clip to the rail, while, kneeling on the deck, he began working on the foresail. He did everything with the utmost confidence and ability. Despite herself, Jessica thought it must be marvellous to have that much expertise, to know just what needed doing, and to do it, in a cold and raw dawn, with no breakfast in his stomach. She almost thought she could admire him, were he not her kidnapper and debaser – not to mention a murderer.

At last satisfied, he dropped back through the hatch, and reappeared in the wheelhouse a few minutes later. 'I'm sopping,' he said. 'Back in a moment.' Jessica sat on the settee berth, and waited. 'Now,' he said, 'breakfast.'

'How often do you have to mess about with the sail?' she asked.

'Not too often. The working foresail is on a roller and can be controlled from in here, just like the mainsail. But it does jam from time to time. So long as it doesn't happen in a storm.' He grinned at her. 'I'm afraid conditions will be pretty grim sometimes. That

110

thought scare you?'

'No,' she said truthfully. She didn't think anything would scare her right now – it was the future that mattered.

They breakfasted, washed up, and returned to the wheelhouse. 'Now,' he said, 'I'm due to call in. So...'

'You mean you're going to use the radio?' She was astonished.

'I must. If I don't report in regularly, they'll begin to think something has happened to me, and send people out to look for me. But obviously I don't want you chattering in the background; I'm supposed to be alone.'

'I'll behave,' she said. 'I promised.'

'Don't let's go through all of that again.'

She sighed, and submitting to being hand-cuffed. This time in addition to securing her wrists to the upright he made her sit on the berth and tied her ankles together as well. Then he produced his roll of tape and gagged her.

All she could do was sit there and watch him, studying what he was doing and what he was saying. He switched the big radio set to the appropriate channel, and called the Lymington Marina Office, had a chat with someone named Peter, gave his position, told Peter all was well, and signed off. Jessica tried to discern anything in Peter's tone which might indicate that the police had traced her kidnapping to Michael, but there was nothing.

111

'There,' he said, closing down the set. 'All seems well. It was tempting to ask after that missing policewoman, but that would have been to give the game away. Anyway, I imagine everyone thinks you're dead in a ditch.' He sat beside her on the settee. 'Do you know, tied up, you are even more desirable than, well, not tied up. I never knew I was into bondage. But it's rather fun, don't you think?'

She wanted to scream at him, but couldn't make a sound as he pulled down her pants and began to stroke her. What made it worse was that he was beginning to get to her; with her ankles tied together she seemed able to feel him much more than the last time he had touched her there. My God, she thought, if he manages to bring me off ... He obviously knew what he was doing.

'I think I've got you going,' he said. 'Let's talk.'

He pulled the tape from her mouth. 'Ow,' she said. 'You are a filthy, perverted bastard.'

'Right-ho,' he said. 'I think that calls for six of the best.' He released the handcuffs to free her wrists from the stanchion, but then immediately clipped them together again, and rolled her on to her face.

'Oh, God!' she screamed. 'No. Please. I didn't mean it. I apologize.'

He merely squeezed the cheeks. 'You are the most accomplished liar. But I forgive you.'

'Please untie me.'

112

'I like you the way you are.'
She burst into tears from sheer frustration.

Yet he could also be quite charming – when not turned on by the mere sight of her.

That evening they sat together in the gloom after supper, the only sound the hissing of the waves. The wind had dropped, and he had, as usual at night, lowered the mainsail, so the motion was very comfortable. Added to the after-dinner brandy, it was soporific. He had been unfailingly pleasant over supper, and she found herself talking to him before she realized she was doing it. 'May I ask you a question?'

'Surely.'

'Do you still claim you are innocent of killing your wife?'

'I am innocent of killing my wife.'

'Even if you were alone in the house with her, were holding the murder weapon, and attacked me when I came to investigate? I hadn't even questioned you yet, much less arrested you.'

'I lost my head. That doesn't mean I killed Mary Ann.'

'Then who did?'

'I have no idea. I do know that she was seeing other men.'

'And you seriously think one of your wife's boyfriends came to call on a Sunday afternoon while you were in the garden?'

'I'm not quite as simple as that. I think it was someone she wanted to stop seeing and

113

she had told him so. I think he telephoned and asked for a last talk, so she allowed him into the house, and he killed her.'

'He was taking a hell of a risk.'

'If he was in a killing mood, through jealousy or whatever, he would have regarded bumping into me as the least of his problems.'

'You never put that theory forward as a defence.'

'I knew the jury wouldn't believe me. Thanks to your evidence.'

'Look, I'm a policewoman. My job is to relate the facts as they were presented to me. That is all I did.'

'And thanks to your dedication to duty, I spent ten years in prison.'

'If you were innocent, I'm very sorry.'

'Sorry? Do you know what they do to you in there? Thirteen years ago I was a good-looking young man.'

'Jesus!' she said. 'Is that why...'

'Yes, that's why.'

'But you came out a rich man. Only now you *have* committed a crime, and as you are on parole you are going to have to go back for the entire rest of your sentence. Plus whatever tariff this carries. Can't you see that's crazy?'

'To some people, maybe. Only, you see, I'm not going back. Neither are you.' He grinned at her. 'Don't worry. When we go, we'll go together. Finish your brandy.' He stood up, checked the course, and took a look at the night through his binoculars; he had switched off the radar, and thus depended entirely upon vision. But there was nothing in sight. 'Come to bed.' He held out his hand.

'After just having been condemned to death?'

'Not for a while yet,' he assured her.

They were, she supposed, experiencing the strangest relationship. Victim and executioner. She had read of such situations, without considering the implications very deeply. But now...

She should hate him and fear him and loathe him, and she did, but she had the terrible feeling that he might just be telling the truth about what had happened. And whether he was or not, she had to experience him, because there was no alternative, and all her life she had made a point of accepting what was inevitable – even while determining to change it as soon as it could be done.

As perhaps he knew; after another unsuccessful wrestling match, which left her bruised and breathless, he again handcuffed her to the stanchion for the night. But she knew this couldn't go on, or one night he was going to explode, and probably take her with him. 'Listen,' she said. 'Perhaps I could help you.'

'How?'

'Well, what's called in the trade a hand relief.'

'You'd do that?'

'If it'll stop you going nuts.'

He gazed at her for several seconds. 'You

really must take me for an idiot. It's a ploy to get your hands free.' She bit her lip, and he grinned. 'The quack tells me it'll wear off – or perhaps wear on would be a better way of putting it – and I'll be as good as new. Wouldn't you like that?'

'No,' she said without thinking. And then hastily added, 'Suppose I were to become pregnant?'

'You mean you're not on the pill?'

'Well of course I'm not on the pill. Not now. I don't walk around with a packet.' She glanced at him. 'You haven't got any, have you?'

'One of the few things I didn't think of. Silly me. I have several packets of sanitary towels.'

'Big deal,' she muttered. But she knew she was going to ask the vital question, even if she might be horrified at the possible answer. She drew a deep breath. 'How long do you plan to sail for?'

'I have no idea. Until everything runs out, I suppose. But that won't be for at least a year.'

Now she was holding her breath. 'And then?'

'We'll cross that bridge when we come to it,' he told her. 'Now tell me what you are planning for lunch.' At least, she thought, he had said 'we'.

'Peter Miller,' Andrea announced.

'Who?' Tom asked.

'Murdered his wife in 1989. Stabbed her twenty times. JJ caught him virtually red-handed,

116

arrested him, and then gave the evidence that had him convicted. He was paroled three years ago.'

'Then how can you possibly relate him to JJ's disappearance last week?'

'Simply because last week he skipped his parole report, for the first time in those three years.'

'That's a very long shot.'

'He's our man, Tom. Motive: he obviously hates the cop who sent him up, and he spent some time in the prison hospital, a psychiatric case, as a result of the sexual abuse he suffered. I reckon that winds a man up. And don't bring up the lezzie bit. That would wind me up even more. Opportunity: he inherited a small fortune when he was in prison. And according to his bank manager, quite a lot of that money has been spent. He doesn't know what on, but Miller was clearly setting things up. Timing: he disappears in the same week that JJ does.'

'So has he been picked up?'

'Not yet. But he surely will be.'

'He could've left the country.'

'With JJ in tow?'

'He could've killed her first.'

'Oh. I thought we were assuming that she's still alive. Listen, if we have his face up on the box...'

Tom shook his head. 'The boss won't go for that. So he's broken parole. That happens every week. We have not a shred of evidence connecting him to JJ, save for that arrest thirteen years ago.'

'You've given up,' Andrea snapped. 'Well, I haven't.'

Gradually they settled into a routine. They

breakfasted, always accompanied by a glass of lime juice. 'Prevents scurvy,' Michael explained. He then checked out various ship matters while she did some cleaning. She cooked lunch, and they siesta'd in the wheelhouse. She cooked dinner, and they went to bed. They had sex, after his fashion: he fondled her desperately and then masturbated himself – which he seemed able to do without fully erecting – but the intimacy engendered by their peculiar relationship at least prevented any more outbursts of despairing rage. Then they slept.

Michael never relaxed his guard for a moment. Jessica came to expect that; she extended her wrists to be clipped into the cuffs whenever he left her alone in the wheelhouse or whenever he wanted to sleep, and never attempted to go into the saloon or galley – and the drawer full of knives – unless he was free to accompany her. By her transparent docility, her apparent acceptance of the situation, as well as submitting to sex whenever he wished it, she kept the peace. There were no more beatings or even a harsh word. And she had that precious 'we' to depend on. That gave her time, to watch, and think, and plan.

He never let her help around the ship, or taught her anything about handling either the sails or the instruments; she presumed he was acting on the principle he had first outlined to her: that if anything happened to him she would not be able to cope, and that therefore it was in her interests to make sure nothing *did* happen to him.

But he talked a lot about the yacht's gear, about things like bottle screws and grommets and standing or running rigging, things she had never heard of and did not understand, and he taught her how to tie various nautical knots, from a simple clove hitch to the somewhat more intricate bowline. And she learned a lot by just watching. He had a satellite navigator, but as this burned battery power, which in turn burned fuel, he relied more upon his GPS, or Global Position System, the simple hand-held position indicator, which worked off various satellites and used its own battery, for which he had several replacements – it was an instrument she had used herself often in her professional career. He would enter their position on the chart, using his slide rule to draw a neat line between one day and the next.

She found the chart fascinating, as it revealed their southern progress. Here again, his knowledge of the currents and winds was awe-inspiring, at least to a layperson like herself. She was also fascinated by the weather fax, would watch the changing patterns by the hour – whenever Michael switched it on. As with everything else electrical, he used it sparingly. And he never used his satellite television at all, as if he had turned his back on the world and wanted nothing more to do with it.

Incredibly, and disturbingly, she realized

that she was enjoying herself. She had never had more than a fortnight's holiday at a time, and then it had been back to the considerable tensions of the Protection Unit, the ever-present knowledge that it was her duty to lay her life on the line to ensure the safety of her client of the moment – whether she liked them or not. Now she had got her sea legs, to be able to utterly relax with not a care in the world, at least for the immediate future...

Even the sex was therapeutic. Due to her and Tom's job commitments, they had shared a bed on a very irregular basis. Now she was realizing how much she had missed a regular partner. But a murderer? Then again, suppose Michael was as he claimed – innocent. And in many ways he was a sensitive, cultured man. It was very easy to suppose that all his faults had been caused by the brutalization he had suffered in prison. So then, had he won after all, bent her to his will, gained the ascendancy he wanted over her mind as well as her body? No way, she told herself.

Sailing as close to due south as they were, once he had gained a sufficient offing into the Atlantic to remain a minimum of three hundred miles off the coasts of Portugal and Africa, they naturally crossed several shipping lanes. But Michael knew where these were as well, and when in the vicinity of other ships at night he used his radar. They saw a good number of ships during the day, but none were allowed to come close enough to have a good look at them – nor did they show any inclination to do so. As Michael had claimed, there was obviously no known link between the disappearance of Jessica Jones and the lone round-the-world sailor: his weekly calls to Lymington revealed no anxiety from either James or Peter.

Meanwhile, the weather grew warmer, while remaining amazingly fair. Michael explained that by leaving England in October they were not only avoiding the really bad autumnal weather north of the Tropic of Cancer, but should also have no trouble with the hurricane season. In any event, hurricanes, while they apparently spawned in the warm waters close to the African coast, never reached any great strength or size before approaching the West Indies, and *Maria Anna* was not heading in that direction.

Going south meant that Jessica could lie on the saloon roof, naked, to enjoy the sunshine, or even better, the rain squalls which began to appear from time to time. Michael obviously felt that she could get up to no mischief up there, nor was he any longer afraid that she might throw herself overboard. And she had no desire to do either. It was such a pleasure to be swamped in fresh water; she washed her hair again and again and again. It seemed to be visibly growing longer by the day.

The sudden abundance of fresh water made a difference in every way. Michael had an ingenious PVC arrangement in the form of a large inverted cone, which he could set in place of the mainsail whenever there was a rainstorm, and which collected a surprising amount of water to be funnelled through a hose into the fresh-water tanks; this meant that they could even wash their clothes, another great relief. Not that they bothered with clothes, most of the time.

When they reached the Doldrums, the wide area of calms that lay close to the Equator, there was a thunderstorm almost every day. By then Jessica had developed almost as much confidence in the yacht as Michael already possessed, and although her first tropical thunderstorm, so much more violent and both nerve- and ear-shattering than anything she had experienced in England, made her gasp in terror, accompanied as it was by rain so heavy it felt like hailstones hitting her skin, and which limited visibility to under fifty yards at times, she soon got used to them and even looked forward to them. The tropical thunderstorms were the first real bad weather they had experienced; she no longer counted the odd gale as anything of importance.

As for Michael ... she daily grew more ambivalent about him. She had always dreamed of adventure, which was why she had become a policewoman in the first place, and here she was enjoying the adventure of a lifetime, in an environment she would never have considered were she not actually experiencing it. Now Michael let her explore to her heart's content, whenever he was available to be with her, and she was fascinated by the way every square inch was utilized for some purpose, and the meticulous care with which all the food was stowed, the predetermined order in which it had to be consumed.

Only the engine room was barred to her. 'You wouldn't find anything of interest in there,' Michael said. The only fresh food they now had were the fish Michael caught by trawling a line astern. But these were plentiful, although they occasionally lost a catch to a predator. Jessica had never seen a shark's fin before, and she found these as fascinating as everything else. 'You don't want to fall overboard,' Michael told her.

When they crossed the Equator, he opened a bottle of champagne, and Jessica became quite giggly. 'There's a ceremony connected with crossing the line,' he told her. 'I have to shave you.'

'Only I don't have a beard.'

'That's a fact,' he agreed. 'I've been looking forward to it.'

For a moment she didn't know what he meant, then the penny dropped. 'You wouldn't.'

'I said, I've been looking forward to it.' He clipped her to the stanchion. She made no effort to resist him. It wouldn't have done her any good, and besides, she was at once curious and excited about the idea. 'Legs wide,' he told her, and knelt between them. 'Now you must keep very still.' He used a pair of clippers and then his own razor, one of the ultra-safety variety, but the feel of the blade scraping over her skin had her heart pounding, especially when he went between her legs to finish the job. 'There,' he said at last. 'Now we know what you really look like.'

She bent over to see for herself. 'Do you like me better with or without?'

'I like you any way,' he told her, but then added, 'I wonder how long it'll take to grow back?'

'Now it's my turn to do you.'

'You must be joking. Do you think I'm going to let you loose, even with a safety razor?'

The sight of her, quite literally naked, turned him on and he wanted sex. She even felt like it herself. The trouble was, it was becoming ever more easy to slip into a relationship with him. Well, she told herself, two people cannot be shut up alone together without forming a relationship. But that meant her sense of outrage at what he had done to her, was still doing to her, was becoming weaker by the day. Her feelings towards him remained ambivalent. What was he? A vicious, kidnapping pervert, or a very lonely man? A father figure, or a rapist? A man living out a fantasy, or a man bent on self-destruction? Or someone with whom she had been thrown together by fate and with whom she might well have to share the rest of her life? That was the grim thought lurking on the edge of her consciousness all the time, even if she daily grew more confident that she would be able to handle the situation when it came – without really wishing that day to arrive.

She felt that if she *was* going to handle it, which might involve having to take his life, she had to be certain of what *she* was, and that was even more difficult to determine; it was something she had never really considered before. She was a woman whose life had been entirely dominated by her profession, which had always required a feminist determination to prove herself as good as, if not better, than her male colleagues. And she had succeeded – until that afternoon she had so carelessly stopped to give a strange man directions, and thus was now being subjected to the most utter masculine domination. She was a victim.

But she was also affectionate and gregarious by nature, and there was only Michael to be affectionate to. Yet she was also, deep down inside, still outraged by what he had done. She was still determined to assert herself, to turn the tables, somehow, sometime. She still waited, coiled like a spring and poised, for him to lower his guard. And she thought he knew that.

A week after crossing the line they experienced their first really severe storm of the voyage. The wind howled out of the southeast, and the yacht struggled through bigger waves than Jessica had yet seen, close-hauled and reefed right down. Their routine went by the board; it was impossible to do more than heat soup in the galley, and the movement was too violent for sleep, or even sex. But thanks to his GPS, Michael was still able to enter their position every day.

'This wouldn't have been possible a few years ago,' he said. 'And with the total overcast we wouldn't have been able to use a sextant, either. We'd have had to operate by dead reckoning. You calculate the speed of the ship through the water, the amount of leeway, the strength of the current, and arrive at a position, based on your last known position. Properly done, it's actually amazingly accurate. They use dead reckoning on board ships like atomic subs, which have to remain submerged for long periods and so are unable to use satellites. Only of course they don't call it dead reckoning; the jargon is inertia navigating, and they use computers to analyse the information fed into them. With all that backup, a sub can navigate to within a matter of yards of its required position.' Jessica didn't really understand. She was too pleased that she was not seasick or afraid throughout the storm. And *Maria Anna* seemed to take everything with a contemptuous toss of the bow.

The storm abated after two days and they were back in calm seas under blue skies. 'Are we going to South America?' Jessica asked, peering over his shoulder as he marked

126

the chart.

'Only in a manner of speaking.' He prodded the end of the land. 'Ever heard of Cape Horn?'

'Yes. You mean that's where we're going?'

'We're going into the Pacific,' he explained. 'That means rounding Cape Horn. Or going the other way, round the Cape of Good Hope and then Australia and New Zealand. That's usually considered the easier route, because the prevailing winds are westerly, you see, so most of the time you're going downhill. But it isn't really. Below South Africa, the winds may be fair, but they hardly ever blow less than a gale; they call them the Roaring Forties. So you can carry them all the way back to the Horn, virtually. That's what the round-the-world racers do. But it's bloody uncomfortable. And if you turn up into the Indian Ocean you can run into all kinds of nastiness, either dead calm or big winds. Whereas if you go westabout, well, you have to beat your way into the Pacific, but it takes a much shorter time.'

'But you have to round Cape Horn,' Jessica said. 'I've read about it.'

'It can be pretty rough. But arriving at the turn of the year we stand our best chance of having good weather; it's summer down here. And once we're round, it's all plain sailing.'

'You've done this before?'

'No. I've read a lot about it, though.' He grinned at her. 'Scared?'

'No,' she said. And oddly, she was telling

127

the truth; he had revealed himself to be a consummate seaman, at least to her inexperienced eyes. She had complete faith in him.

A few days later they were awakened from their siesta by a tremendous roaring noise, and the yacht began to heave about as if in a gale. 'What the hell...' Michael ran up the companion and peered out of the wheelhouse windows. 'Holy shit!'

'What is it? Let me up.'

He came back down to release the handcuffs, and Jessica scrambled up behind him, stood at his shoulder to look out. It was a beautiful day, with blue skies and only a light breeze, and the yacht was under full canvas. But all around them the sea seethed and tossed in white foam, while huge plumes of water soared upwards and fell across them. 'Is it a reef?' she asked, although she couldn't believe they had run into a reef in the middle of the ocean.

'Worse,' he snapped. 'Whales.' He began dropping the mainsail, and then furled the jib.

Jessica climbed into the hatch the better to see, and now could make out the great greybrown bodies moving through the water to either side, enormous heads emerging briefly to spout, even more enormous tails thrashing the water into foam. 'They won't attack us, will they?'

'Not intentionally.' Michael was panting as

he worked the winch to wrap the foresail round its stay; the yacht came virtually to a halt, rolling in the disturbed water, with only the mizzen for stability. 'But if a flick from one of those tails, or a bump from one of those heads, were to open a seam, we'd go down like a holed bucket.'

Jessica swallowed. She hadn't been afraid since getting her sea legs. Now she was terrified. 'Shouldn't we try to get out?'

'Best to keep absolutely still. They don't bump into each other, so hopefully they won't bump into us. And they're moving away from us.' He stood behind her and put his arms round her waist, clasping her against him, and without thinking she brought up her hands to hold his. Although for the moment she was free, she had no desire to do anything about it. She needed the comfort of his arms and his strength. It was that dreadful simile he had used; down like a holed bucket. Suddenly the yacht was all the security in the world.

Slowly the school moved away from them, without touching them. Even after the last whale had left their vicinity, and the water had calmed, they remained standing, holding each other, watching the maelstrom vanish. 'I was scared,' she said.

'So was I.' He released her, went down into the saloon in search of the brandy bottle, while Jessica sat on the settee. It was the first time he had left her alone in the wheelhouse, unhandcuffed, since their last fight, weeks ago. But still she didn't have any urge either to try to use the radio or to wreck something. She was suddenly feeling very vulnerable.

Michael brought up two glasses. 'At three o'clock in the afternoon?' she asked.

'That was the nearest you have ever come to sudden death,' he told her, sitting beside her. 'Or me.'

She sipped. Actually, she had come closer to death than that, more than once, but she didn't feel like telling him that. And when previously she had been in danger, she had also been on duty, keyed up, ready to kill or be killed. This had come on her when she was totally relaxed, feeling totally secure. 'Are we likely to run into them again? Like maybe at night?'

'I shouldn't think so. That was a chance in a thousand. A mischance.' He kissed her. 'Tell you what, though. I'm going to alter course, just in case.'

Now, as if the whales had been a portent, the weather changed. The blue skies disappeared, and instead there was leaden grey. Even the sea looked grey. They were now south of the Tropic of Capricorn, and while it might be summer in the southern hemisphere, it was not very welcoming. The wind was fitful, sometimes quite strong and at others dead calm, while it came from a variety of directions. But they were slowly approaching the Horn. 'Look there.' Michael held her arm one morning and pointed to the south-east, then

130

handed her the binoculars. She focussed them on low hills. 'Those are the Falklands,' he said. 'So no funny business. Or have you got over that?'

'Of course,' she lied. But he didn't believe her, and it was back to the tying-up routine. He didn't call the islands, but she knew enough about radar by now to be sure they would almost certainly have been seen. But no one had any reason to stop them.

They celebrated Christmas a week after seeing the Falklands. By then they were again in an empty ocean, with not a ship in sight. Jessica heated up a plum pudding and Michael opened a bottle of champagne, and they both got quietly drunk. She wondered where she would be next Christmas. If anywhere.

Four days later they sighted land again, this time to the south-west. Jessica was in the head when Michael called her on deck. 'Argentina,' he said. She didn't like the look of it at all, as she could see nothing but serrated mountains – she gathered they were well south of places like Buenos Aires. And the wind was quite fresh and the sea lumpy. She shuddered, and he held her breasts to feel her nipples, which were as hard as ice-picks. 'I think you need to put on something warm,' he suggested, nuzzling her neck.

She dressed in a tracksuit and added the heavy sweater he had also bought for her, then joined him on deck to watch the approaching land. 'How far south of it do we go?' she asked.

'We need to give it a good berth. Something like twenty-five miles.' He peered ahead through the binoculars. 'Doesn't look too bad.'

'How long will it take?' she asked.

'A couple of days.'

This time she refused to admit she was scared, but it was certainly awe-inspiring as the land steadily came closer, and although the wind remained fresh rather than strong, it was from the west, which meant they were beating and therefore plunging, while the seas grew bigger. But the swell was very long, and they rose and fell with some regularity. Having bound and gagged her, Michael called Lymington. 'Just approaching the Horn,' he said. 'I'll probably be out for a day or two.'

'Good luck,' James told him.

Michael released her. 'Food,' he said. 'Make a big stew, something we can dip into whenever we're hungry.' As always, he accompanied her into the galley while she prepared the food, just so she'd not be tempted to try anything. But she could tell he was nervous. This was something outside of even his experience, no matter how much he might have read about it. 'What's the worst that can happen?' she asked.

'The seas are always big off the Horn,' he explained. 'If the weather's fine, that's not a problem. If it's bad, and the waves begin to break, you can be pitch-poled: the stern gets lifted up, the bow digs in, and the whole ship goes ass over tit. You very rarely experience something like that without sustaining serious damage.'

'But you said the weather would be good this time of year.'

'I said it *should* be.' He grinned at her. 'We'll make it.'

'*Got him!*' *Andrea announced triumphantly.*

Tom raised his eyes to heaven. 'Where?'

'*He's off Cape Horn.*'

'*Would you care to say that again?*'

'*You know all that money he spent over the past two years? Well, it had to go on something; there is no record of his living it up. So I checked into his pre-prison background, and found out that his hobby was sailing. That's where the money went. He was building a boat.*'

'*You said something about a quarter of a million.*'

'*It's a big boat. Equipped to go anywhere. Listen, I tracked down the shipyard, simply by chasing up every sizeable yacht built in the past two years. And guess what? I came across one named* Maria Anna.'

'*So?*'

'*Miller's wife, the woman he murdered, was named Mary Ann.*'

'*And you think he'd have a boat built and name it after a woman he stabbed twenty times?*'

'*Well, he always claimed he was innocent. Maybe he was.*'

133

'And he managed to have this boat built without his parole officer or his bank manager knowing about it?'

'Sure. For the purposes of the boat, he changed his name to Michael Lomas, and transferred funds from his Miller account to a Lomas account by means of cheques made out to non-existent people, which he then endorsed and paid into his second account. I traced the boat to a Lymington marina. They remember him well, because he set out to sail round the world, so he said, last October. And guess when he left? The night JJ disappeared.'

Tom stroked his chin. 'And you think JJ might be on board? How? You're not suggesting she went willingly?'

'Of course not. Miller/Lomas told everyone he was sailing single-handed. How he got her on board I have no idea. But he did. That he should leave the night of her disappearance is just too much of a coincidence.'

'Unless he took off because he had just murdered her.'

'Well, we'll never know until we stop that yacht, will we?'

'And you think he's off Cape Horn? How do you work that out?'

'He calls in every week, reports his position.'

'Would he take that risk if Jessica is on board, a prisoner?'

'Yes, he would, because he has to. It's standard procedure, and if he didn't, Lymington would have all the emergency services in the world out looking for him. Besides, he obviously feels he's in

134

the clear, having taken all that trouble to cover his tracks. The one problem is that Lymington has to wait for him to call in to contact him, and the last call was made several days ago. So he could have covered quite a distance by now. But the next time he calls...'

'We can tell the Chilean navy and air force where to find him. The trouble is, they are going to require proof that Lomas and Miller are the same man, and that we don't have.'

'We do have proof.'

'Such as?'

'Lomas forgot to garage his car. When the dock master on duty the night he left, James Martin, reminded him of this, he apparently got quite confused, then asked Martin to hold it for him till he returned. Martin agreed, if he was given a letter of authority. This Lomas gave him, and Martin still has the car. He showed it to me. I noted the number and got on to Traffic. That car is registered in the name of Peter Miller.'

Tom got up. 'Let's go see the boss.'

Jessica had never felt such a sensation of the sinister as they rounded the Horn. Michael had, as usual, been entirely right in his calculations, and the wind never got above twenty knots, force five on the Beaufort scale. Just to be safe he closed all the ports inside their steel shutters, rendering the interior of the yacht quite gloomy. But that compared well with outside of it: the skies remained grey, the seas even greyer, and the swell was bigger than she had anticipated, four to five hundred feet between each crest, while the crests themselves were fifty and more feet high. Changing course every two hours as she made deep tacks to work to windward, *Maria Anna* surged up the back of these monsters and then slipped down into the immense troughs beyond with a stomach-dropping slide. Even in force five there were quite a few breaking waves, and every so often the yacht was smothered in spray.

The worst aspect of the big seas was that once the yacht was in the troughs, the crests were high enough to rob her of the wind, so that she lost way and wallowed until taken up the back of the next monster. It wasn't difficult to imagine what it would be like were those immense walls of water being hurled about by a gale force wind.

And always to the north were the grey mountains of Tierra del Fuego. 'There's quite a big seaport somewhere there,' Michael told her. Out of which next morning there came a sizeable fishing fleet, some of which came quite close to them. 'Please don't try anything stupid,' Michael said. 'This simply isn't the place for it.' He gave one of his grins. 'They wouldn't understand you anyway, unless you speak Spanish.' But he kept her out of the wheelhouse so that none of the fishermen could possibly see her. Obviously they would make out the name of the yacht and be able to confirm that she had been sighted, and Michael was supposed to be alone.

★　★　★

Two days later they were sailing away from land and into the immense empty reaches of the Pacific. The skies were blue and the wind was suddenly fair and light. It was like stepping out of a vast cavern into broad daylight. 'That's the hard part of the voyage over,' Michael said. 'Nothing but blue skies and soft seas from here on.'

'What happens when we cross the Pacific?' Jessica asked.

'Do we want to cross the Pacific?' he replied.

She wasn't sure how to take that. She had understood from the very beginning that he didn't mean to return to England to face the inevitable charges that would be brought against him, unless he murdered her first, but over the months they had lived in such intimacy that that realization had become dulled. They still had sufficient food on board for another nine months. Did he really mean just to cruise about the Pacific for all of that time, and then...

But he would have to maintain his radio links with Britain, or they would become worried about him and send out search ships. He couldn't afford to risk that. Wouldn't they know where the signals were coming from? The trouble was, from a listener's point of view, he would be sending them from where he should be, somewhere in the Pacific.

He had been studying her expression. 'Relax,' he told her. 'Enjoy yourself. Do you know how many girls would give their eye-teeth, or a lot more, to be in your position?'

'I think I've given quite a lot,' she riposted.

He chucked her under the chin. 'And you've loved every minute of it. I know *I* have. Now it's calling time.' She sighed, sat on the settee berth, allowed herself to be trussed and taped. If she survived this voyage, the thing she would remember most, more than the sex or the beatings or the storms or the whales or even Cape Horn, would be being tied up at least once a day. And of course, gagged, on the days he used the radio.

He spoke with his friend Peter as usual, told him that he had rounded the Horn and was now in the Pacific. 'Would you give me your position, please?' Peter asked.

Michael frowned. 'Don't I always, old son?'

'Of course you do.' Peter was apologetic.

'I'll just check it to make sure.' Michael bent over the chart, used his dividers and slide rule, then turned back to the mike and gave the latitude and longitude.

Peter was apparently writing it down, and no doubt checking it with a chart of his own. 'That can't be right,' he said. 'Shouldn't you be further north?'

'I've abandoned that idea,' Michael said. 'I'm making for New Zealand.'

'You were going to lounge about the Central Pacific for a while.'

'So I've changed my mind. Call you next week. Over and out.' He closed down the set. 'Bastards.'

'Would you mind telling me what is going

138

on?' Jessica asked when he took the tape away.

'They're on to me.'

'What? How?'

'How the shit do I know? But he's never been that curious before.'

Jessica experienced a violent flutter of her heart. But wasn't this what she had always told him was bound to happen? What she wanted to happen? On the other hand, she was still alone with him on the yacht. And if he was backed into a corner... 'What are you going to do?'

He grinned. 'Give them a run for their money. I've given him a false position and a false track. What we need to do is get as far away into the Central Pacific as we can. Then we'll be a needle in a haystack.'

'They'll still find you. *Us.*'

'No way. They've only traced us this far because I've been calling every week. Well, no more calls. If they send out the emergency services, we'll be no worse off. Anyway, you'd better hope they don't find us.'

'Because if they do, you mean to murder me? Is that it?' No sooner had the words been spoken than she was biting her lip; she had never intended to bring that out into the open. But it was done now.

He took his hands away and stood up. 'I think you need a drink.' He pointed. 'Don't move.'

She sat with her hands between her legs, muscles tensed, until he returned with two glasses of rum and lime. 'I don't feel like alcohol,' she muttered.

'And I say you need it.' She took a sip. He leaned on the console. 'I don't want to murder you, JJ. I have become really fond of you. I think I have fallen in love with you.' She stared at him with her mouth open, and hastily took another sip. 'Have you nothing to say to that?' he asked.

'What am I supposed to say?' she snapped. 'That I have fallen in love with you?'

'That would be very nice.'

'You have got to be stark, staring mad. I suppose you are, or you wouldn't have dreamed up this idea in the first place. You have stalked me like a creep, hit me, injected me to lay me out, kidnapped me, beaten me, raped me – all but – kept me trussed up like a chicken for the pot, humiliated me ... and I'm expected to fall in love with you?'

She had expected a violent response, but he continued to regard her thoughtfully. 'It's a shame you still feel like that,' he said at last. 'I had hoped you might get used to the idea. Anyway, that is your twenty-first century woman spouting her usual nonsense. Because men, at least in Western Europe and North America, have been growing more and more wimpish with every generation, you women have been allowed to grow far too big for your pretty little pants. You ought to take a long look at history. Since the human race began, with the cavemen, women have been kidnapped for sex and children. And they got on

140

with it.'

'And you think they loved the men who did that to them?'

'There's plenty of evidence that they did. Have you never heard of the Sabine women?'

'I think so.'

'Well, just to refresh your memory, a whole lot of them were kidnapped by the early Romans for sex and children. Their menfolk naturally took offence at this, and attacked Rome. The two armies were all set to destroy each other when the Sabine women rushed from the city to throw themselves between the opposing forces, begging their fathers and brothers and presumably even erstwhile husbands to stop fighting their new husbands. And they succeeded. Jean-Louis David painted it. And there is no evidence that any of the Sabine women ever went home.'

'As you say,' Jessica remarked, 'that was a very long time ago.'

'Well, then, think of all the queens and princesses, even the great heiresses, who have been married off, willy-nilly, to someone chosen by their father.'

'You were not chosen by my father,' she pointed out coldly.

'I could have been. A hundred years ago. And you would have said to yourself, shit, I'm being sacrificed to that old man, probably for a few acres of land. But you would have accepted the situation, because you would have been brought up to accept it.'

'A hundred years ago. You must be the only

141

person in the world who doesn't recognize the injustice women suffered for thousands of years. But that is all history. We are living in the here and now. And no argument or evidence you can produce can alter that fact. And by the standards of the here and now you are the worst type of criminal, a man who should be locked away for the rest of his life.' She paused for breath, again biting her lip in case she had said too much.

'There's one little point you have over-looked,' he said. 'As you say, we are living in the here and now. And the here and now for us is this ship, on which I make the rules. And the rule I have made is that you are my woman, for as long as I want it that way.'

'And then?' Now she was in a fully defiant mood.

'It never pays to cross bridges until you come to them, just in case when you do come to them, they're no longer there.' He grinned. 'Our first business is to get the hell out of here. When we are safely lost, we are just going to loll in the sun for the next few weeks. Maybe the next few months. Then we'll talk about the future.' He handcuffed her to the stanchion, and went on deck to set the spinnaker.

She didn't dare press any further ahead than that. Presumably she should be reassured that he didn't want to kill her, that he had said he loved her. But she couldn't believe that. He loved her body, but she was just an object to him, his living blow-up doll – which he would one day puncture.

So, after three months, nothing had changed. She was no closer to gaining her freedom or guaranteeing her life. He had never dropped his guard for a moment, and she did not now suppose he ever would. That was the seaman in him. Sailors became so used to watching and checking and mistrusting the weather it became part of their lives; watching and checking and mistrusting his captive was no big deal to Michael.

Jessica studied the chart. *Maria Anna* was sailing north west, making excellent time before a very pleasant wind, and judging by the chart, she was heading towards a huge number of islands, atolls, coral reefs, some individual, others in clusters. Obviously, as this particular chart had a small scale, there was a lot of water between each island or group, but in the course of time they had to pass fairly close to some of them. Islands meant people, people meant fishing boats ... and she had at least six months to play with.

So, for the time being, obey Michael's orders, lie in the sun, cook, eat, sleep, and have sex – always without completion. She was surprised she was not getting fat.

'Do you believe him?' Tom asked. He and Andrea had gone down to Lymington together to listen to the radio conversation, which Peter, at Andrea's request, had recorded.

'I think he gave a false position,' Peter said.

'Has he ever done that before?' Andrea asked.

'I don't know. They always seemed reasonable before. There was no reason to doubt them, before.'

'What you mean is, you don't actually have a clue where he is. He may not have rounded Cape Horn at all, and be sailing in quite the opposite direction. He could be in the West Indies.'

'I think he'll be looking for empty water, not inhabited islands, if what you say is true, Miss Hutchins. But I agree, that may not necessarily be the Pacific.'

'Can't you trace where his signal is coming from?' Tom asked.

'Yes, I can, Mr Lawson. But there are two problems. One is I need more time than he usually spends on the air. The other is that I can't try until he calls again.'

'Shit!' Tom commented. 'You mean there is nothing we can do?'

'Well, you know, I'm sure he does listen to the radio. Why don't you put out a sort of general APB, telling the world, but especially him, that we know what he's up to, and that the sooner he turns himself in the better.'

'Can't be done,' Andrea said. 'And mustn't be done.'

'Why not?'

'It can't be done because we have no proof, even if we now know that he is actually Peter Miller, other than a set of coincidences and now this phoney position, that he has committed any crime greater than breaking his parole. Until we recover Miss Jones, we have nothing that would stand up in a court of law. Our boss would never go for a *public accusation. And it mustn't be done, because if he does hear it, the first thing he'll do is murder JJ.'*

'Don't you think he's already done that?' Tom asked miserably.

'No, I don't. Because if he has, the way he has covered his tracks, there is nothing to stop him from sailing into any port in the world. Like I said, without JJ we have nothing but suspicion.'

'So what do we do?'

'We can still mount a search,' Peter suggested. 'It would be quite reasonable for me to put out a general call, informing all shipping that I urgently need to contact *Maria Anna,* and asking them to contact this office in the event of any sighting.'

'You're on,' Andrea said.

The next fortnight was idyllic. The weather just got better and better, and warmer and warmer, as they cruised north-west. And Jessica's tan got deeper and deeper. And she felt strangely relaxed. The future was still a dark cloud, but they were looking for her. That was what mattered: they hadn't given up, and they were on her trail. 'Are we going to cross the Equator again?' she asked Michael.

'Maybe. Why?'

She giggled. 'I was wondering if you'd shave me again.'

He peered at her pubes; as usual, they were both naked. 'Might be an idea. I'd say you've grown back thicker than before. Would you like me to do it again?'

'Whatever turns you on.'

145

'Well,' he said, obviously turned on, and then frowned at the sound of the boom moving above his head. He went to the hatch and looked out. 'Wind's dropped.'

She also looked out. 'What an odd sky.' The blue had turned to a sort of burnished bronze, in which the sun appeared to be shining through a vast filter.

'Jesus!' Michael muttered, and went to the barometer. 'The glass has gone down three millibars.'

'Big deal.'

'Darling, this isn't England,' he reminded her. 'Three millibars in these latitudes means a blow. A bloody big blow.'

'We haven't had too much trouble with gales before.'

'I'm not talking about a gale.' He switched on the weather fax – something he hadn't done in the last couple of weeks – studied the printout for a few moments, then gave a low whistle. 'We've got a typhoon coming up our ass.'

The Storm

'Is it going to be very bad?' Jessica asked.

'I don't know,' Michael confessed. 'I've never been in a typhoon. But we'd better prepare for the worst.' He released the handcuffs. 'Do the same as before the Horn; prepare a big stew. I'll put up the shutters.'

Jessica went down the steps into the saloon. It was the first time she had been allowed in here, alone. Almost instinctively she opened the galley drawer to look at the knives. But to attempt something now, with the whole world apparently about to drop on them, didn't make sense; she needed Michael, at least until the storm was past. However...

She bit her lip as she looked at the largest of the knives. This was for gutting fish, and had an eight-inch-long blade. And she was naked. But if she couldn't conceal the knife about her person, she could still hide it where only she would know where it was, and where it would be readily accessible when she needed it.

Did she really want to use it? Actually to cut a man in whose arms she had lain every night for the past three months? But a man who was also a perverted kidnapper, a convicted murderer, and a continuing threat to her own life. She took the knife from the drawer, thrust it beneath the seat cushion on the settee berth where she invariably sat to eat, then began opening tins.

By the time she had the stew cooking Michael had joined her to screw down the last of the deadlights. 'That's as tight as I can make her,' he said. 'Save for the wheelhouse door. But that can wait until things actually start to happen.' There was still no wind, and although the yacht had all sails up she was rolling gently in the swell; he had handed the spinnaker several days before. Jessica left the stew secured with bungees to the stove rails, and went on deck. It was extremely odd, because although it was coming up to noon, the sky was gradually getting darker, yet there was no actual bank of cloud to be seen. And there were no whitecaps, either. It was as if the whole world had been put on hold, and the air was oppressively hot.

But she observed that the swell had increased to something like Cape Horn proportions, carrying the little ship up and then down, down, down, into troughs where the horizon was invisible. Michael was also on deck, aft, where he was bending several warps together. She joined him. 'Sea anchor,' he explained. 'I actually do have a patent sea anchor. I mean a large canvas thing to tow astern and reduce our speed. But from what I've read, they carry away quickly enough and you're left with nothing. Whereas if you tow a good length of warp astern, in a bight, it has practically the same effect.'

Jessica couldn't understand why he was worried about their speed; apart from being motionless at the moment, the fastest the yacht had ever sailed was about eight knots. When both ends of the warp were secured, and the centre, after being looped round the mizzen-mast, was coiled against the after window of the wheelhouse, from where it could easily be released, he went down to the engine room and brought out four gallon cans of oil. 'Heavy duty stuff,' he said. 'Stops the waves from breaking, so they say.' He strapped them together in the after head.

'How are you going to let the oil out?' she asked.

'At the appropriate time, if necessary, I'll pump it out through the loo. Now,' he said, 'I think we should both put some clothes on, as protection; there's a chance we may be thrown about. Two layers would be best.'

Jessica dragged on two tracksuits, one on top of the other. By the time she had done that, she was sweating heavily, and now it seemed closer and hotter than ever. Michael studied his various instruments, made calculations. 'The storm is going to carry us to the west,' he said. 'But as near as I can figure, we are four hundred miles from the nearest land. No matter how hard it blows, I reckon we have about four days before we're in any danger of hitting anything.'

She peered over his shoulders. 'What is the nearest land?'

'Don't get excited. It's just a coral atoll. Uninhabited. Wouldn't do us any good to run into it.'

'Those look pretty close.' She prodded the chart. 'The Marquesas.'

'But they're south-west of us, and a very long way away. The storm is going to carry us north-west.'

'Towards the Christmas Islands,' she suggested.

'Given enough time, perhaps. But as I say, even when pushed by hundred-mile-an-hour winds, we're not likely to get there for a week or two. No storm is going to last that long.'

'How long are you expecting?'

'Ten to twelve hours, I suppose. Depends how fast it's travelling.' He grinned at her and asked his usual question. 'Scared?'

'Yes.' Because for the first time he was so obviously scared.

They lunched as usual, but neither felt in the mood for a siesta today. Instead they watched the weather as the sky slowly turned from brown to black, spreading out of the east. Michael furled the jib down to the size of a handkerchief, and reefed the main right down as well. He even took a reef in the mizzen. The yacht continued to roll sluggishly, the log showing almost no movement. Jessica kept looking out of the wheelhouse door, the only port still unsealed, enjoying the sensation of having her arms free.

She was where she was when, in the middle of the afternoon, there was a sudden flash of lightning which seemed to cut the entire sky in two. For a moment she was blinded, and before she had recovered there was a tremendous peal of thunder, seeming to be immediately over the ship. The door was wrenched open and Michael, who had been on deck, tumbled into the cabin. She closed the door behind him, and helped him fit the steel plate in place. 'What happens if we're struck?' she asked. That possibility had never bothered her in the 'ordinary' thunderstorms they had experienced in the Atlantic.

'It'll be the mast. There's a conductor.'

Through the small clear-view screen let into the steel shutter above the wheel – it was made of thick glass which, when switched on, would rotate so rapidly as to throw all water off – they could see that the lightning was almost continuous, as was the thunder, an unending roar, but even this was now deadened by the thudding of the rain on the cabin roof. Looking through the screen Jessica watched the drops digging into the surface of the yet calm sea, although the swell was bigger than ever. 'Well,' she said, 'so far so good.'

'There's an old sea saying,' Michael said. 'When the rain comes before the wind, then masts and spar and sails must mind.'

'Doesn't really scan,' she pointed out.

He went below to the saloon and returned

with two glasses of brandy.

'You think this is a good idea?' she asked.

'Essential.' He had also brought up the bottle, which he stowed in one of the drawers in the port locker. 'We're going to need a lot of that before the night is out.'

It was uncanny, to be sitting in semi-darkness in the wheelhouse, surrounded by the noise of the rain and the thunder, dazzled by the flashes of lightning, and with the yacht hardly seeming to be moving at all. It gave Jessica a sense of unreality. That the yacht *was* going to move, violently, and sometime soon, was certain. But she knew she couldn't remain tensed and poised until it did. The brandy certainly played its part in relaxing her. Michael had said the storm would not last more than twelve hours. She didn't know if he counted it as actually having begun with the thunderstorm. But even if it hadn't...

She had early in her life evolved a method of dealing with crises, such as going to the dentist, where one was passively at the mercy of outside forces. The secret was to think right through whatever lay ahead. Thus, if the dentist's appointment was for half past three, and you knew it would last half an hour, one set one's mind, like the automatic cooking time on an oven, for four o'clock. Whatever happened in between had no reality. And it had worked in the past. Suddenly it would be four o'clock, and all the pain and discomfort that had gone on before was just a bad dream.

She needed that approach now. It was just coming up to four in the afternoon. She needed to set her mind to dawn tomorrow. Surely the storm would have passed by then. Dawn tomorrow.

'You okay?' Michael asked.

'I'm fine. What exactly is the drill?'

'There's not a lot we can do. I'm going to helm, for as long as I can. But after that ... it's a matter of keeping one's head down.'

'Can't you heave to and sit it out?'

'Not if it's a real blow. Because after a while the wind will be too strong, and we'd have to run off. Trying to do that after having hove to could be risky. No, I'm prepared to run before it from the start. But I can manage on my own. Why don't you lie down. Make sure all the leeboards are up.'

'I'd rather stay here for a while,' she said.

He raised his eyebrows, then kissed her. 'We'll make a great team.'

Jessica sat on the settee berth, checked her watch. Four thirty. Just over twelve hours to dawn. Where the fuck was the storm?

It came so suddenly she was taken by surprise. The first thing she heard was the loudest screaming noise she had ever experienced. It made her think of an express train entering a tunnel with its whistle at full blast. Added to the thunder and the rain, it left her ears feeling like someone had blown a bugle into each of them at the same time. And it

153

didn't abate, but kept up the shrieking howl, immediately above her head.

There was no immediate response from the sea, but the yacht first went over on to her side, and then, coming back up, slowly gathered way. Michael immediately seized the helm, peering through the clear-view screen to oversee the waves. Soon *Maria Anna*, even under her almost non-existent sails, was rolling and pitching, and creaming along at several knots.

'Whee!' Jessica shouted. It was certainly exhilarating. But then she went to the tiny view port in the door, having to hang on to the grab-rails to stop herself from falling over, and looked out at the sea. The afternoon was still entirely overcast, and very dark, but she could make out the whitecaps surging by, each one picking up the yacht and driving it forward.

She glanced at Michael, hunched over the helm; even through the thick sweater he was wearing she could see his muscles straining. But so far he was in control.

At dusk she went below and brought up two mugs of the stew, and fed him with a spoon, hanging on to the console. By then the violent motion had become almost normal, but she gasped when she looked at the log and saw that *Maria Anna* was travelling at twelve knots down the reverse side of each swell, slowing to almost nothing in the troughs. This was when the following waves caught up with her, picking her up and hurling her onwards. But always she regained speed sufficiently to draw away from them before they could lift her stern. They could do this forever, she thought. As long as someone was on the helm. 'Would you like me to spell you?' she shouted.

'Do you know anything about helming boats?'

'You never taught me,' she pointed out. 'But I can try.'

'Forget it.'

'You can't hold her all night.'

'Yes, I can. Look, go below, or something.'

Jessica bit her lip as she went down to put the empty mugs in the sink, then sat on the starboard berth. The motion was easier down here, and she drew up her legs and secured the leeboards to stop herself from being thrown out. She moved to and fro with the roll, but with a reassuring sense of safety; from where she was she couldn't see out, and the noise and the motion had settled into a pattern.

By eight o'clock it was utterly dark, and Michael had switched off the light in the wheelhouse to avoid being dazzled. Jessica was surprised to discover that she had dozed off, and what had awakened her was a louder than usual noise from astern. 'Shit!' Michael muttered. 'Hold on!' he bawled. Jessica clutched the strap for the leeboard, as suddenly the yacht fell away from beneath her, at

155

the same time as she heard a terrible crash from aft; she realized that a wave coming up astern had actually broken on them. Oh, my God, she thought. We're going down, down, down. It could only be a matter of seconds before the steel plates buckled to allow the ocean to come rushing in.

She released the leeboards and scrambled out of the berth and up the steps to the wheelhouse. Michael was wrestling with the helm, shouting curses. 'I've lost steerage!' he shrieked. As he spoke the yacht turned sideways to the seas, and went over. Jessica found herself lying on the wheelhouse floor, feeling as if she had been trampled by an elephant. Then she realized that it wasn't the wheelhouse floor. It was the wheelhouse roof. The yacht was upside down!

Jessica screamed, even as she became aware that books, charts, cushions, accompanied by the half-empty brandy bottle, were cascading about her, followed by a splintering crash as the big radio broke loose and came smashing on to the roof, fortunately missing her, but exploding into a mass of valves and transistors and other components. Where Michael was she had no idea, and before she could gather her wits she was sliding again, down to the port shutters, and then actually finding herself sitting on the deck as the yacht came back up, surrounded by another cascade of debris.

Again before she could determine exactly what was happening, *Maria Anna* was struck by another wave and knocked down; this time she did not go right over, however, but lay on her side for a few seconds before righting herself. At the after end of the wheelhouse, Michael was opening one of the shutters just far enough to release the warp. In that brief second, however, Jessica saw a whole succession of monstrous, rearing, white-topped mountains of water, black in the darkness, but streaked with foam. If one of those broke while the after window was open ... but a moment later it was slammed shut and bolted. Michael looked round. 'You all right?'

Jessica felt bruised from head to foot. 'I think so,' she said. 'My God, we were upside down!' Even as she spoke there was another rush of sound, and the yacht went over on her beam ends again. Jessica found herself hanging on to the helm to avoid being thrown into the windows once more. Michael was not so lucky, landed with a crash that left him dazed. Jessica inhaled the smell of the stew; there was no way the pot – even strapped in place – would have stayed on the stove in the capsize.

The yacht came upright, and Michael slid down the after companionway to start emptying oil into the loo and pumping it out. He was gone for some time, but the motion definitely eased. Then his head emerged at the top of the ladder. 'Damage control,' he said. 'I'll check aft and the engine room. You check forward. Use a flashlight.'

There were two in the locker by the helm, and this had remained shut, thanks to its

157

safety catch. Jessica found her light, shone it down the steps, on to the chaos she had anticipated. The pot had indeed upended and there was meat stew everywhere, stuck to both the roof and the carpet; the mugs in the sink together with several cups and plates had broken loose and were shattered; the cool box – which they still used for overnight storage as the daily electricity charge kept the temperature down – had burst open to add its contents to the general chaos; the knife she had secreted beneath a cushion had flown away, with its cushion, and was embedded in the bulkhead. Hastily she pulled it out and restored it to its drawer; time enough to regain it later.

At the next lurch of the yacht she was thrown on to the port berth, but the ship came up again fairly rapidly this time, and she deduced that the oil was having an effect. How long would the oil last? She looked at her watch; it was nine o'clock. Dawn seemed an awfully long time away, and the wind was still howling as loudly as ever.

She closed the cool box, dragged the carpet up to raise a floorboard and look into the bilges; they were almost dry, the various plastic bottles still intact. She stuck a finger into such moisture as there was and tasted it; it was faintly salty but not enough to be sea-water, therefore it was either condensation or something that had got in from above.

She crawled forward, thrown left and right as the yacht rolled and pitched, but the movement was perceptibly easier than before. She opened the door to the forward sleeping cabin, and was bombarded by various tins and packets that came pouring out. Getting into the forepeak took time, because the spare sails and a good deal of the additional stowed food had also broken loose in the capsize and lay in every direction. She scooped them out to add to the mess on the saloon floor, and again groped up a floorboard – and was again relieved to find the bilge was dry. This was some ship.

As the stew was obviously irrecoverable she tucked a tin of Christmas pudding into her tracksuit and made her way back to the wheelhouse on her hands and knees, as the yacht was still rolling to her scuppers, but Michael had not returned. She put the tin on the deck and crawled down the after companion, to find the cabin in as great a chaos as forward, sheets and blankets and duvet and pillows tossed about, but at least it was not all stuck up with food; she didn't feel like investigating the head at that moment. But Michael was in there, pumping away. 'That's the last,' he panted. 'But it should keep things quiet for an hour or so.'

'Is the engine room all right?'

'Boy,' he said, 'are we lucky. Not a pipe burst. Not even a battery displaced.'

'Whee,' she said. 'I'm afraid there's no hot dinner. But I have some Christmas pudding.'

'Instant energy. Sounds great,' he said, and returned to the wheelhouse.

★ ★ ★

Jessica was amazed at how the human mind could adapt to the most outrageous circumstances. The noise, the motion, the knowledge that they had had the most narrow escape, all settled into a pattern. They sat on the wheelhouse floor, as it was the safest place to be, and ate Christmas pudding with their fingers. They didn't say much, as they had to shout in any event. When Jessica looked at her watch again it was midnight. Only four hours to go, surely. But the storm was showing no sign of abating. 'Have we still got sails up?' she shouted.

'I have no idea,' he confessed. 'We'll have a look when it's daylight. But we have spare sails.' He had regained both his nerve and his confidence, no doubt because they were still alive and coping. And his confidence spread to her. Only four hours. How she was praying for daylight.

The next hour passed without any great increase in the motion. The yacht was being held before the wind, careering onwards, but both its speed and its direction were controlled by the warp trailing astern and acting as an immense rudder.

Then there were several violent rolls and jerks, and Jessica gathered that the last of the oil was no longer having an effect. She looked at her watch: two fifteen. Less than two hours to go. But there was still no sign of the wind dropping. She endured the nerve-shattering

160

feeling of the ship being picked up, and up, and up by a wave breaking under the stern. 'Oh, Jesus!' Michael shouted.

Jessica knew they were going over again. She turned on her knees and threw both arms round the steel upright for the steering chair, pressing her face against the metal. She wasn't aware of praying, but she knew she was. She was lifted from the deck, and hugged the steel tube tighter. Her legs were flailing in the air, but there was something wrong with their direction. She panted, still hugging the tube, and realized what was wrong: the yacht was not rolling over as before, but was being pitch-poled, as Michael had described it: her stern being thrown so high that her bows were driving down and catching in the water, so that she was about to capsize, stern over bow.

Jessica screamed, again and again, more to release the tension than because she was terrified. But she was terrified as well. She heard a succession of sharp, dramatic noises, and conceived that the hull was splitting asunder. Then the wheelhouse roof was again the floor, and she was still hanging on to her tube, panting and weeping. It has to come back up, she thought. It simply has to. And it did, but in a different manner than after the capsize. Jessica found herself again sitting on the deck, still with her arms wrapped around the tube, even if rivers of pain were running up and down her muscles. And again the yacht was rolling to and fro, but unlike earlier, the movement was neither as fast nor as violent. Oh, my God, she thought. We must be taking water. We're sinking! 'Michael!' she screamed into the gloom. 'Michael!'

There was no reply. She released the tube and slithered across the wheelhouse deck, moving her arms from side to side. The darkness was intense, and she had no idea what had happened to the flashlights. Or to Michael, as she did not encounter him. But he couldn't have been knocked overboard, not from a totally enclosed cabin. She reached the after companion before she realized it, and fell down the steps to the corridor between the fuel tanks. It was dry. There was no water anywhere inside the hull. And the ship's rolling had a liveliness she had not known before. She understood what had happened: the masts must have gone. That left *Maria Anna* helpless, but also buoyant, tossed about like a cork by the waves, but also, like a cork, certain to stay afloat unless something gave way and the ocean got in.

She crawled into the cabin, and lay on the floor, because down here the motion was marginally less violent. And although she was sliding back and forth between the bed and the head door, in the middle of a mass of debris, she didn't think she would come to any harm. As to whether she had already come to any harm, that would have to wait. She was a mass of bumps and bruises, but she didn't think she had broken anything – yet.

And suddenly she was utterly exhausted.

And almost relaxed. There was nothing she, or Michael, could do now. She was aware of the yacht being picked up and rushed onwards by breaking water, all sound obliterated by the tremendous hiss of the waves. But then each wave passed on, and *Maria Anna* was left tossing in its wake. She was also aware of a bumping on the hull; that had to be one of the masts. The sound was muffled, and she supposed it was still wrapped in its sail. In any event, there was nothing she could do about that, either, even if there was a risk of them being stove in. The yacht would either survive, or it would sink. If it survived, they would survive with it. If it sank...

Her head drooped.

When Jessica awoke, she was for a moment uncertain where she was, aware only of pain and movement. But something was missing from her nightmare. Noise! There was a lot of sound, but it was mostly slurping water hitting the hull. The dreadful cacophony of the thunder and the lightning, and above all the wind, was gone. And for all the steel shutters, there was enough light getting in the view port and the clear-view in the wheelhouse to tell her it was daylight. And the storm had passed. Leaving what behind?

She sat up, pushed hair from her eyes. She felt utterly battered, both physically – she dared not imagine what kind of bruises she had accumulated – but also mentally; her brain felt absolutely dead. All she wanted to do was sleep for a week. But there was so much to be done. Like enjoying the fact that she was alive!

She blinked around herself. The cabin was a total chaos, mattress and bedclothes flung helter-skelter, books and videos lying everywhere; at least the television set and the recorder were still in place. The door to the head had burst open and she could see a similar mess in there. And always there was the steady thump-thump on the hull, but much less violent than before.

She held on to the mast to pull herself up, and promptly fell down again. She gritted her teeth, and crawled to the companionway, then up the steps into the wheelhouse. Here the chaos was no less, composed mainly of cushions and navigational instruments and shattered pieces of radio, all overlaid with brandy. And in the middle of the mess there lay Michael, on his face, arms thrown out, legs curled up. Oh, my God! she thought. She knelt beside him, turned him over. He was breathing, but there was a huge bruise on his forehead, and she supposed there were as many bruises on his body as she knew were on hers. She looked left and right for something to revive him with, then crawled back to the after companion to gain the head, and filled a tooth mug she found on the deck with fresh water. She was back at the foot of the steps before she checked herself, and sat on the bottom step to think.

What was she doing? Michael was the man

who had kidnapped her, raped her – as far as he was able – tied her up, beaten her ... and now he was helpless. He was also the man she was required to arrest. She was utterly relieved that he wasn't dead; she didn't know what she'd do without him out here in the middle of the ocean on a wrecked yacht that might be about to sink. But this was the first opportunity she had had to gain her freedom and establish her authority. At least until she had discovered whether the yacht *was* about to sink or not.

She went back up the steps. Michael had not moved. But his breathing was even, and he would soon recover consciousness. She knew where he kept the handcuffs, in a drawer beneath the console. This had as strong a latch as any of the others, and had stayed shut throughout the various capsizes and knockdowns. She took out the cuffs, put one on his right wrist. Then it was a matter of dragging him across the deck to the settee berth. He was a big, heavy man, the more so as he was inert, but, panting and pouring sweat, she made it until she could carry his right arm up to the upright, bring up his left wrist, and then cuff that as well, round the steel stanchion. Then she sat on the floor and panted for several minutes. She wondered how long he had been out. Since the pitchpole, which had been at least three hours ago. That was a long time. Suppose he had brain damage? But there wasn't a lot she could do about that. And it was more likely that he had

165

just passed out from tension and exhaustion – as she had done.

Her throat was dry, and she went below aft and pumped some fresh water into the tooth mug, drank it, and felt better. She would have loved a cup of coffee, but she didn't feel up to facing the saloon at that moment. It would have to be done, but she reckoned it could wait until after she had found out her exact situation.

With some effort she unbolted the steel panel covering the wheelhouse door, pushed them both back, and inhaled the fresh air which immediately filled the yacht. She climbed out and stood on the deck, overseeing a scene of even more complete chaos than below, a mass of cordage and steel rigging and collapsed aerials; as she had guessed, both masts had gone – the satellite, radar and radio aerials with the mizzen – but remained connected to the yacht by their various stays. Although the wind had dropped there was still a fresh breeze, and the swell remained enormous, quite shutting out the horizon except for brief moments when they were on a crest, and there was still a good deal of breaking water; almost immediately she was soaked in spray.

The yacht rolled whenever a wave broke close to it, but as far as Jessica could tell, *Maria Anna* was still perfectly buoyant. Cautiously, holding on at every step, she picked her way through the mess, round the wheelhouse to the port side. The masts, as she had surmised, remained wrapped in their sails, but they were still striking the hull and she couldn't allow that to continue. But how to get rid of them?

She crawled back round the deck and into the wheelhouse. Michael, slumped on the floor with his arms above his head and secured to the stanchion, was groaning and making abortive tugs. She stooped beside him. 'Michael! Wake up!' His eyes opened, half-focussed, and then closed again. She wondered if he had a concussion. She went down to the after head, filled the tooth mug with water again, and brought it into the saloon. She knelt beside him, and stroked water on to his lips and eyes.

Again his eyes opened, more positively. 'God,' he muttered. 'What happened?'

'We survived,' she said. 'Aren't you happy about that?'

He blinked at her, then looked right and left, then again tugged on his arms. 'You little bitch.'

She kissed him on the nose. 'Sauce for the gander.'

'Listen,' he said. 'You let me go or I am going to take the skin from your ass.'

'What you need to understand,' she said, 'is that if the skin is going to be taken from anyone's ass, it is going to be yours, if you annoy me. Now listen. Both masts have gone, and are threatening to hole the hull. I have to get rid of them. Do you have an axe? You must have an axe.'

'Fuck off,' he said. She rocked back on her heels. 'Why don't you face facts?' he suggested. 'You're helpless without me. You don't know one end of a boat from the other. Now, just release me, and we'll forget this happened. I'll get rid of the masts.'

Jessica stood up. 'If that's the way you want to play it. Right.' She considered. He simply had to have an axe, or some powerful cutting tool other than a kitchen knife. She was pretty sure it wasn't in the after cabin, and he had never seemed too bothered about her going forward on her own. There was only one compartment on the ship into which he had never allowed her, whether on her own or with him.

She went down the after companion. 'Hey!' he said. 'I need something to drink. And my head ... Jesus!'

'You'll have to wait,' she told him, and opened the engine-room door. It was utterly dark in here, but when she tried the light switch, the bulbs glowed. As Michael had said they would, the batteries had survived the double capsize, strapped into their trays as they were. She paused in the doorway, amazed at the intricacy both of the engines and their various fuel pipes. It was all remarkably clean and well cared for. She was glad of that. These two were her only hopes of survival. Michael had said they were only four hundred miles from the nearest land. Surely there was sufficient fuel left to take them four hundred miles.

But first, the axe. And there it was, secured in a wall bracket which had been strong enough to prevent it from flying loose. And beside it ... She stared at the guns. There were three of them, also firmly secured in place: a shotgun, a rifle, and a revolver; beneath them were satchels of bullets and spare magazines for the rifle, and this was an Armalite M-16 Mark II, her very favourite weapon, while the revolver was a Smith and Wesson thirty-eight, another gun with which she was totally familiar. Suddenly she had the whole world at her feet. She freed the axe and returned to the wheelhouse. 'Quite a smarty-pants, aren't you,' Michael remarked.

Clearly he realized that if she had found the axe she had also found his armoury, and was furious at the way things had turned out. Well, he had every reason to be: she wasn't going to forget anything he had done to her in a hurry. 'I'm happy,' she told him.

'When do I get a drink?'

'When I have nothing better to do.'

She went on deck. There were six links connecting the masts to the ship: the forestay and three amidships stays retaining the mainmast, and two aft holding the mizzen; the backstay had parted. Both main and mizzen had snapped off about six feet above the deck, carrying with them not only the aerials but also the various connecting lines for the instruments – not that she had much use for the aerials, as the main radio was in pieces.

169

But having considered the situation, she went below again and switched off the electrics to avoid any risk of a shock. 'Listen,' Michael said.

She ignored him, hunted in the seat lockers, and found a length of stout line. Then, as the morning was growing hot, she stripped off her tracksuits and replaced them with a safety harness, which secured her like a corset. To this she attached the line. 'You look as pretty as a picture,' he told her. 'Now listen.' She continued to ignore him, and returned on deck. 'Listen, for God's sake!' he shouted.

She closed the wheelhouse door behind her so she wouldn't have to do that. Then she tied the length of line round the base of the mainmast, went forward, and began hacking at the forestay. She had never used an axe before, and she quickly realized that the real danger was to her toes, followed by the toe-rail. Meanwhile, as the stay itself was metal, even when she connected it was more a matter of sparks than any immediate reward. But she gritted her teeth and kept swinging, until she collapsed to her hands and knees with exhaustion. Then she realized that the stay was actually fastened to the deck by means of an elaborate steel screw. Was this the bottle screw Michael had talked about?

The screw was secured at each end by a nut, and consisted of a long thread through a metal body which she supposed could be compared to a bottle. It could therefore be lengthened or shortened to adjust the tension on the stay and thus the mast; all she needed to do was release it altogether. But the nuts were too tightly turned for her fingers. She got up, and went below. 'You wouldn't listen,' Michael said.

'Oh, shut up,' she recommended, and hunted through his tool drawer to find a wrench. By now she was again dripping sweat, so she abandoned work while she went down to the head and showered. Michael watched her to'ing and fro'ing with brooding eyes. He had pushed himself up until he was sitting on the settee berth, but there was no way he could get free of the handcuffs. Having bathed, Jessica examined herself. As she had supposed would be the case, there were massive bruises on her back and hips; even her breasts felt tender. She found some soothing cream and rubbed it on, then dressed herself in a clean tracksuit and a pair of trainers – now that the sun was out the deck was becoming quite hot – added the harness, and went back to work, armed with the wrench.

It was still very tiring, as the nuts seemed almost to have seized. She returned to the engine room to find a can of lubricating oil and smothered all the screws, but it took her an hour to free the forestay and two of the midship stays. By then she was again exhausted, and her hands and fingers ached. She had another shower, changed her tracksuit, and sat on the settee beside him to rest. 'Bitch,' Michael mumbled.

'Would you like an early lunch?' she asked.

171

'I am dying of thirst.'

'Oh, yes.' She filled the tooth mug, sat beside him, and held it to his lips.

'Listen,' he said. 'Let's be sensible about this, JJ.'

'I entirely agree,' she said. 'You just sit there, and let me get on with it. Don't worry, I'm not going to kill you. What I *am* going to do with you we'll talk about when I've tidied up the ship.'

He kicked at her in reply. She had to throw herself away from his flailing feet, as he brought up one and then the other, thrusting with such force that she fell off the settee on to the deck with a thump. She reacted with instinctive anger, scrambling up, evading the next kick to get inside his legs, and hit him across the face, once, twice, a third time, panting. He brought up his knees to attempt to hold her against him, but she avoided them easily enough, staggered across the cabin, and without thinking picked up the axe.

He gazed at her in consternation, seeing the fury in her eyes. His mouth opened, and then closed again. Jessica had raised the axe. Now she slowly lowered it again. 'Well,' she said. 'Now we know where we stand. I might even use this, the next time.'

In Control

'You can't blame me for trying,' Michael said. 'You tried, when you first came on board.'

'I can blame you for everything,' Jessica said. 'And I do.'

'I need to go to the loo.'

'Keep your legs crossed,' she recommended. She went on deck and continued twisting away with the wrench. It was nearly noon by the time she had freed both masts; they promptly sank. Then she used the axe to cut away the warp that was still trailing from the remains of the mizzen; she didn't reckon it could possibly do them any good now. By then the wind and the sea had gone down some more; she reckoned even the swell was subsiding, although she could still have been within a hundred yards of land or another ship and not known it.

Utterly exhausted, she returned below and sat on the steering chair. 'What a mess,' she remarked, looking around her.

'You'll have even more to clean up if I don't get to the loo,' he told her.

Jessica went below and crawled into the engine room. She chose the pistol, on the grounds that either the rifle or the shotgun, if she had to use them, would cause too much damage. She returned into the wheelhouse, the pistol in her hand. 'You want to be careful of that thing,' he said.

'Just don't do anything stupid,' she recommended, and unlocked one of the handcuffs. He brought his hands together to rub his wrists. 'Down you go,' she said. 'Moving very carefully.'

He looked at her, then at the gun. 'You ever fired one of those things?'

'Yes,' she said. 'It's my job. I thought you were in a rush?' He went to the after companionway. 'Slowly,' she said, moving behind him.

He went down the companion. The yacht was still rolling, and he had to clutch at the door to stop himself from losing his balance. But she knew what was in his mind and thrust out her foot past him, kicking the panel away from him. He turned, eyes blazing, lunging at her, and looked into the barrel of the pistol, held in both hands, and aimed straight between his eyes. For a moment they glared at each other, Michael evaluating whether or not she would actually use it, Jessica considering the same point. But the risk was all on his side, and he turned and went into the head. Jessica stood in the doorway to watch him, the pistol still levelled. 'Kinky,' he remarked.

'Maybe I am,' she said. 'You'd enjoy that, wouldn't you?'

His trouble was, he couldn't tell when she

174

was serious and when she was having a private joke. He ran his hand over his chin. 'I need a shave.'

'Later,' she said. 'But you can clean your teeth.'

'What about a shower?'

Jessica considered. 'Why not. You could use one.' He stripped, stepped into the shower stall. 'Leave the curtain open,' she said.

'It'll make a mess.'

'So what's new?'

'Why don't you join me?' he asked.

'Just do it, before I change my mind.'

He showered, then she let him find some clean clothes, always keeping the pistol levelled at him while at the same time remaining six feet away from him. She could tell that his brain was buzzing like a saw as he tried to make up his mind whether he could risk tackling her or not. But as she had anticipated, he decided against it. He would likely be thinking the same thing she had at the beginning of the voyage: that a better opportunity must arise, when she relaxed her guard. But he had never done that, so why should she?

She locked the handcuffs back into place once he had reseated himself on the settee berth in the wheelhouse. 'That feels a whole lot better,' he said. 'When do we eat?'

'Now,' she said. She was also hungry. 'But it'll have to be some more of that plum pudding, cold, until I can get things cleaned up.'

She sat on the berth beside him, the pistol

175

tucked into her waistband, and fed him with a spoon, alternately with herself. 'You look like a gangster's moll,' he remarked.

'And you look like a gangster,' she retorted.

'What do you mean to do?' he asked. 'You won't get any joy out of even the VHF without an aerial.'

'I reckoned that. Well, first I'm going to clean up this God-awful mess. Then I'm going to start those engines, and drive us to the nearest land.'

'Just like that?' he sneered. 'You don't know how to navigate. Or how to steer.'

'I reckon I'll pick it up,' she said. 'But it would be simpler if you'd tell me how to do it.'

'And go to gaol? Do you take me for an idiot?'

'You probably are an idiot,' she agreed. 'For attempting this caper in the first place. And yes, you are going to go to gaol. But how you go to gaol, and on what charge, and thus for how long, might depend on how much you cooperate with me.'

'Get lost,' he said. 'You're going to have to turn to me, eventually, to get anywhere.'

'Don't hold your breath,' she advised him, and went forward.

She needed to start with the saloon, not only because it was the biggest job, but also because it was important for cooking. But that wasn't practical until she had attended to the fore cabins, because the contents there had spilled out.

Patiently she restored the spare sails in the forepeak – not that she could visualize their ever being used again – and then the various tins and plastic bottles. Then she tackled the forward cabin. But she already had the germ of an idea, and left the forward head vacant. Repacking the tins without using this space involved a slight list to starboard, but she could sort that out later.

It was mid-afternoon by the time she had restored order, and she was again exhausted and bathed in sweat. And Michael was again shouting from the wheelhouse. 'I need to use the loo.'

'Anyone would think you had a bladder problem,' she grumbled. But of course, going to and from the head, which involved being released from the berth, was his best chance of overpowering her if she made a mistake. That was where the spare head came in handy; she didn't really want him watching her all the time, anyway. And there was a stout metal grab-rail in the forward head. She climbed to the wheelhouse and released him, pistol levelled. 'Use the forward head.'

'That's full of food.'

'Not any more.'

'This is a big job. You going to watch me do that too?'

'I don't think that will be necessary. Go down and sit down.' He obeyed, frowning, and she clipped the handcuffs round the grab-rail, then pulled down his pants. 'There

177

you are,' she said. 'Now you can go as often as you like, for as long as you like.'

'You can't keep me chained up down here,' he complained. 'I never did that to you.'

'Probably because you never thought of it. Don't call me. I'll have a look-in when I've nothing better to do.'

'Bitch!' he shouted. 'When I get free...'

She ignored him, went up to the wheelhouse, lay on the settee and had a nap. She hadn't realized how tired she was. When she woke up it was all but dusk, but Michael had subsided and she felt quite fresh again. There were so many questions hammering at her brain, questions she would have to answer for herself, as she could expect no cooperation from Michael. Such as, how much electric power did she have? The sun was low in the western horizon now, but it had shone quite brightly from time to time during the day. And anyway, she had read somewhere that it was the ultraviolet rays, which penetrated any cloud cover, that mattered, not the actual sunlight.

She went on deck, made her way aft. The decks were now reasonably clear, as everything that could possibly move had been swept overboard; only the stumps of the two masts remained, with some scattered stays, and the life-raft strapped into position on the cabin roof. And the solar panels let into the after deck. They were not even cracked, and there was no evidence that any water had got in. As she had very little use for electricity in

178

her circumstances, save to start the engines, she reckoned she might be all right. But she wished she could be sure.

She went below and forward to begin work on the saloon. Michael heard her and started shouting, so she shut the head door on him. It was like dropping the cover over a parrot's cage. Then it was a matter of getting down to hard work. As she really had no idea of their fresh water situation – or when it would rain again – she felt obliged to use salt water, which made things even stickier than they already were. But she gradually got all the by now dried food off the roof. There was very little she could do about the carpet, so she pulled it up, rolled it up, and with a great effort lugged it through the wheelhouse and up the steps on to the deck. She was reluctant to actually throw it away, so she left it spread on the wheelhouse roof over the life-raft. She might be able to do something about it the next time it rained. She washed the cooking pot and did what she could with the stove. The berths were also a mass of dried food; she laid these cushions also on deck, on the cabin roof, and strapped a line across them to hold them in place; although the wind had dropped almost to a flat calm, she had no idea when it would be back.

By now it was utterly dark, so she switched on the saloon and wheelhouse lights, and then flushed the toilet under Michael, who was very morose. 'You going to leave me here all night?' he inquired.

179

'Yes. Are you hungry?'

'Fuck off.'

'Suit yourself.' She made herself some package soup, which she drank while chewing salt biscuits, then opened a fresh bottle from the liquor cabinet, which was undamaged, and had a glass of brandy. If she was now feeling quite played out, she also had a growing sense of exhilaration. She was her own woman again. More than that. She was on top.

She stood in the head doorway. 'I am going to sleep now,' she said. 'I recommend you do the same. I know it's not very comfortable, but it's better than you deserve. Let me make one thing perfectly clear: I'm going to leave this door open to give you some air, but if you start any kind of a ruckus, I am going to tape up your mouth and tie your ankles together. You get the idea. We'll get some kind of routine going tomorrow.'

The wheelhouse remained in a mess, but that also would have to wait until tomorrow: she still had the cabin to put back together. This was relatively easy, as it was just untidy, not food-stained, and the head was less difficult than she had feared it would be; if various bottles and tubes were scattered about the place, and of course the toilet had emptied itself during the capsize, it had been nothing more than salt water slightly mixed with oil. She replaced the various items in their drawers, then had a long shower, standing under the water for a good ten minutes until she almost fell asleep.

She knew she was utterly drained, as much emotionally as physically. She felt that she wanted, needed, to sleep for as long as possible. She went forward and had a second glass of brandy. Then she dried herself and went to bed. It was the first time in three months she had lain in this bed without being handcuffed. It felt tremendous.

She was asleep in seconds, and regained consciousness in the middle of the most erotic dream she had ever had, a kaleidoscope of naked penises, surrounding her, whacking her, thrusting at her...

She sat up, thrusting her hands into her hair, and looked at her watch. Two o'clock. She listened, but the only sound was the slurping of the water against the hull. Even so she got up, and went up to the wheelhouse, moving as quietly as she could. But there was no sound from forward, and the night was quiet, a huge moon sending a swathe of light across the slowly settling sea. Maybe it had been the moon that had awakened her, although its light had not penetrated the cabin. Then, the dream?

She went below and back to bed, lying on her back with arms and legs outstretched, again glorying in her freedom. It could have been the dream. She tried to rationalize. For the past three months, she had been forced to have sex every day, at least once a day. Down to two days ago. Her body hardly less than her mind had become used to it. And now wanted it?

Her instinctive reaction was to reject such a concept. But as she lay in the dark, her naked buttocks moving gently on the sheet and her breasts and pubes rubbing against the duvet to the motion of the yacht, she realized she had no reason to react in such a conventionally moral way. She had no idea if she was going to survive this incredible voyage any more now than in the beginning. Although she now felt that she could prevent herself from being murdered, she knew that much of what Michael had said to her was true: if she failed to find land before their fuel ran out, or if there was to be another storm as fierce as the last, she would probably die. He would die too, of course. But he seemed prepared for that.

And in the meantime, she had been forced over the edge of conventionality into a world where only passion and lust mattered. And survival, of course. But the first two were active; survival was passive. And as she was being perfectly honest with herself, she could admit that, once she had got over the initial revulsion of being a sexual prisoner, she had learned to enjoy much of what Michael had done to her. So much so that she now craved it? But why not? On this ship, in the middle of this vast ocean, she had become the supreme goddess, mistress of everything she surveyed.

She had always been an avid reader of

historical romances, had often envied the power of Cleopatra or T'zu Hsi, or Catherine of Russia or Zenobia. They were women who had simply pointed at a man and said, I will have that one. Zenobia, she recalled, had been somewhat chaste, and only permitted herself to have sex once a month; she had always thought that a waste.

Now she was in their position. After a lifetime of careful discipline, both mental and physical, she could wear what she liked, eat what she liked, drink what she liked, do what she liked ... and have a man whenever she chose. Of course, it would always have to be the same man, which was a bit of a bore. But it was better than nothing.

What a concept! What a crazy dream! But it wasn't a dream. She was here, and he was there, and to all intents and purposes they were the only two people in the world. And she was the mistress. Who owed him nothing but vengeance. It was certainly not a concept to be rejected out of hand.

When she awoke, Jessica had no idea where she was for several minutes. It was daylight, and the slow movement of the yacht brought her back to reality. The slight fuzziness in both her mouth and her brain made her realize that she had actually been drunk. But not merely with that second glass of brandy. It had also been the headiness of survival. Which had induced a sexual euphoria. Trouble was, that had not entirely gone away.

She had actually been awakened by Michael shouting. Maybe something was wrong. She went forward, and he blinked at her. 'Christ, what a night. Every joint seems to have seized. Listen, JJ, let me go and I'll be as good as gold. I'll be your slave. You can do anything you like to me. Just get me out of here.'

'You look pretty grim,' she agreed. 'But you'll have to hang on a little while longer.'

'Bitch!' he shouted. 'When I get my hands on you...'

She let him run out of breath while she went on deck. It was a magnificent morning. The sun was rising out of an empty eastern horizon, the swell had gone right down, and there was not a whitecap to be seen: the ocean looked like a blue carpet. She went below to fetch Michael's binoculars, then sat on the wheelhouse roof and slowly swept the horizon. But there was nothing in sight. Today was the day she had to make her move, decide where she was going, and get to it.

Trouble was, she just felt like sitting on the wheelhouse roof and enjoying the sun's heat seeping through her skin. And feeling as randy as hell. She had been on deck, naked, often enough before. But before had been a different world, Michael's world. This was hers.

She went below, poured two glasses of concentrated orange juice, and held one to his lips. 'Now listen,' she said. 'I am going to have a shower and generally clean myself up. Then

I am going to tidy the wheelhouse. Once I've done that, we'll be all shipshape. Then I'll cook us breakfast.'

'While I sit here with my arms dropping off.'

'Be a good boy and we may be able to sort something out after I've showered. Misbehave and I'll tape you up.'

She decided to work on the wheelhouse first. Putting everything back together that could be put together wasn't difficult; even the smell of the spilled brandy had almost gone. But the big Sailor radio was a total wreck. On the other hand, she was reluctant to throw so valuable a piece of equipment overboard; she pushed all the bits and pieces into a corner. Then, more from curiosity than anything else, she tried the VHF. It was working all right, but there was nothing but crackle. She thumbed the mike; there could be another ship within a mile or so, even if she hadn't been able to see it. 'Hello,' she said. 'Hello. This is the yacht *Maria Anna*. I am dismasted and drifting and need help. Hello.' Time enough to explain the exact situation when help came. She repeated her call several times, but of course there was no reply. It had been wishful thinking.

She showered, cleaned her teeth, washed her face in fresh water, instinctively reached for her clothes, then threw them on the bed. She didn't need clothes; it was a beautifully warm morning. And being naked was essential for her mood, for what she was trying to

185

work herself up to do. It was simply an act of will. On board *Maria Anna*, she was the mistress of the world.

She went below with the pistol, unlocked the handcuffs. Michael moved so slowly and painfully she reckoned she didn't really need the gun, but she kept it pointed at him, anyway. 'Up,' she told him. He staggered out of the head and aft to the companion. 'Keep moving nice and slow,' she recommended.

'I don't believe you have the guts to use that thing,' he remarked.

'Any time you feel like finding out. But it may interest you to know that I have shot several people in my time, in the line of duty. On the settee,' she commanded, and clipped him into place.

'I'm starving,' he said.

'Breakfast coming up.' She left him and cooked smoked bacon and tinned tomatoes, then sat beside him on the settee to feed him.

'You've done a great job,' he said.

'Thank you.'

'You're a great girl, JJ.' His eyes drifted up and down her body. 'Did I ever tell you that you are quite the most beautiful woman I have ever seen?'

'You may have done.' She took the plates down to the galley, washed up, brewed coffee, and gave him some.

'You said we'd come to some kind of arrangement,' he said.

She nodded. 'I've been doing a lot of thinking.'

'That's my girl. I mean, you need me, and I need you. Right?'

'Not entirely. I don't need you. But I *have* you, right?'

She washed the coffee cups, then opened one of the seat lockers and took out a length of thin line. She tied a loose bowline in one end of the line, and returned to the wheelhouse. Michael frowned at her. 'Just what are you going to do with that?'

'Tie you up,' she said, and dropped the bowline over his right ankle, drawing it tight. Immediately he kicked at her with his left leg. She avoided the blow, but as he continued to kick it took her several minutes to loop the line round his left ankle as well, and draw the two together, tying them tightly. By then they were both panting.

'What the fuck are you playing at?'

'I'm not quite sure yet. I'm just amusing myself.'

'Bitch!'

'You have a limited vocabulary.' She opened the drawer and took out a roll of tape.

'Now listen,' he began.

'You listen. There are things I want to say, and perhaps even do, and I don't want you calling me names while I'm doing them.'

'Okay,' he said. 'I won't say a word. I apologize for calling you a bitch. From here on I'll speak only when spoken to.'

'I don't think you have enough self-discipline for that.' Jessica stood behind him. He moved his head to and fro, but she chose her moment and slapped the tape across his mouth, carefully smoothing the ends on to his cheeks. 'There we are.'

As she spoke, she realized that the sun had gone in. Hastily she climbed into the hatch, and saw a huge black cloud rising out of the east. Oh, Lord, she thought. Not another storm. She didn't think she could cope with that. She slid down the steps and ran to the barometer, watched by Michael; the weather fax was of course useless without an aerial. He had said that a drop of three millibars meant trouble. But the needle had actually *risen* a millibar. Dared she believe the instrument? She had to. She had taken down several of the shutters to give herself maximum light – discovering to her amazement that while several of the glass ports were cracked, none had actually broken – and she didn't think she had the strength to get them back into place.

But at the very least, the cloud should mean rain. Heavy, tropical rain. The masts might be gone, but there were still the stumps, each some six feet above the deck. And Michael's water-catching arrangement was still stowed in the forward cabin. With a great effort she lugged it out and pulled it on deck. The shrouds were all gone as well, save for their lower lengths, but some stanchions for the handrail were left. Using several yards of line she connected the funnel between them and the two stumps, attached the tube, then found the right spanner and unscrewed the

188

cap for the fresh-water tank. She inserted the end of the tube into the aperture, using more yards of electrical tape to secure it in place. Then, pouring sweat, she returned to the wheelhouse and dried herself with a towel. Michael continued to watch her, the tape moving against his lips as he tried to say something.

'Now, what were we doing?' she asked. 'Oh, yes. We were going to have a little chat.' She swung her leg over his and sat on his lower thighs. 'You justified your kidnapping of me on historical grounds, on the basis that the old sea captains used to press most of their men. And I suppose those poor kids were as subject to rapes and floggings as I was. Who am I to argue with history? But now there's been a mutiny. You, the old-time sea captain, are now a prisoner, and I, the old-time press-ed seaman, am now in command. Histori-cally, you're a dead duck, Mr Lomas. As a matter of fact, I have got so many options it's quite making my head spin. There are so many things I can do to you, or with you. So many things I *want* to do to you, and with you. There are limits, of course. I can't make you walk the plank, because I don't have a plank. And I can't hang you from the yard-arm, because I don't have a yardarm, either. When it comes to killing you, I suppose the simplest way would be to cut your throat and roll you over the side.'

His head jerked in consternation. 'Don't you think I'm that kind of woman?' she

189

asked. 'Do you know, I never thought I was, either. But then, I never thought I'd be kidnapped and raped, again and again and again, either. Things like that can effect a personality change, don't you agree?'

His nostrils flared as he reached for breath. 'However,' she went on, 'before you're executed, you have to be punished for what you did to me, and obviously I will get more satisfaction out of punishing you myself than by merely sending you to prison, even if you do get beaten and buggered by your cellmates. Anyway, if I sent you to prison, you wouldn't be executed at all.'

Now his chest was heaving as well. 'The obvious way to punish you, and make you understand just what you have done, I suppose, would be to cut it off.'

She unbuckled his belt, released his zip, and pulled down his pants and drawers to expose him. Now the heaving had reached his stomach, but he was also half-erected. 'I thought that might turn you on,' she said. 'Yes, cutting it off would be fun. But then, I think to myself, you'll probably die, as I wouldn't know how to stop the flow of blood. And anyway, it's quite a handsome one, don't you think? Would you believe that I have grown quite fond of it? Much fonder of it than I am of you. But then, I can always put a bag over your head and have it all to myself. I could do things to you. I could put red pepper on it. That would make you squeal, wouldn't it?'

Now his whole body was surging. Would she do it? *Could* she do it? He was entirely at her mercy. But although her profession had conditioned her to violence, it had always been committed in self-defence, and even if she had, on occasion, known the consuming anger that will destroy, it had always been in hot – never in cold – blood. Shit! she thought. And was distracted by the rumble of thunder, followed almost immediately by the thud of the raindrops.

She got off him, climbed into the hatchway and closed it behind her, went on to the roof, and sat on the carpet spread across the life-raft, allowing the heavy drops to thud on to her flesh, and more important, into her hair. It was clearly going to be quite a shower. She went back below, got a bottle of shampoo, returned on deck, and washed her hair: it now stretched halfway down her back. When she was finished, she fetched up a scrubbing brush from forward, and began working on the carpet.

The rain was pouring now, limiting visibility to a hundred yards, while the thunder crash-ed and every so often a searing flash of light-ning would cut through the gloom. Michael had said they had been in no danger from electrical storms because there was a light-ning conductor from the top of the mast. But that had gone overboard, and the yacht was made of steel. She thought it would be rather amusing if she were struck by lightning and killed, and he was left, bound and gagged in the saloon, slowly to starve to death. But as she had no desire to be struck by lightning, she went below.

The rain and the thunder and the lightning had done nothing to allay her mood; rather, it had enhanced it. The teeming water took away her horizon as well as the sky, left her world intensely limited – but even more her world. She was drunk with a sense of power – and with lust as well. So she would do it, do it, do it. All of it. Everything she could think of.

He was staring at her with enormous eyes, still half-erected. She was still wet and gleaming, her hair a deep yellow stain right down her back. She delved into the rope locker and found another length, considerably thicker than the cord binding his ankles. The end of this she knotted. 'Roll over,' she said.

He continued to stare at her. 'I'm going to begin by paying you back for all the beatings you gave me,' she told him. 'I'm going to start in three seconds. If you don't roll over and stay rolled over, your sexual problems will be ended forever, because you won't have anything left.'

Still he stared at her, for a second longer, then he rolled over. In almost a frenzy now, she started flogging him with the knotted rope's end. Her swings were wildly inaccurate, and landed anywhere from the back of his knees to the middle of his back, but most of them found the naked buttocks in between. He writhed and made high-pitched moaning noises, but she kept on hitting him until she ran out of breath and his flesh was red and raw.

She had no idea how many blows she had delivered, but it was time to go on deck and stand in the rain for a while. This had now slackened to a drizzle, and the electric storm had passed on. My God, she thought, what am I doing? What am I becoming? But she didn't regret a moment of it, and although her mood was temporarily assuaged, it was still lurking. She had become what he had made her become.

Yet, maddeningly, she felt sorry for him. And she still admired him, for the way he handled the yacht, the way he had faced the storm.

She went below, poured a glass of brandy, drank some, and then took off the tape. 'Not a word,' she said. 'Or I'll start all over again.' She held the glass to his lips.

He drank greedily; he was still unable to keep still, and rolling on to his back was clearly very uncomfortable. When the glass was empty, she taped him up again. 'Just lie there,' she told him, 'while I think of what I'm going to do to you next.'

She went below, dried and dressed herself; despite her exertions the rain had left her feeling chilled. And for the moment, having flogged him, her mood had quietened. She could think straight, and she had a lot of thinking to do, as well as decisions to make.

She wrapped her head in a towel, and returned to the wheelhouse, took out the chart, and
studied it. Down to the storm, Michael had,
faithful to his routine, marked their noon
position with an X every day. So she knew
where they had been two days ago. And the
GPS would tell her where she was now. But
where the hell was it? She hunted through all
the drawers without success. Then a terrible
thought crossed her mind. Michael had
usually left it lying on the console, so when
they had capsized and then pitch-poled...

Yet it had to be in the cabin. Panting, she
went to the corner where she had swept the
debris, dropped to her knees, and sifted
through the wreckage. And there it was. It
must have fallen off the console at an early
stage of the storm, unnoticed by Michael on
the helm, and had lain on the deck, directly in
the path of the crashing radio set. Now it too
was a broken mass of microchips.

She wanted to scream. She looked at
Michael, and then looked away again. Had he
known all along that it was smashed, and that
without it she would be helpless? Well, fuck
him, she thought. She was surely as capable
of calculating as he was. The storm had come
out of the east, with easterly winds. So they
had drifted for two days. How far would that
be? she wondered. They had probably been
driven and then drifted something between
fifty and a hundred miles. Michael had told
her that one degree of latitude measured sixty
nautical miles; she used the dividers, and

made a mark on the chart approximately seventy-five miles due west of his last marked position, understanding that it was a wild guess. But, as far as she could make out, the nearest land – apart from that infinitesimal dot which was now by her reckoning just over three hundred miles distant – were the Marquesas to the south-west, and as far as she could figure it, something like fifteen degrees of longitude away. She looked for a scale for longitude, but there was none, so she went below to see what she could find in his various nautical books, but without success. So, she thought, if a degree of latitude measures sixty miles, a degree of longitude must be the same, at least here, virtually on the Equator. She had no idea how one calculated when the lines started to close up towards the poles.

However, allowing sixty miles each up here ... that was nine hundred nautical miles. 'Jesus,' she muttered. And that was supposing she didn't miss them. But she couldn't miss them, surely. According to the pilot book she checked, the principal island, Hiva Oa, consisted mainly of a four-thousand-foot-high mountain.

So, nine hundred miles. She went down the after companion and studied the two sight gauges on the fuel tanks. Each was still more than three quarters full, and he had said they each held two hundred and fifty gallons. That meant there had to be something like two hundred gallons in each tank, a total of four hundred gallons. He had also said that the engines burned a gallon an hour each at a cruising speed of six knots. That gave her a present range of twelve hundred miles. Waves of relief swept up through her system.

She returned to the wheelhouse and studied the chart again. Of course she couldn't miss the Marquesas, but just in case she did ... just south-west of them – at least 'just' as it appeared on this small-scale chart – was another group called Tuamotu. If she missed the one she would surely hit the other. And beyond Tuamotu were the Society Islands, one of which was Tahiti. What a scream if she were to steer this boat into Papeete. Now that would cause a worldwide sensation. But she didn't have the range for that. So, the Marquesas it had to be.

Her first business was to plot a course. Michael had talked a lot about currents and so forth, and by again hunting through his navigation books and charts she found a small-scale chart of ocean currents. He continued to stare at her, but was less restless than before as the pain eased.

Jessica studied the chart, and discovered that the South Equatorial Current, in the grip of which they presumably were at that moment – his last X had them only just south of the Equator – moved almost due west, and at a fairly good speed. Just before it reached the Marquesas, however, a branch turned south-west, at a somewhat reduced speed. But that all seemed to be going her way. The only problem was if she missed the Marquesas to the north, there was another nine hundred miles or so to the Christmas Islands, and she certainly could not make that, even with the assistance of the current.

She got out a notepad and ballpoint pen to calculate. At six knots, she would make just under a hundred and fifty miles a day – more with the current. Which meant she would cover the nine hundred miles in approximately six days. Or even less, if the current was as strong as it appeared. She looked at Michael. 'I reckon we can be in this place Hiva Oa in six days,' she said.

His stare became a glare. She blew him a kiss and got back to work. So, she thought, if I steer due west, two hundred and seventy on the compass, for two days, then say two hundred and sixty for another two days, then two hundred and fifty for the last two days, I should be spot on. It all seemed very simple. Too simple. But she had nothing better.

Now for the big moment, on which all her plans were based. She studied the console, and the switches; the ignition keys were in place, as they had been throughout the voyage. And the levers were in the neutral position. The whole console did not look very different to a car dashboard, except that there were two switches and two sets of dials instead of one. Therefore all she had to do was turn them. She held the first switch between thumb and forefinger, drew a deep breath, and turned it. She could hear the engine growl beneath her, and again. But it did not kick. Oh, shit, she thought. But of course, it would have taken a buffeting, and been upside down at least twice during the storm. Perhaps it was flooded.

Did diesel engines flood? And if it had flooded, she had no idea how to clear it. She knew that the way to start a flooded car was to press the gas pedal to the floor and then turn the engine over, releasing the pedal the moment it caught. But she couldn't put the throttles full ahead and attempt to start this engine; she didn't see anything resembling a clutch.

Michael was thrashing about on the settee, watching her. Was he trying to tell her something? She tried the port engine, with the same lack of any result. Shit, shit, shit! It had all seemed so simple. Michael was still thrashing about. She pulled off the tape, and he grimaced with pain. 'Give,' she commanded.

'Why should I?'

'Because if you don't, I am going to flog you again, and this time I'm going to draw blood.' She kept her face and her eyes as hard as flint.

'You have to use the heat-start,' he muttered.

'Eh?'

'The engines have to be heat-started. That is, you turn the key halfway, press it in, and hold it there. You'll see a red light glowing on the console. When that goes out, turn the key the whole way and it should start. Also, if you

198

pull the throttles out to the side, they'll slip permanently into neutral, and you'll be able to gun them without being in gear.'

'Thank you.' She took out another role of tape.

'Hey,' he protested. 'I'm cooperating.'

'And the next time I want you to cooperate, I'll take the tape off again,' she promised, slapping a piece across his mouth. Then she turned the switch, held it on heat-start until the light faded, heart pounding in both anticipation and apprehension, then turned it the whole way. Instantly the engine came to life. 'Wheee!' she shouted, pulling the lever out as instructed and then thrusting it forward to gun the power.

She started the port engine in turn, got them both going really well, and throttled down. Then she simply had to go below and watch them working. The noise was tremendous in the confined space of the engine room, but she didn't see anything actually moving.

Feeling like a combination of Einstein and Watt, she returned to the wheelhouse, placed her hands on the two levers, brought them together so that they clicked into gear, and pushed them forward. The yacht slowly gathered way. 'Wheee!' she shouted again.

Now for the autopilot. But this was a very straightforward affair. It was simply a matter of switching it on, then lining up the yacht on the compass course she wanted, two-seven-zero, and throwing the lever. It took her three goes to get it quite right, as the yacht kept wandering off before she had actually set the course, but at last she was satisfied, and was then immediately alarmed as the compass needle drifted five degrees north. She debated calling on Michael's knowledge again, but before she had made up her mind to do that the needle yawed the other way, to five degrees south, and then adjusted itself back again, all the while with the pilot making a high-pitched whining sound. But it slowly settled down, moving to and fro within a seven or eight compass-point spread. She reckoned that was good enough.

She remained staring at it for some minutes, listening to the growl of the engines, feeling the movement through the water. Six days! In six days' time ... She sat in the steering chair and peered through the window at the waves seeming to part before her. She couldn't see very far because of the drizzle. Six days, and then? People! Cameras! TV interviews! Police! Lawyers! And at the end of it, Tom, and Andrea ... and the Commander! Suddenly she felt quite sick. The questions they would ask. Would they believe any of her answers?

She had to be nuts, she told herself. She had been dragged on board this ship, gagged and bound, abused, beaten, and to all intents and purposes raped. And now she was afraid to end it? But she was. She had grown to love this boat. She had seen how secure it was, even when completely at the mercy of the elements. And now it was hers, as her life was entirely hers. For six days! Her hand moved, involuntarily, as if she would have switched off the engines. But then she pulled it back. It had to be done. She couldn't drift around the Pacific for the rest of her life.

But there was so much she still wanted to do while she was entirely in control, and hadn't yet dared to do. She turned to look at Michael, who was, as always, staring at her.

Six days! Or forever!

The Fish

If she didn't do it, she would regret it for the rest of her life. But then, perhaps, if she did do it, she would equally regret it for the rest of her life. Yet the fact remained that these coming six days were unique, and would remain unique, for her. She would never be in such a position again, as long as she lived. She had to make the most of them, and it was simply a matter of will. There was no power on earth that could gainsay her will for these final six days.

She continued to stare at the compass for several minutes, watching it yaw back and forth, then she got up and stretched. Time for lunch. She cooked a good meal, brought the plate up, and took the tape from Michael's mouth. She put the plate on the console, went back below, and fetched some lime juice, which she mixed with rum and water. She drank some herself, gave some to him. 'Hungry?'

'Very.'

She fed him, alternately with herself as usual, using a spoon. 'Ass still sore?'

'Yes.'

'Then you have some idea how I felt when you were tanning me.'

'What else are you going to do to me?'

'I haven't quite decided yet,' she replied, truthfully enough. 'Would you like to offer an opinion on how I'm doing, navigation-wise?'

'You seem to be doing very well. You're a bright girl.'

'Do you wish to use the head again?'

'Yes.'

'Okay.' She had left the gun on the console. She picked it up, and rested the muzzle on his left temple while she unlocked one of the cuffs. He sat up to rub his hands together, then pulled up his pants. Jessica backed across the wheelhouse, the gun levelled. 'Use the aft one.'

The drill was as before, only this time he made no attempt to close the door on her. 'Can I shave now?'

'I like your little beard. But you can shower.'

He obeyed. 'Don't bother to dress,' she told him when he had dried himself.

He raised his eyebrows. 'I like looking at you,' she said. 'You really have a very attractive body. Up you go.' He hesitated, obviously debating whether or not to attempt to take advantage of her apparently lighter mood, then climbed the steps. 'Now back to the settee.'

'Aren't I cooperating?'

'Just do it.' He hesitated, then shrugged and obeyed, and she handcuffed him. 'Back in a while,' she told him, and went below to have a shower herself, clean her teeth, add some perfume, and generally make herself as fresh and sweet-smelling as possible. She didn't know why. He wasn't going to touch her. But she felt it was important.

Yet she still couldn't bring herself to commit so wanton an act, and instead went on deck. The rain had stopped, and she even thought it might be going to clear. She stood in the stern to watch the bubbling wake. Despite the constant movement of the autopilot, the white streak was remarkably straight. She felt her usual sense of exhilaration at being so much in command of her situation, and with it, another surge of sexual energy. She went down to the wheelhouse. 'Well?' Michael asked. 'What's happening up there?'

'Not a lot.' She took the tape from the drawer.

'Oh, for God's sake,' he grumbled. 'Look, I won't talk. I won't say a word unless you invite me to.'

'As I said, I doubt you have the will-power for that.' She taped his mouth, then took off

203

another length. He gazed at this in some alarm, but he knew he couldn't resist her, and kept his head still while she taped his eyes as well. By now he was becoming interested, both from apprehension and anticipation, she reckoned. She stood in the centre of the wheelhouse for several minutes, watching him. Now, she told herself. Now, now, now! If you don't do it, you are never going to do it, and you are going to hate yourself.

But she had never done anything like this before. In fact, she had only ever had 'real' sex with four men in her life: the almost forgotten teenager who had been her first boyfriend, her husband – from whom she had been divorced for nearly ten years – Tom, and that handsome hunk of an aristocrat with whom she had become involved while attempting to rescue his sister from her drug baron husband. And she still felt guilty about that. I am a rather strait-laced thirty-eight-year-old police sergeant, she told herself. I don't do things like this.

You *were* a strait-laced police sergeant, she argued. Now, you are Cleopatra and Catherine, Semiramis and Zenobia, rolled into one. Forget Zenobia, she thought, remembering her once-a-month limitation on sex. And in a few days' time you are going to be once again a strait-laced police sergeant – supposing that is possible. But whether it is or not, you will never have this power again.

She took a deep breath, sat astride his thighs, began to play with him, caressing his shaft, taking his head into her mouth for quick, stimulating licks, even giving him little nibbles from time to time. His body moved under her ministrations, and he slowly hardened. And kept on hardening.

It had to be now, she told herself. Now, now, now! Or never. Drawing another deep breath she eased herself forward, one foot on the deck to balance herself, the other leg kneeling on the berth on his inside. She held him in both hands, placed him in position, and... 'Wheee!' she shrieked as she felt him sinking into her, initially hurting her, but going in and in and in. He was moving now, up and down, and she did the same, gasping in a mixture of discomfort and ecstasy.

Then it was done.

'There,' she said. 'See what you can do if you try?'

But she didn't want him to be able to see her, or say anything, right that minute. She fetched a wet towel from the head to clean him up, then had another shower herself ... and discovered that the event had in no way allayed her desire, because there hadn't been all that much for her. Save some fairly sharp discomfort: it had been a long time.

Michael lay with his head lolling on the cushion. But he was clearly a very relieved man – in every possible sense. Well, she was a relieved woman. Because now that he had managed it once, he would manage it again, she had no doubt at all. And the next time she might even enjoy it. She went down to the

205

cabin, got into bed, and fell into a deep and, remarkably, dreamless sleep.

It was five o'clock before she returned to the wheelhouse. Michael was awake, and clearly listening. But she still didn't feel like either looking at him or talking to him. Her imagination had only taken her this far. Now she had to work out what happened next. What she wanted to happen next. Because she still had five and a half days of omnipotence. At the end of which it would be his word against hers. But he wouldn't have a hope. Everyone would have expected him to rape her, again and again and again. His claim that *she* had raped *him* would be laughed out of court.

Meanwhile, she felt on top of the world. She had proved that she could do anything, be anything she chose. Then why not eat anything? There had to be fish out there.

She got out the fishing line, hooked a piece of tinned meat on the end, and let it trawl astern, as she had seen Michael do time and again. By now the sky was entirely blue, and it was a delightfully balmy afternoon. She sat on the cabin roof, leaning against the aft wheelhouse window, watching the wake and the line sinking beneath the water. It was hypnotic, and with the breeze playing gently over her body, she almost fell asleep. Then, just as it was getting dark, she saw movement in the water. She sat up, shading her eyes. There had been a fin. But if it had been a shark, she didn't think she had caught it, because the hook was well below the surface, she was sure. Anyway, she had no desire to catch a shark. She went below to fetch the binoculars, focussed. It was definitely a fin, large and black. In fact, it was larger than any fin she had ever seen in her life. And it was doing nothing but swim alongside the trawling line. As if it was tracking the yacht. Tracking her.

She began to feel uneasy, her awareness of her own omnipotence disappearing. There were still forces out there that could destroy her. But not so long as she was on the yacht and the fish was in the water. Yet the fin was coming closer. She retreated to the wheelhouse hatch, left the cover back and closed the door so that she could stand on the top step and look out and yet be perfectly safe from any risk of falling overboard. Then she levelled the binoculars again. The fin was definitely approaching. And it seemed to be growing larger every second. And now she thought she could make out some of the body beneath: it looked like a submarine. She found herself thinking of Jules Verne's novel, *Twenty Thousand Leagues Under the Sea*. *The Nautilus*, as Captain Nemo's submarine had been called, had been mistaken for a large fish. But that had been a fantasy.

She realized she was panting as she slid down the steps and pulled the tape from Michael's eyes and mouth. 'Ow,' he said. But his eyes were lazy. 'You're quite a girl,' he remarked.

'Listen,' she said. 'How big do sharks grow? How big do great whites grow?'

He raised his eyebrows. 'Company?'

'It's a whopper.'

'Well, a great white can run to about fifteen, twenty feet, so they say.'

'This is bigger than that.'

'You've been at the bottle. Something out there is bigger than twenty feet?'

'I'm sure of it.'

'Then it's not a shark. It's a whale.'

'It's not a whale.' She went back up into the hatch. The fin was now only about fifty yards astern.

'Could be a basking shark, I suppose,' Michael mused. 'Now, they grow pretty big. Forty-odd feet.'

It was very gloomy now, but she was sure she could see the huge movement just beneath the surface. It certainly looked bigger than the hull of the fifty-foot yacht. 'I think it's more than forty feet,' she said.

'In that case, it has to be a whale shark. Now, they grow to seventy feet, so I've heard.'

'A whale shark. Jesus! Are they dangerous?'

'Well, they don't eat meat, so far as I know. They live off plankton. But I suppose any creature that big can be dangerous if it gets in a bad mood. Let me up to have a look.'

'No way. Listen, I'm trawling. Haven't caught anything. Do you think that attracted him? I mean, would it be an idea to bring the line in?'

'I'd leave the line. I shouldn't think that interested him. More likely the engines. Sharks are very susceptible to noise.'

Jessica licked her lips as she studied the monster. 'You mean, if we stopped the engines, he might go away?'

'Could be.'

Now she chewed her lip. If the noise was attracting the big fish then it did make sense to stop the engines. But she didn't like the idea of just lying there, inert in the water, while that monster was swimming close by. As long as the engines were going, she felt that she retained a certain command of the situation. But then she remembered how Michael had dropped the sails when in the middle of those whales, and the whales had gone away.

She went down the ladder and switched off the engines. *Maria Anna* slowly lost way, and the evening became silent, save for the faint moan of the wind and the slurp of the sea on the hull. Jessica stood in the hatch, and watched the fin slowly come abeam of the yacht, although remaining some thirty yards distant. Oh, God, she thought, he's lining up to attack.

Still moving comparatively slowly, the fin went round the bow of the yacht, which had now fallen away from her course line and was rolling gently in the swell. Then the fin came down the other side. 'What's happening?' Michael asked.

'He's having a look.'

209

'You look scared stiff,' he commented.

'I *am* scared stiff. And so would you be, if you'd seen him. He's abeam your side now. Try looking out of the window.'

Michael blinked into the gathering gloom. 'Jesus,' he commented.

Jessica went below and into the engine room, took down the rifle from its bracket, together with a magazine, and returned to the wheelhouse. 'What the fuck are you going to do with that?' Michael inquired.

'Shoot it, if it comes too close.'

'You can't shoot a whale shark,' he protested.

'It's flesh and blood, isn't it?'

'Oh, sure, but you're very unlikely to kill it. And if you just wound it, and madden it...'

'If it comes any closer than it is,' Jessica said, 'I would say it's already mad.'

She rested the rifle on the top of the door, fitted the magazine into place. 'Please don't shoot it,' Michael begged. 'It'll wreck us.'

Jessica squinted into the gloom. She couldn't see the fin any more. But she couldn't doubt that it was *there*. She descended the steps, laid the rifle on the deck. 'Do you think it can see lights?'

'God knows. Probably not.'

'Well, I think we'll leave them off, for the time being, up here.'

The appearance of the shark had quite put her off sex. She went below and dressed herself, and when next Michael had to go to the head, she let him dress himself too. 'Just

210

when we had something going,' he remarked.

'Listen, shut up,' she suggested. 'Or it's back to the tape.' She settled him, went below, and started cooking supper. To compound her agitation, halfway through cooking it the gas bottle ran out. But she had seen Michael change the last one, and had no difficulty switching to number three, frowning as she did so. He had said each bottle would last two months. But they hadn't yet been at sea four months. Maybe she'd been using too much. It didn't matter; they were going to be in harbour in five days' time, anyway. If that shark stopped making a nuisance of itself.

The quiet was uncanny, and disturbing. She had never known anything like it. The wind had dropped right away and was not making a sound. The yacht rolled gently, silently. The only sound was the odd gurgle of water around the hull. But these were more disturbing than anything, because she kept imagining they were caused by the shark. In any event, she found that she was listening, all the time, for some sound outside and beyond the boat. The thought that there was a living creature, bigger than the yacht, lurking, waiting...

She made them their evening drink. She really needed hers. Then she sat beside Michael and fed him. 'What's your plan?' he asked. 'Just to drift for the next few weeks? Mind you, I'm all in favour of that.'

'We'll be moving on as soon as he's gone,'

she assured him.

'Sure. Listen, I didn't have a chance to tell you, but I really am grateful for what you did.' She didn't know what to reply, and was herself grateful for the darkness that prevented him from seeing her face. 'I really never thought nice girls did things like that,' he went on.

'I'm not a nice girl any more,' she pointed out. 'You took a nice girl, and twisted her inside out.'

'Would it do any good to say I'm sorry? But you know something – I'm not. Sorry, I mean. I wanted a last adventure, with the most beautiful woman I have ever seen. So, no matter what happens now, I've had that adventure. And I've even had my fuck. I'm happy about that. When are we going to have another?'

'Are we?' She took the plate below, washed it, then returned into the hatchway. There was no moon as yet, but the clouds had gone and it was a bright and starry night. The water flickered and moved all around her. And there was no fin to be seen. Yet the beast could still be there.

She closed the hatch. 'Now listen,' she said. 'I'm going below to lie down. I'm not going to tape you up tonight, because I want you to call me if you hear anything. But if you make yourself a nuisance, I *will* tape you. You got me?'

'You're a real toughie,' he sneered. 'I bet you dream about sharks.'

She was only too afraid that he might be right. She gathered up the rifle and the revolver and took them to bed with her; the occasional touch of the cold metal was reassuring. But she really didn't expect to sleep, as she lay there, listening, expecting any moment to have to leap out of bed and face the shark ... then awoke to bright daylight.

There was no sound, save for the slurp of the water against the hull. Jessica rolled out of bed, and ran up the companion. Michael was fast asleep on the settee berth. The wheelhouse was exactly as she had left it. She grabbed the binoculars and climbed into the hatch, throwing the cover back with a bang. It was another glorious day, with the sun just climbing out of the eastern horizon, the sea so calm it might have been solid, undulating in a long, low swell. There was not a whitecap to be seen – and certainly not a fin.

She went on deck, and aft to where the line still hung over the stern. She reeled it in. Both bait and hook were gone, but there was no way of telling if that was the work of the shark. The important thing was that it had gone as well.

Michael opened his eyes when she returned to the wheelhouse. 'Any sign of our friend?' he asked.

'Not a sausage. That's what we're going to have for breakfast – sausages.' She felt on top of the world again, went below and opened the tins, then cooked the meal. She brought it

213

and the fruit juice into the saloon, and fed him.

'Listen,' he said. 'After yesterday, well ... Do you still have to keep me chained up? We have something going now. You wanted it. I wanted it. We want each other.'

She sat in the steering chair to drink her coffee. 'My plan is to take this boat into the Marquesas. What's yours? Supposing you were free?'

'Well, if that's what you really want to do...'

He would promise anything to get those cuffs off, she knew. But she remained curious. 'Tell me what the original plan was. I mean, you know that if you ever return to civilization, you'd be locked up. For quite a while, I reckon. That is, unless you returned without me. Did you mean to murder me when you were ready?'

He licked his lips. 'I never intended to murder you,' he said. She raised her eyebrows. 'I wanted this voyage, with you. I wanted to sail, with you, for a year. Then ... I had it in mind that I would just fall over-board, and you would be able to go home.'

'You expect me to believe that?'

He shrugged. 'It's the truth.'

'Okay,' she said. 'But you're talking in the past tense. That plan has changed. Hasn't it?'

'I'm not sure that it has,' he said. 'I couldn't hurt you now, JJ. You must realize that.'

She wanted to believe him. She wanted to be rid of this antagonism. But if he was just saying that to get free... 'So what would be your plan, if I released you now?'

'I would like us to keep on drifting for a while. Or at least, look for some deserted island, like that atoll, where we could shack up together. You know we could get on together.'

Which was absolutely true. There was a big part of him she actually liked, and some more that she admired. But that did not alter the fact that he was a kidnapping rapist, and that she was a police officer. Does a leopard ever change its spots? 'We'll have to talk about that,' she said, and turned the first key to heat-start.

'But you're going to keep me tied up and make for the Marquesas anyway,' he said.

'I am going to keep you tied up while I consider the matter,' she told him. 'As for the Marquesas, as far as I can make out, they're the nearest land of any description. And between them and us is that atoll you're talking about. So it makes sense to keep going in that direction, right?'

The light had gone out, and she turned the switch the whole way. As before, her stomach was rolling with apprehension, but the first engine fired immediately, as did the second. She lined up the autopilot, and the yacht moved smoothly through the water. 'So you see,' she said. 'We have time to think about things.'

It was nine o'clock. She climbed into the hatch with the binoculars and swept the horizon, and felt she was about to be sick.

215

Smoke! To the north. What to do? There was a Verey pistol in the wheelhouse, but she didn't think anyone would see the rocket at such a distance, especially on a bright morning. Perhaps the VHF...

She slid down the steps, and reached for the mike. 'Hello,' she said. 'This is the yacht *Maria Anna*, dismasted in a storm. Can you see me? I am to your south.'

Nothing but crackle. 'Where is it?' Michael asked.

'Too far,' she muttered.

She considered altering course towards the distant vessel. But it would be travelling far faster than the yacht, and would be gone long before she reached its present position. Then she wondered if it might be possible to rig a jury aerial. Of course it was possible – if she had any idea how to go about it.

She could work on that, obviously not in time for this ship, but where there had been one there would surely be others. Michael had carefully kept away from the designated shipping courses as shown on his chart, but the presence of the ship suggested they could have drifted on to the edge of one.

She returned to the hatch, watched the smoke through the glasses. She even thought she could make out the superstructure beneath it. But it was steaming away to the north-east. Next stop San Francisco, she supposed. Or somewhere like that. No one on board had any idea how close they had come to a genuine sensation. She sighed, then

216

swept the rest of the horizon, swinging right round to cover every point of the compass, and finally looking astern – and gave a shriek of the sheerest terror. Coming up behind the yacht, and moving at considerable speed, was the huge black fin.

Jessica half fell and half tumbled down the ladder to the wheelhouse deck. 'What in the name of God...?' Michael asked.

'That thing!' she screamed. 'It's attacking!' She reached her feet and staggered to the console to alter course. But as she took the yacht off autopilot it was struck a violent blow. She gave another scream as she was spun round and fell full length on the deck, all the breath knocked from her body.

'Jesus Christ!' Michael gasped. He had been half-thrown out of the settee berth, and was dangling from the upright by his hand-cuffed wrists as he tried to get to his feet.

Jessica scrambled up. There was a funny noise coming from below, and the yacht was turning in a slow circle. She looked left and right, but there was nothing to be seen, save for an area of disturbed water. But they were still afloat. Michael had said if a whale hit them they'd sink like a holed bucket. He had underestimated the strength of his craft. Thank God for that. She seized the helm, turned it to bring the yacht back on course, and nothing happened. 'There's no steering!' she shouted, twisting the wheel the other way. 'Oh, Jesus!'

The fin had reappeared, some forty yards away, on the other side. And it was moving forward again. 'Kill the engines!' Michael shouted.

Jessica turned off the switches, but it was too late; the giant fish had already launched at them, and a moment later there was another massive crash. This time Jessica's hands were wrenched from the wheel and she was sent flying across the wheelhouse to cannon into Michael and fall at his feet, while the yacht rolled almost on her beam ends before coming up again.

'Shit!' Michael gasped. 'He means to get us.' Jessica scrambled to her feet and ran down the after companion, seized the rifle, and dashed back up to the wheelhouse. 'You think that'll stop him?' Michael demanded, straining on the cuffs.

'It's all we have,' she retorted, climbing into the open hatchway and looking right and left, the rifle thrust forward, resting on the closed door. But although the water was disturbed all around them, the shark had again disappeared. 'Do you know how to fire that thing, anyway?' Michael asked.

'It's my favourite toy.' Although she was still terrified, she was also filled with a white-hot determination to sell her life dearly. 'Come on, you bastard,' she muttered. 'Come and play.'

But nothing happened. The yacht rolled idly to and fro. Jessica went down the steps. 'Won't he have hurt himself, banging us like that?'

'About as much as I'd hurt myself hitting someone with my fist. I'd bark a knuckle, maybe. That wouldn't stop me hitting him again, if I felt it was necessary.'

'So he's likely to keep coming.'

'When he's ready.'

'I'd prefer it if he did it when *we're* ready. He'll come back now if I start the engines again.'

'Maybe,' Michael said. 'But I think we need to project, very accurately.'

'What do you mean?'

'He's hit us twice, real hard. We have to find out what damage he's done. He's certainly done something to the rudder. There's no point in starting up again, and getting involved in a shoot-out, which you may or may not win, while we have no means of going anywhere if you *do* win. Right?'

Jessica considered. But she knew he was making sense. She was letting emotion get the better of logic. She put down the rifle. 'How do we tell what's happened to the rudder?'

'You'll have to go aft, on deck, and look over the stern.'

Jessica swallowed. She had no desire to be on deck if that beast charged again. 'I've a better idea,' she said. '*You* try the after deck. Anyway, you'll know more of what we're looking for.' She grinned at him. 'Don't worry, I'll cover you.'

'Big deal,' he grumbled.

219

'Will you do it?'

It was his turn to hesitate. Then he shrugged. 'Okay.'

'Just remember,' she said. 'The rules haven't changed.' She thrust the pistol into the waistband of her tracksuit, unlocked the nearest cuff, and then stepped back, picking up the rifle as she did so. Michael took a long breath, seeming to be pulling himself together, then went up the hatch and cautiously looked around. 'Do you see it?' Jessica asked.

'I can see where it's been.' The water around the yacht was still disturbed. Michael opened the door and stepped on to the deck, dropping to his hands and knees for greater stability, as the yacht was still rolling from the last attack. Jessica went up the steps and closed the door. 'Hey!' he protested.

'It'll be open when you come back,' she assured him. Through the glass she watched him move aft, and then stood in the hatchway herself, rifle resting on the wheelhouse roof. Carefully Michael crawled to the very stern, where he lay on his stomach to peer over the side. Jessica looked from right to left, fore and aft. The sea was slowly calming. But she did not doubt the beast was still there. 'Can you see anything?' she called.

'Yes.' Michael raised his head. 'It's a shitting awful mess. The rudder is half-adrift.'

'Can you fix it?'

He peered again, hanging so far over that his head was only just above the water. Jessica could feel her whole being tense as she stared at the slowly undulating blue. It was *there*, watching. She knew it. Michael raised his head. 'The top is secure. The bottom bolts have gone. I reckon I can get it back into place. But it'll mean going over the side.'

Jessica gulped. 'With that thing knocking about?'

He pushed himself to his knees, and crawled back to her. 'I told you, whale sharks don't go for human beings, or any kind of meat. They don't have the teeth for it. All that's bothering him is that we're a strange kind of fish making a strange noise in his territory.' Jessica opened the door and retreated down the steps to let him in. 'If you want to get anywhere, JJ, it has to be done. Anyway, you'll cover me, right?'

'Yes, I'll cover you.'

'Okay. I'm going to have to get my gear.' She nodded. 'So will you take these off?' He held out his left wrist, from which the handcuffs still dangled.

Jessica gave him the key, and he freed himself, then went down the forward companion. She followed, the rifle levelled. Why am I doing this? she asked herself. This man has more guts than I could ever have. But he was also a kidnapping sex maniac. She had to keep reminding herself of that.

'Get dressed in the wheelhouse,' she told him as he dragged the carry-all containing the wetsuit gear from the forepeak. She backed away from him and up the steps. He followed, laid the suit on the deck, and began

221

pulling it on. With his goggles and the cylinder he had brought up his diving knife. 'You won't need that,' she said. 'I'm going to cover you, remember?'

He zipped himself up. 'Just so long as you do.' He strapped on the cylinder. 'I'm going to need some tools.' She nodded. He opened the tool drawer beneath the settee berth, took out a screwdriver, a hammer, a pair of pliers, a wrench and a small bag of nuts and bolts. The tools he placed in his waistband, the bag of bolts in his thigh pocket, which he zipped into place. 'This may take a little time,' he said as he spat into his goggles.

'Time is one thing we have a whole lot of,' she reminded him.

He went on deck and aft. There he sat down to pull on his flippers. Then he put in his mouthpiece, checked his regulator, gave her the thumbs-up sign, and went in. There was more of a splash than she had anticipated, but after that there was silence. She stood in the hatchway as before, rifle at the ready, looking left and right. She could see nothing, but when the yacht gave a slight lurch she thought she was going to have a heart attack. That was before she realized that had to be Michael pushing the rudder back into place.

Then there came a clang, and another. He was using the hammer. But how loud the sound seemed.

Jessica made a visual sweep of the surrounding sea, and experienced another sudden lurch of her heart. The fin was back, amidships and perhaps a hundred yards away, but moving towards them and gathering speed; it must have heard the clang of the hammer.

'Michael!' she screamed, even as she knew he would not be able to hear her. But surely he would hear the sound of a gunshot. She levelled the Armalite and fired a single shot. She knew she hadn't hit anything, as she had only the fin to aim at, but it made her feel a whole lot better.

She lowered the gun, and saw the fin ever closer, travelling now like an express train. 'Michael!' she screamed again, and saw his head break the surface, several feet forward of the stern – and on the side of the yacht away from the shark. Jessica gave a sigh of relief, even if she knew he was still in danger. But they both were. A moment later the yacht was struck another tremendous blow which drove her over on her side. Jessica was thrown so hard against the door that she was winded, and lost her footing. She clattered down the steps and sprawled on the wheelhouse deck, the rifle landing on top of her.

The yacht was upright again. She scrambled to her knees and then her feet, went back to the hatch. The fish had dived; she could no longer see the fin, but the disturbed water indicated that it was some fifty yards off and still moving away. 'Michael!' she shouted.

His head appeared at the toe-rail; a hand thrust up to grasp one of the remaining stanchions. She pushed the door open and knelt on the deck above him, digging her fingers into the wetsuit. But she couldn't budge him. 'My leg,' he said.

'It's hurt?'

'No. Grab it when I throw it up.'

He made an immense effort, and his left leg came out of the water, tossed nearly as high as the toe-rail. Desperately Jessica grasped the ankle, having to use all her strength to hold it. 'Don't let go,' he gasped as he pulled up on his arms. A moment later he had hooked the leg itself round another stanchion, while his arms were wrapped round the first one he had grabbed. Jessica released his ankle and grasped his upper thigh, and between them they managed to roll him on to the deck.

He lay on his back, panting, while she sat with her back against the wheelhouse. 'Shit!' he commented.

'No joy?'

'I was getting it. But that fucking beast sent all my tools away. Anyway, going back down...' He shuddered. 'Where's the cylinder?'

She pointed. Still more than half-full, the oxygen cylinder was floating some thirty feet from the yacht. Michael sat up. 'I have to get it back.'

'No way,' she said. 'That would be suicide.'

'Can't you get it through your thick skull that he's not attacking me? It's the yacht he's taken exception to, whenever it makes a noise.'

Jessica stood up and looked around. As earlier, the sea was still disturbed. But again as earlier, the shark had disappeared.

'We had a hell of a job getting you back on board just now,' she said.

'That's because we were caught on the hop, and I'll confess I was scared shitless. Now listen. Fetch up a length of rope. Make a bowline in one and secure the standing end to that winch. Hurry now.'

Jessica went below, and heard the splash as he went overboard. He had *guts*. Her hands were shaking as she pulled out a coil of rope from the forepeak and dragged it on deck. It took her three attempts to tie the bowline. Then she wrapped the standing part round the winch on the stump of the mainmast as instructed. By then he was back alongside, pushing the cylinder in front of him. 'The cylinder first,' he said. 'Lower the bowline.' She did so, and he pulled the loop round the neck of the bottle and drew it tight. 'Take it up.'

She turned the winch handle and brought the bottle up. She rolled it on to the deck, freed the bowline, and dropped it back down to him. He put one foot in it and nodded. She winched him up in turn. This was harder work, but as soon as he was level with the deck she took a turn on a cleat, then hurried back to the security of the wheelhouse and picked up the rifle.

She could feel the tension oozing away from her muscles, even if she knew the crisis was far from over. Then, without warning, she felt his arms go round her waist, pinning her own arms to her sides. 'Jesus!' she shouted. 'You bastard! Now's not the time.'

'Listen,' he said. 'Will you marry me?'

The Catastrophe

'Marry *you*?' Jessica asked, shrugging herself free when she realized he was not intending to recapture her. 'You need your head examined.'

He sat on the settee berth. 'What's so crazy about that idea? We know each other very well, we get on well together, we have great sex together...'

Jessica sat on the steering seat. 'Are you talking about before you go back to prison, or after you are out? By then we'll both be past it.'

'You're not seriously going to turn me in after what we've been through together?'

'So you're a hero. But I'm not going to have any choice. They're on to you, Michael. No matter where you go, they'll catch up with you.'

'Do we have to go anywhere?'

'You mean we'd spend the rest of our lives on this boat?'

'Why not?'

Oddly, that sounded very attractive. But she had to keep a sense of perspective. 'This boat is a wreck. It isn't going anywhere.'

'That's the idea.'

'You are also a kidnapping rapist bastard,' she reminded him.

'I fell in love with you at first sight.'

'You mean thirteen years ago, while I was holding you on the floor?'

'Can happen. Dante fell in love with Beatrice at first sight, and remained in love with her all of his life, although he never even spoke to her. I dreamed of you every night for ten years, and then even more when I got out. But I knew that if I simply walked up to you and asked you to go out with me, you'd suppose I only wanted sex with you.'

'You *did* only want sex with me.'

'That doesn't mean I can't be in love with you.'

'And if we married,' she said, arguing with herself now, 'I suppose you think I wouldn't turn you in when we eventually reach civilization.'

'It would be unusual, wouldn't it?'

'But we can't be married *until* we reach civilization. That means we can't be married until after I've turned you in.'

'You have tunnel vision,' he said.

Jessica picked up the rifle. 'Most women do, when it comes to rape.'

'I never raped you,' he said. 'You raped me.'

'Tell that to the judge. Now just don't do anything stupid.' She moved towards him, the rifle levelled.

'You can't be serious,' he protested. 'You're going to tie me up again? After what we've been through? Listen, I could've knocked you about just now, and I didn't.'

'That's your business. This is mine.' She passed the handcuffs round the upright and clipped his wrists together. 'I think we could both do with something to eat.' She grinned. 'Don't go away.'

'Bitch!' he said. 'Bitch!' he shouted, then added, 'You never did say yes or no.'

'I think you can assume that my response is negative. Ask me again when you come out of gaol.'

She took a look around the sea. No fin, and even the disturbed water was settling. Of course, that didn't solve their problem of how to get the yacht moving towards where she wanted it to go. Or even, supposing they managed to fix the rudder, if she would dare start the engines again. But her brain was teeming with ideas. There had been that ship. If she could rig up some kind of jury aerial for the VHF, then the next time a ship was within twenty miles or so, she would be able to contact it. So what if it didn't come for a couple of weeks, or even a couple of months? They had enough food to last well beyond that, and as long as it rained from time to time, enough water too. She felt quite buoyant. But as she looked at the sea, she frowned. It didn't seem quite right. For a moment she couldn't decide what was different, then she realized it was the angle that had changed, very slightly.

'Listen!' Michael said, his tone also quite changed. 'Christ! I think we have trouble.'

Jessica listened to the faint gurgling sound from aft. She ran across the wheelhouse and almost fell down the companion into the cabin, landing on her hands and knees ... in about an inch of water. 'Oh, Jesus!' she gasped. 'Michael!' she shouted. 'We're sinking! What do I do?'

'Start the pump.'

'Where?'

'It's up here in the wheelhouse. The switch is under the console.'

Jessica found the switch, flipped it on, and knelt beside it as the gentle hum started, followed in seconds by the swish of water exiting from the ship. She leaned out of the wheelhouse door to watch the thin stream emerging from the drain in the hull. 'Oh, thank God! Will it do?'

'That depends on how big an opening it is. Can't be more than a strained seam from where that bastard butted us, or we'd have gone down by now. But it has to be fixed, for two reasons. Leaks that aren't fixed have a habit of getting bigger, and that pump is burning more battery juice than we are likely to take in through the solar panels.'

'How long do we have?'

'Maybe twenty-four hours. But once those batteries go flat, you'll have a hell of a job getting them charged up again without starting the engines, and you can't start the engines without battery power. And if you start the engines now, that might just bring his nibs back again.'

Jessica felt like having a good cry. This was mostly emotional exhaustion, she knew. But every time she seemed to have things under control some fresh crisis faced her. 'Listen,' Michael said. 'Let me free and I'll have a look and see if I can patch things up.' She knew she had to; there was no way she could cope with this all by herself. She picked up the rifle, unlocked one handcuff, backed across the wheelhouse. 'One day you just have to get tired of pointing that thing at me,' he said. 'You have to learn to trust me.'

'Like I said, I should need my head examined,' she said. 'Get on with it.'

He went down the steps. 'Jesus!'

She stood above him, pointing the rifle at his back. 'How much is there?'

'Maybe an inch over the floorboards.'

'Then at least it's not gaining.' But it wasn't going down, either, and when she looked out of the window there was an even more pronounced angle: *Maria Anna* was definitely down by the stern.

Michael had rolled back the carpet and was taking up the floorboards. The bilges were certainly full of water, in which various plastic bottles were floating. He took these out and thrust his hand in, and felt around. Then he moved and tried another section.

'Got it. Right aft,' he said. 'When he struck the rudder, I guess. Can you pass me down my goggles?' She did so, and he put them on and thrust his head into the dark water. She didn't believe he could see anything, even with the goggles, but a few seconds later he brought his head up. 'As I thought, there's a seam opened up.'

'Can you fix it?'

'Maybe. But I need to get rid of this water. Look in the port locker by the helm, and you'll see a hand pump. We'll have to use that as well.'

Jessica did as instructed, and passed the cumbersome apparatus down to him. 'Feed this hose over the side,' he said. She did this through the wheelhouse door, and watched the steady stream of water emerging from the exit for the electric pump. That was reassuring, and if they could double that...

'Okay?' Michael called.

'I think so.' He began to pump, moving the handle to and fro. After a few seconds water began to issue across the deck, and this was in a greater volume than from the lower exit. But it was dependent upon Michael's muscles. Whatever would she do without him? 'Is there anything I can do to help?'

'In a while. Do you think you can handle this pump?'

'I would say so.'

'Right. You can take over from me as soon as I've broken the back of it.' Jessica looked out of the window. The last trace of the foam

231

that had accompanied the final attack had gone. There was no sign of the shark. But he had done enough damage. Even after being dismasted in the storm the yacht had still seemed utterly secure. But now it was wounded, perhaps mortally. And they had nowhere to go. 'Right,' Michael said. 'Take over.'

She knelt beside him. The bilges were almost dry, but water was constantly seeping in through the strained seam, and now she gasped when she saw that the gash was several inches long, the crack opening and shutting to the movement of the yacht, each opening allowing water to enter. 'Keep pumping,' Michael told her.

He left her. The rifle and the revolver were in the wheelhouse, but she couldn't believe he was going to try anything right this minute.

Nor did he. When he returned a few minutes later he was equipped with a couple of blankets together with various tubes of instant filler. He lay on the deck beside her while he tore the blankets into strips and stuffed the home-made caulking into the crack, then poured the filler on top of them. 'Will that hold?' she asked.

'Let's hope it does.'

He continued to add material, sweat pouring down his cheeks. But sweat was pouring down her cheeks as well, and soaking her tracksuit, as she worked the handle to and fro, arm muscles burning now, knees aching from kneeling. But at last Michael was satisfied. 'I think we could both do with a drink,' he said.

They went up into the wheelhouse and he switched off the pump. Then he mixed them each a rum and lime cocktail. Jessica sat on the settee berth, too exhausted even to think. 'Seems to me you said something about lunch,' he remarked. 'Would you like me to get it?'

'Would you?'

'No problem.' He went down the forward companion while she sipped her drink. The alcohol restored some of her energy. She knew she couldn't just drift away. Michael had been magnificent as usual when it came to the boat. But that didn't change what he was, what he had done. And above all, it wouldn't change his determination not to go to gaol.

The revolver remained on the console, the rifle on the floor. She picked them up, put them where she could reach them. 'Grub up,' he called.

She left the rifle, put the revolver in her waistband, and went below. The meal both smelled good and looked good, and he had opened a bottle of wine. 'Armed to the teeth, as always,' he remarked.

'Seems a good idea.' She ate hungrily. 'So what happens now?'

'Not a lot. We can't go anywhere. Even if you risked the engines, you can't steer her.'

Jessica had been thinking about that. 'Yes, I can steer her,' she said. 'With the engines. If I line her up in the direction we want to go, and keep both engines at the same revolutions, we should travel in a relatively straight line.'

His eyes narrowed. 'Who's a smarty-pants, then? That's supposing the props aren't damaged.'

'Well, are they? You went down there.'

'Why should I tell you?'

'All right,' she said. 'Be macho. I can always test them and find out. But the first thing is to rig a jury aerial for the VHF.' She actually was in no hurry to start the engines. She wanted to be sure the shark had gone for good.

'Fat lot of good that'll do you. It only has a range of fifty-odd miles, even with an aerial at the top of the mast. The best aerial you can rig on that stump would give you perhaps twenty.'

'Twenty miles will do fine. That ship we saw yesterday certainly wasn't more than twenty miles away. If that.' She watched him finish his meal. 'So, will you help me? I'm sure you know more about it than I do. But if you won't help me,' she said, studying his expression, 'I'll do it myself, even if it takes time. We have the time.'

He glared at her, then grinned, and refilled her cup with wine. 'What I would like to do, JJ, is have another sex session. You have no idea what an effect the last one had on my libido.'

'I hadn't noticed anything wrong with your libido,' she remarked. It had certainly had an effect on hers.

'You'd be surprised. So, how about it? You can tie me up and blindfold me again if you wish. Although I'd rather you didn't. I'd really like to watch you getting off.'

'I'm not in the mood,' Jessica said. Besides, she was still thoroughly ashamed of what she had done, no matter how much she had enjoyed it.

'So it's back to undeclared warfare,' he suggested.

'I think the warfare has been declared for some time,' she said.

'Well, then...' He lunged at her, and found himself looking down the barrel of her revolver.

'Bitch,' he commented. 'Do you realize that if you were to shoot me, you'd be done? You couldn't have coped with that leak by yourself.'

'I think I might have.' But she knew she was lying. 'Anyway, I don't have to kill you, you know. I can shoot you anywhere I like.'

'God, what a conversation,' he grumbled. 'So what you really mean is, it's back to the settee up top.'

'Yes,' she said. 'But you had better use the head first.'

Once she had handcuffed him to the stanchion, Jessica went below to the cabin, knelt, and peered into the bilge, which they had left exposed. There was a little water in there; she couldn't remember how much had been there before. But the patch seemed to be holding.

She took off her sweat-soaked clothes, had a shower, and climbed on to the bed, lay down, and was asleep in seconds. She felt that she had never been so tired. She had not, in fact, really had a chance to recover from the exhaustion of the typhoon. Now she just wanted to sleep and sleep and sleep. There were so many problems, so many aspects of her situation, which needed to be addressed. But they could wait until she was fully recovered.

She awoke to a clap of thunder that seemed to be right over the boat. 'Shit!' she shouted as she sat up. She ran up into the wheelhouse without stopping to dress herself.

Michael was awake and staring out of the window. 'Kind of caught us unawares,' he remarked. The entire sky was black, and now there was another crash of thunder, and a few minutes later the rain began to fall, huge drops which hit the sea like bullets and drummed on the wheelhouse roof to shut out all other sound. Except for the peals of thunder.

Jessica ran to the console, checked the barometer. It had fallen, but only one millibar. 'Do you think it's going to blow?' she asked.

'Yes.'

She bit her lip. 'Should I put up the shutters?'

236

'Can you?' She released him, and followed him around with the revolver while he shuttered them in. By the time he was finished it was dark, and the wind had risen. But it did not have the terrifying force of the typhoon. 'Just a gale,' he said.

She made him return to the berth, and cooked dinner. The rain continued to pound down and the wind to howl; big waves began to buffet the derelict yacht. Some of them seemed to break right over them. 'Do you think she'll capsize again?' she asked as she fed him.

'There's no top hamper to pull her over,' Michael said. 'I think we've a good chance of staying upright. It all depends on whether we get picked up by a real big one.' He grinned. 'But you're not afraid?'

Oddly, she wasn't. There was just too much to be afraid of. Instead, she felt in a mood of wild defiance. But when she went below to try to get some sleep, she was horrified to find water over the cabin floor. 'Michael!' She scrambled back up into the wheelhouse. 'That leak's opened up.'

'Had to happen, with this buffeting,' he agreed. 'Start the pump. No, start the engines first, to make sure the batteries stay topped up.'

'But that shark...'

'Fuck the shark. We're going to sink anyway if you don't get that water out.'

Jessica knew he was right. She drew her usual deep breath before starting the engines.

237

This time there was a slight hesitation before they turned over – the batteries had begun to run down. She put the gear levers in neutral and half-throttle ahead, so that they would both give a useful charge, then turned on the pump. She went aft, equipped with a flash-light to reinforce the cabin lights. Water drifted to and fro over the floorboards as the yacht rolled. The handpump lay where they had left it. But they had had to close the wheelhouse door in order to put up the shutters, and to open it while the storm lasted would probably let in as much water from above as there was coming in from below. She went back up to the wheelhouse and sat on the floor. 'Any joy?' Michael asked.

'I can't see any yet,' she confessed.

It was the longest night of Jessica's life, even longer than the night of the typhoon. She kept going aft to check the water. She was sure it was gaining, but kept telling herself that it wasn't. On the other hand, it certainly wasn't going down. She sat down again, head drooping between her drawn-up knees. Please don't sink, *Maria Anna*, she begged. Quite apart from the small matter of survival, she had become very fond of the yacht. Please don't sink.

When she awoke, amazed at having slept, the storm had passed and a brilliant moon was shining across the water. She looked at her watch. Four o'clock. In another hour or so it would be getting light. She scrambled

238

up, and skidded across the wheelhouse because of the list. 'Oh, my God!' she gasped, and thumped Michael on the shoulder.

He awoke with a start, took in the situation instantly. 'Get me out of these,' he shouted. Jessica released the handcuffs, this time taking them right off. He grabbed the flashlight and went aft. 'We're done. We'll never get that lot out.'

'The hand pump ... We can open the door, now.'

'Too late for that.' He brushed past her as he ran on deck, released the harness for the life-raft and threw it over the side. Jessica stood in the hatch to watch. A jerk on the lanyard, and the canister burst open to allow the bright orange raft to unfold itself. Jessica thought she had never seen a more beautiful sight in her life. 'We've only minutes,' Michael said. 'Get some plum puddings.'

Jessica dashed forward, sliding down the companion, hurling herself into the forepeak to gather up half a dozen of the tins, then found a bag to put them in. All around her were creaks and groans, and the slurp of water. My God, she thought. If she goes down with me in here...

She scrambled back into the wheelhouse, and saw that both the rifle and the revolver had gone. Her head jerked, and Michael grinned at her from the hatch. 'I put them in the raft. I didn't think you'd want to be separated from them.'

'Bastard,' she said. 'I've six tins.'

'That'll have to do. Abandon ship.' The yacht was certainly low in the water.

'We can't live on six tins of Christmas pudding.'

'It's a help. There are emergency rations in the raft. You coming, or drowning?'

'What about clothes? I can't leave in the nuddy.'

'I'll fetch you some clothes. Just get off the ship.' Jessica gave him the bag of tins, went up the ladder to the deck – with some difficulty because of the list – and sat on the toe-rail. The raft's canopy was now fully erected, and the flap was open, allowing her to enter. But to go in there … It looked so small and flimsy, rising and falling on the swell. 'It's a six-man raft,' Michael told her. 'So there's room for two.'

'It looks as if it's about to turn over,' she protested.

'It'll be better with our weight in it,' Michael assured her.

Jessica drew a deep breath, timed her moment at the top of a swell, and dropped through the aperture. She landed on her hands and knees, bounced, and rolled over. Which was just as well, she reflected, as Michael threw the bag of tins behind her. Then he was gone. Suppose the yacht went down before he came back up? But he was back in a few seconds, handing her an armful of clothing and two lifejackets, together with a spare magazine for the Armalite. Then he climbed into the raft himself, and cut

240

the painter.

Instantly they drifted away from the yacht. 'Suppose she doesn't sink?' Jessica asked. 'Can we get back?'

'There are paddles,' he said.

The darkness was fading, and now they could see the yacht quite clearly. She was about fifty feet away, and while the raft was bobbing on the waves, up and down, *Maria Anna* was hardly moving at all. Her after deck was now only a few inches above the surface, and the water was churning from the exhaust exits. The engines were still running! But a few minutes later there was a puff of steam and a small explosion, and then *Maria Anna* went down like the holed bucket Michael had once used as a simile. Her stern went under, her bows went up, and hung there for a moment, and then slid beneath the waves.

Jessica burst into tears.

The sun came out of a cloudless horizon to play on an empty ocean. The sea was going down all the while, and the wind had dropped. Jessica imagined them as a little orange speck, seen from afar or above. But who was going to see them, from afar or above, where no one was looking?

Michael sat opposite her, staring at her. 'Damn and blast and fuck,' he remarked.

'Has that aspect of the situation just occurred to you?'

'I forgot to collect the GPS. Now we won't know where we are.'

'What would you like first, the bad news or the bad news?'

'What?'

'The GPS was smashed four days ago. But does it matter where we are when we die?'

'We are not going to die today. Or tomorrow. There is sufficient food and biscuit, used sparingly, on board the raft to last six men three days. Ditto cans of water. Therefore it should last two people nine days, right?'

'If you say so.'

'And then we have six plum puddings. Then there is also a fishing line and some hooks, so we should be able to catch some fish. Add to that some rain, and I'd say we have at least a fortnight.'

'How do we cook these fish you are going to catch?'

'We eat them raw.'

'Ugh!'

'You'd be surprised what you can do when you're sufficiently hungry. Anyway, raw fish is very good for you. The Japanese eat it all the time.'

'In case it has escaped your notice,' Jessica said, 'I am not Japanese.'

She was being thoroughly disagreeable, she knew. But never had she felt so devastated. Every plan was shot.

'So, would you like breakfast?' Michael asked.

'I couldn't eat a thing.' She was actually feeling quite seasick, for the first time since her initial days on board *Maria Anna*. That was partly because her stomach was still tied up in knots at having to abandon the yacht, but also because the raft had a totally different motion, which was uneasy even for someone who had been at sea for more than three months.

'Suit yourself,' Michael said. 'Just remember you need to keep your strength up, for as long as possible.'

'My watch has stopped.'

'Wasn't it water-resistant?'

'I don't think it has anything to do with water. The battery has gone dead.'

'Well, there's damn all we can do about that, my love.'

Just one shitting thing after another, Jessica reflected.

There was a long PVC carry-all secured to one of the side sections of the raft. This Michael unzipped with great care. There seemed a good deal of stuff in there, as he had told her, but she wasn't at that moment sufficiently interested to look, although she accepted a sip of water from the can he opened. It tasted very stale, but was better than nothing.

Michael opened a container of biscuits and munched one. 'I suppose you're quite happy,' she said. 'This is how you always intended it to be.'

'Not quite. This has been rather forced on us by that goddamned fish. I had hoped to be more able to choose my time. And I hadn't reckoned on it being so soon. But man proposes, and God disposes, right? I'm only sorry it's happening to you as well.' She drew up her knees, clasped them in her arms, and rested her head. 'And as you know, I was seriously considering abandoning all of Plan A,' Michael went on, 'in favour of Plan B. How would you like to change your mind about marrying me?'

'Oh, shut up,' she said.

'Or at least forgiving me, for everything.'

She raised her head. 'Forgive you? For God's sake, you kidnapped me, beat me, raped me, made me your slave, and now you've got me in a situation where I have nine days to live, and I'm supposed to forgive you?'

'Actually,' he pointed out, 'as I said, we have more than nine days. Because of the plum puddings. Remember?' She glared at him, then could not stop herself from bursting into laughter. She felt pretty hysterical anyway, but this situation was beyond her wildest imagining. Or her wildest nightmare. 'That's my girl,' Michael said, and took off his shirt.

Jessica didn't pay much attention to that, but when he took off his pants as well, she raised her head again. 'Just what are you doing?'

'Taking off my clothes. For one thing, it's getting pretty warm in here, or hadn't you noticed?'

She hadn't; she still felt chilled to the bone. If her clothes weren't wet from the condensation in the bottom of the raft, she'd have

244

put them on. 'And for another,' Michael went on, 'as you have just reminded me, we have only perhaps a dozen days to live. In that time there's not a lot we can do. I thought we could spend most of it making love.'

'You mean having sex. Love has nothing to do with it.'

'A rose by any other name...'

'Well, you can forget it.'

'Are you claiming to have a headache?'

'As a matter of fact, I do have a headache. And a bellyache and backache. And I'm depressed as hell. In any event, it's not practical, not on this surface.' Every time she moved, the rubber undulated beneath her.

'I'm sure we'll manage,' he said, crawling towards her. 'Have you never made love on a waterbed?'

'In that case, I'll get dressed,' she said. 'And catch pneumonia.' But he was kneeling on her clothes. 'Do you mind?' she asked.

'I do mind. Come on, JJ, be a sweetheart.'

She sighed, and relaxed, and let him get on with it. As she had pointed out, it was quite impossible for him to enter her without the most complete cooperation from her, but actually he made no attempt to do so. He just wanted to stroke her and caress and kiss her, all over. It occurred to her that for a man who was about to die he certainly had a one-track mind. Or maybe he did love her, after all.

Jessica lay with her body half out of the opening, her hand trailing in the water. Michael lay beside her, but he had got over his bout of passion, and was paying out the fishing line astern. 'What happens if we catch a whopper?' she asked.

'Maybe we'll live longer,' he suggested.

Eating raw fish! But she didn't really expect him to catch anything. 'What will we do when we run out of food?' she asked.

'What do you want to do? I mean, we can just lie here and dwindle, or one of us could kill the other. Would you like me to kill you? I'd do it absolutely painlessly. Cut your throat. Then I could perhaps live off you for a day or two longer.' He squeezed her backside. 'Nothing like a good ham.'

'Oh!' She flung herself away from the opening, and bounced in the bottom of the raft. 'You are obscene! Horrible! But you have always been obscene and horrible. You are an obscene and horrible man!' She burst into tears, of anger, and frustration ... and despair.

'You're upset.'

'Oh, you...' She swept her hand over the bottom of the raft to find something to throw at him, and encountered the revolver, which slipped easily into her hand.

'Okay,' he said. 'You kill me instead. I won't be as tender as you, but I should still be good for a meal or two.'

Jessica put down the gun, hunched herself into a ball. 'I don't want to die, Michael. I really don't want to die.'

'I know,' he said. 'Neither do I. I would like to drift here with you forever and ever. Maybe, if we wished for that long enough, and hard enough, it might happen.' She realized that he was as light-headed and close to hysteria as was she ... and there was nothing either of them could do about it.

He did not catch a fish that day, or the next. They spent the time lying beside each other, sometimes touching, sometimes stroking, most of the time just staring at the canopy. It was very hot and close within the raft, and neither of them had the slightest inclination to get dressed. They chewed biscuits and sipped water, but neither had much of an appetite, either. 'If it's going to happen,' Jessica said, 'shouldn't we make it happen? Like have a real blow-out, eat all the food, drink all the water, and then commit suicide? Joint suicide,' she hastily added.

'I'd rather string things along awhile,' he said, and kissed her.

Jessica supposed she should start composing herself for death. This was difficult, when she felt as healthy and as strong and as *vital* as at any time in her life. And yet death was inevitable, and in only a few days' time!

She found it difficult to think of her life as a police officer, or at home with Tom. The past three months had been so packed with a mixture of tension and utter relaxation that her previous life had faded into a nether world which might never have existed. Her actual death would make no difference to

Tom, or Andrea, or the commander, because they would go on searching for her, with every day that passed having to accept, more and more, that she had to be dead. Then there would be a memorial service, and tears from her friends, and statements on television from the police that they were still pursuing useful lines of inquiry ... while all the time they would not have a clue.

While she would have disappeared forever. The life-raft had the name of the yacht painted on it, and she supposed it would eventually be picked up or drift ashore. But having established that it came from the *Maria Anna*, which had so tragically disappeared on its voyage round the world, the fact that there would be two skeletons in it would merely close the file; they would be able to trace her identity through her dental records and perhaps DNA. So she'd go out with a bang after all. And Tom and Andrea would never know the truth, whether she had been abducted or whether she had been carrying on a secret romance and finally run off with her lover, straight into tragedy.

But what was the truth, she wondered? She glanced at Michael, lying beside her with his eyes shut. After that first surge of sexual energy he had not come at her again, save for the odd stroke. He too was having to come to terms with the fact that the end of his life was at hand.

She wondered what he thought about that. She had seen no evidence that he was a practising Christian, but surely everybody, as the end approached, had to at least consider what might be waiting for them, even if it was to turn into a dissolving cloud of nitrogen. She had attempted to hold that belief herself, for most of her short life. It was difficult to be certain about it at the very end.

So, if Michael was no different from anyone else – and she was sure he wasn't – then he would have to accept that if there was any kind of retribution waiting in the hereafter, he was going to get it. She wondered if he was afraid of that.

But what of herself? As she had thought before, it was impossible for two people to be shut up together with no other company whatsoever over a period of nearly four months and not form some kind of relationship. Michael and she had formed a very definite relationship, love-hate on her side, maybe, but none the less valid. She had actively hated him in the beginning. Then the hatred had been, if not replaced, certainly softened by both familiarity and her admiration for him as a sailor. Yet when she had had the opportunity to turn the tables she had seized it with both hands ... and then proceeded to go right over the top. She still could not believe that she had done what she had, mounted him like the most casual whore – or the most aggressive lover! What's more, she had gloried in her power, her ability to do anything she wished, to him or with him.

She suspected that for a day or two after the

typhoon she had not been entirely sane. And now they were going to die, lying naked beside each other. Shit, she thought, now is no time for hatred. She nudged him. 'You awake?'

'Yes.'

'What are you thinking about?'

'Remembering.'

'Oh! I've been thinking about what happens next.'

He opened his eyes. 'Are you saying you know something I don't?'

'Not really. But it seemed important. Listen...' She raised herself on her elbow. 'I want you to know that I forgive you for everything.'

'That's very nice of you. I'm grateful, believe me.'

'It's simply that I don't want us to die at odds.'

'Absolutely.'

'Well...' She leaned over and kissed him. 'Do you think that'll make any difference?'

'To what?'

'To your reception in the hereafter.'

'I really wouldn't know. I don't believe in a hereafter.'

'Not at all?'

'Not a sausage.'

'Oh.' She lay down again. 'Then that was a waste of time.'

He rose on his elbow in turn. 'I think it was a very sweet thing for you to say. And, having said it, how about marrying me?'

'Oh, all right.'

'Great. Then, as captain of this ship, I proclaim us man and wife. And we even have some wedding cake – well, the nearest thing to it – to celebrate with.'

She supposed they were both mad. Well, that figured. But she thought it was rather fun, and even consummated the event with some pleasure.

She awoke to a distant rumbling sound. For a moment she thought it was Michael snoring, then she realized it was coming from outside the raft. Thunder! Shit! she thought. All they needed was another storm, which would throw the raft about like a cork and then probably capsize it, with them inside it.

She rose to her knees and peered through the flap. She could see nothing but stars, so low she thought she might be able to touch them. The flap faced east, thus the thunderclouds must be coming from the west. She pulled herself up to sit on the rubber gunwale, and peered round the tent squinting into the darkness. Again, nothing but stars. Except ... She frowned as she narrowed her eyes even further, trying to identify the long line of white that filled the horizon.

She had no idea what it could be, but she didn't like the look of it. 'Michael!' She dropped back beside him. 'Wake up. Something's happening out there.'

'Eh?' He sat up and shook his head. 'What's happening?'

'That's what I want you to tell me. Listen.'

He did so, frowning. 'It's coming from the west,' she said.

He sat in the opening, and like her, peered round the canopy. 'Holy Jesus Christ,' he muttered.

'It looks like a huge wave,' she said. 'It's not coming this way, is it?' Although she couldn't imagine why she was worried about that: a tidal wave would finish them off very smartly.

'No,' he said. 'It's not going anywhere.'

'Eh?'

'That's surf, JJ. Surf. Just over there is a coral reef. And where there's a reef ... there's almost certainly land.'

Andrea was excited. 'Peter just called.'

Tom looked up. 'Something?'

'You bet. A Japanese freighter en route from Yokohama to San Francisco picked up a call just over a week ago. It was very faint, but they did get the name: Maria Anna. *That's why he reported it. And, wait for it: their operator swears it was a woman's voice.'*

Tom stood up. 'What did they do?'

'Nothing. They entered it in the log.'

'What?'

'They didn't think it was a distress call. Whoever was speaking didn't use the word "mayday". And it was so faint they thought it had come from a long way away, sort of maximum VHF surface range, maybe fifty miles.'

'Shit.'

'But we do have their position when they

252

received the call.'

'From fifty miles away. That's a big ocean.'

'Peter has an idea. He thinks that the call may have been made from much closer than that. Seems there was a typhoon in that part of the Pacific only a day or two before. The freighter had a rough time. Peter suggests that if the yacht was caught in the storm, and lost its aerials, that call could have come from as close as twenty miles of the freighter's position. Maybe less. If he's right, we know pretty accurately where she was a week ago. And we know she's alive.'

'Andie, you are a genius. I'm going up to Adams.'

'Do you think he'll let us mount a search?'

'If he doesn't,' Tom said, 'I am resigning and going on my own.'

The Island

Jessica felt sick. She had prepared herself to die, had accepted the inevitability of it. And now...

'Of course, getting through that surf isn't going to be easy,' Michael said, studying the horizon through his binoculars. 'It's big stuff.'

Jessica slipped down into the bottom of the raft. Her emotions couldn't cope with such an on-off situation.

Michael sat beside her. 'So, are we going to

go for it, or not?'

'What do you mean?'

'Well, if we just sit here and do nothing, there's at least a fifty per cent chance that the current will carry us right round the island.'

'And where there's one island there could be another.'

'There *could* be. Although this looks more likely to be that isolated atoll I spotted on the chart before the typhoon. But even if there is another atoll about, there'll still be surf.'

'What's the alternative?'

'We can try to get ashore. We can get the paddles out when we get closer, and paddle ourselves towards the reef. Eventually we'll get caught in the inshore current, and that'll suck us into the surf.'

'And?'

'We try to keep control of the raft until we're carried through it. There'll be a lagoon beyond. But I wouldn't rate our chances of getting through as more than fifty-fifty.'

'So,' she said, 'we either die today, by drowning, or in about three days' time, by starvation. I'm for today.'

'It won't be today. More likely first thing tomorrow morning.'

'Can you see anything?' Jessica asked.

Michael sat on the gunwale in the flap opening, studying the horizon. It was afternoon now, and he was looking into the sun, but they had appreciably closed the surf during the past few hours. 'Yes. Land.'

'You mean it's really there? Let me have a look.'

He draped the binocular strap round her neck, and gave up his place. She wanted to stand up, but didn't dare on the undulating rubber base. So she sat on the gunwale and focussed the glasses. She first of all picked up the surf, and gulped. She could now make out that while there was a tremendous mass of foam out there, it was the breaking crests of waves being drawn up by the shallowing water. They looked enormous, as big as anything off the Horn.

And beyond the surf there were palm trees, on a hill, she reckoned. The hill looked quite extensive, so maybe the rest of the land, presently hidden behind the surf, might also be fairly extensive. 'Do you think there'll be people?'

'I shouldn't think so. This atoll is too far from anywhere else. But if there are, you won't forget that we are now married. That means you cannot testify against me.'

'What you mean is,' Jessica corrected, 'I cannot be *forced* to testify against you. Whether I do or not is up to me.'

'I would regard that as an act of betrayal.'

'Seem to me we're putting the cart well before the horse,' she pointed out. If he really thought she accepted they were married because he had pronounced them to be, he needed his head examined. She had gone along with the farce because she hadn't wanted them to die hating each other. Now

255

there was a whole different ball game. But she didn't want to fight with him again until she knew whether she was going to live or die. 'Let's get ashore first, and worry about everything else after.'

In any event, conversation was becoming increasingly difficult as the noise of the surf grew steadily louder. 'What causes it?' she shouted. 'There's not a lot of wind.'

'There's a hell of a long way to any land looking east,' he said. 'The movement of the sea just builds over big distances. Could be there's a storm off the west coast of America, and this is the swell from it. Or even left from that typhoon.'

She supposed that going to sea on a long voyage in a small boat was a lesson in humility that few people who spent their lives ashore could grasp. Of course there were things like earthquakes and volcanoes and floods on land, but most people felt that they were in control of their lives, and if one of those catastrophes occurred, providing one wasn't personally involved, everyone went into a state of shock for a few days and then came to and reflected, well, it'll probably never happen to me. It would be impossible to live otherwise.

But at sea one was deliberately challenging the greatest forces in the universe. Once one left the sight of land, one was constantly made aware that there really was something bigger than oneself, an enormous power which one was attempting to utilize but

256

which every so often shrugged its shoulders and said, remember, I call the shots. It had taken a long time for that to sink in, in her case.

Jessica was surprised when Michael touched her arm. She had been sure she wouldn't sleep, but she must have gone off into a doze, because he had apparently been sitting in the opening without awakening her. Now the darkness of the night was just beginning to fade, and the noise was deafening. 'I think we should get ready,' he shouted. 'First thing, we need to eat.'

She opened a tin of plum pudding, although she wasn't in the least hungry, and her stomach was tied up in such knots she didn't know if it would accept food. 'May as well drink the last of the water, too,' he said, dropping beside her. They shared it out. 'Right,' he said. 'Now get dressed.'

'To go swimming?'

'It's the only way you're going to get any clothes ashore.'

Jessica pulled on her knickers and tracksuit.

'Now these.' He gave her one of the life-jackets, showed her how to put it on, and tied the straps in front and behind.

'I feel I may float away at any moment,' she commented.

'That's the idea.' He tied on his own. 'Now, we have to get rid of the canopy. We can't use the oars with it in place.' It was actually secured by clips, and these were easy to

257

release. The PVC settled about them and they rolled it up and secured it to one of the gunwales.

While they were doing this, Jessica looked up and gasped. The surf was now only half a mile away, immense walls of water, rising up and up, moving away from them and then tumbling over. They could not possibly survive such monsters. 'Are we going to tie ourselves in?' she asked.

Michael shook his head. 'If we tie ourselves in and she capsizes, we may well drown. If we get thrown out, we get thrown out. Make for the shore.' He frowned at her. 'You *can* swim?'

'What a time to ask. I'm great in a pool. And I once swam a river in South America. A small river.'

'Well, moving the arms and legs works in the sea as well. The jacket will keep you up.'

'What about the reef?'

'We can't foresee everything, JJ. You said go for it. You can still change your mind. If you do it right now.'

She chewed her lip. The surf looked terrifying. But so was the thought of lying in this raft waiting for death. 'We go for it,' she said.

'Right. Now here's what we do. We take a paddle each, and we move the raft towards the white water. You ever paddled before?'

'You mean, as with an oar? No.'

'Okay, so we may have to practise a bit. It's very important that we act in unison, otherwise the raft is just going to turn round and

258

round and we are going to get nothing but exhaustion.'

She nodded. He could be so masterfully sure of what needed to be done.

'I reckon that when we get to within about a quarter of a mile of the surf, we'll be into the undertow, and after that we won't be able to get back out. Whatever happens after that is going to happen very quickly. What we have to do is attempt to keep the raft under control, and, if we see anything that looks like a break or a passage, head for it. There is certain to be one. Okay?'

'Okay.' She was trembling with a combination of fear and excitement.

'Last thing. We must anticipate being thrown out. In which case we head for the beach, as I said. That means everything in the raft that isn't tied down is probably going to be lost. I'm going to put this revolver in my belt and hope it stays there.'

'I think I should have the gun.'

He grinned. 'You don't have a belt. And if you stuff it down your tracksuit pants it might just go off and spoil your figure. You can have the knife.'

She pulled up her tracksuit leg and he strapped the diving knife to her calf, drawing the buckles tight, including that holding the haft to the sheath. 'That should stay put,' he said. 'I don't think we can carry anything else. I'd like to take the binocs, but they'd just be a hindrance. However...' He did his best to secure all the gear, including the rifle, to the

259

various panels, put the binoculars and the spare magazine for the rifle with what remained of the survival kit into the PVC carry-all attached to the inside gunwale, and zipped it up. 'You never know your luck. Ready?'

'As I'll ever be.'

'Then give us a kiss.'

She obliged. She was still trembling, but now the apprehension had been overtaken by the excitement, the desire and the determination to be up and doing.

'Well, then,' he said, 'as I am sure someone said in similar circumstances: Geronimo!'

The sun was just rising as they started paddling. As Michael had suggested would be the case, they didn't do at all well at first, and merely spun round and round. But after about an hour they got the raft under control. By then Jessica's tracksuit was soaked in sweat and she was already feeling exhausted. 'We're in the undertow,' Michael said. 'Just keep her steady, until we really have to paddle. On my count.'

On his count of three they dabbed their paddles together. Now they were being sucked down a gigantic trough. There was a wall of water behind them, and another wall in front of them. Neither was as yet breaking; it was just a steadily increasing swell, yet Jessica felt they were about to be crushed. Then they were going up again, on the back of the wave in front. Up they went, up, as if in an elevator, before they peaked the swell, and Jessica gasped in the sheerest terror of her life.

In front of them was another valley, then another hill. It was two hills away that the crest of the swell was beginning to tumble over, hurtling down the far side like a snow avalanche. Beyond that was another breaking crest, and then another. Then she was sure she could see the darkness of the reef, visible for just a moment as the water was sucked away from it. And beyond that, the breaking water continued on its way for perhaps a hundred yards, then it dissipated into the calmest of lagoons, perhaps another quarter of a mile across, before, as Michael had promised, there was a stretch of golden beach, backed by a fringe of coconut palms, behind which there was thick green jungle, and out of which, at a distance of perhaps a mile, there rose the hill they had first seen.

It looked incredibly peaceful and beautiful, a glimpse of the most utter heaven – but they must first of all plunge into the most utter hell to reach it. As for a break in the reef ... She thought she could see a patch of blue in the middle of the foaming white, but it was several hundred yards to the right; they were never going to get over there.

'Get ready!' Michael shouted as the view disappeared and the raft sank into the following trough, and then began its slow surge up the far side.

'Stand by!' Michael yelled. Jessica knelt,

paddle held in both hands ready to thrust it over the side. The raft reached the crest and spray flew past them. Immediately ahead was the maelstrom, white even before the crest with the spindrift thrown back by the breaking wave.

'Paddle!' Michael bellowed. 'Together now.' Jessica dipped her paddle into the water, and again, as hard as she could, conscious that he was doing the same on the other side. The raft gained speed as they shot into the trough and up the next wave.

'Don't stop!' Michael screamed. Panting, sweat rolling out of her hair, Jessica dug the paddle in as fast as she could. Now they were really going very quickly, and it was obviously Michael's hope that the momentum would carry them up the far side. Actually, it did, but that was no great help. The wave was already breaking when they reached the crest, and they were sent flying downwards, reminding Jessica of the last time, many years ago, she had tried tobogganing and lost control, and gone careering down the shallow hill in a cloud of snow.

This time she could not merely jump out of the sled on to firm ground. Beneath them seemed a bottomless pit, into which the raft was capsizing. This realization drifted through Jessica's mind almost casually as she felt herself being propelled from her knees and out of the raft to fly through the air. She drew a deep breath, and was then in the water.

Around her was a totally green world. She

didn't think it was a case of her going down very far so much as the water coming up so very far to embrace her. Desperately she flailed her arms and legs, knowing she was rising, as much by the buoyancy of the life-jacket as by her own efforts. Yet her lungs were bursting when she emerged into the sunlight. She tried to look left and right, but could see nothing but flying white water, rising all around her, throwing her about as if it were a giant amusing himself. There was no sign of the raft or of Michael.

The wave moved away from her, and the water was again green. She took huge breaths, still slapping the surface with her hands. The entire world was a mass of roaring sound, but there was an even louder noise immediately behind her. She looked round, then up at the huge, twenty-foot-high wall of water coming at her, its crest over-toppling to create a foaming mass an additional eight feet high. She knew she screamed in sheer horror, then it was on her, driving her down, down, down. Her foot struck something solid, and she wanted to scream again, but knew she had to hold her breath.

Suddenly she knew she wasn't going to be able to do it. She had to breathe, while being rolled over and over in the depths of the wave. She had to breathe, and die. And disappear forever. Now her body would not even be found. Pains were shooting away from her chest and behind her eyes. It had to be now, now, *now*...

She opened her mouth and her nostrils, choked, and vomited violently as the salt water found its way down her throat. But it was mixed with air.

Jessica lay inert in the water, coughing and vomiting. Dimly she heard the roaring behind her, and a few moments later she was picked up and thrust forward again. But this time there was no violence, and she didn't even go under, supported as she was by the life jacket. And above her the sun was shining out of a clear blue sky.

She was aware principally of exhaustion, mental and physical. She felt she could lie in the warm embrace of the now calm sea forever. But her brain was still working, and she kept remembering Michael's words: to get ashore as rapidly as possible. Michael's last words!

She twisted her head to and fro. Behind her the waves still thundered on the reef before dissipating themselves in the lagoon. In front of her the palm trees beckoned, rustling in the breeze. To either side of her there was only the lagoon. She was the only living creature in the world. On top of the water, anyway. Then she remembered swimming that Brazilian river, which might, or might not, have been full of piranha. But she had survived that. So she would survive this too.

She began to swim, with slow, positive strokes. The life-jacket was a hindrance now, preventing her arms from swinging properly, and was also acting as a brake as she tried to move through the water. But she didn't dare discard it yet; she'd sink like a stone. She ran out of breath, and flopped in the water. Behind her the surf still roared, but ahead of her the beach was appreciably closer. How marvellous it would be if people were to appear, rushing forward to rescue her, and succour her, and bring the whole nightmare to an end. But the beach remained empty.

She started swimming again, arm over arm, moving her legs as well as she was able. Never had she felt so exhausted. Her feet touched something before she realized how close she was to the shore, and her heart seemed to come up into her mouth as she wondered what it was beneath her. Then she was kneeling on sand, and the gentle waves were caressing her back. She stared at the trees and the thick undergrowth beneath them. She was so thirsty. But first she had to get ashore.

She tried to stand, and fell to her knees again. So she crawled the rest of the way, slowly emerging from the water, her soaked tracksuit seeming to weigh a ton. She reached the dry sand, and stood up. Immediately the entire world seemed to revolve about her; it was nearly four months since she had set foot on dry land. She staggered to and fro, constantly putting her foot down to meet the rising deck; only the deck wasn't there, and she fell, with a thump that knocked all the breath from her body. Jessica fell asleep where she lay.

⋆ ⋆ ⋆

She awoke to complete disorientation, like that first awakening on the yacht. In the first instance, there was the continuous noise, as if she were on a train. Then there was the hardness of the sand, and the heat of her body; her clothes, and her flesh, had been dried by the sun, and she could almost feel the skin on her face getting ready to peel. But the sun had lost its heat now, and was drooping below the trees behind her.

She was thirstier than ever before in her life; her tongue seemed glued to the roof of her mouth. Slowly and painfully she moved it, trying to find some saliva. But she had to drink, something.

Then she became aware of movement close at hand. Her exhausted heart still managed to skip a beat. She turned her head, and gazed at a pair of pincers, only inches from her nose, moving gently to and fro. She gave a shriek, and rolled away from it, and the crab scuttled off and into the sea. Jessica did not remember ever having seen a crab before, in the flesh. Certainly not that close or that big. She sat up, panting, and gazed at the lagoon, and beyond at the tumbling surf. Memory flooded back, and she shuddered. She stood up, and promptly fell down again. The earth had been shaking even before she had tried that, and it was obvious that standing up or attempting to walk was going to be a problem for a while yet. But she could crawl, surely. Even that was difficult. She fell over several

266

times before she reached the grass. Each fall made her realize just how buffeted her body had been by the waves; she was in pain from head to foot. But it didn't appear as if anything was broken. It also made her realize that she was still wearing the life-jacket. The cords were solidified with salt and water, and she could not untie them. Then she remembered the knife, pulled up her pant leg, unclipped the knife, and cut the cords. She threw the jacket away, feeling as if she had been released from a straitjacket.

She sat on the grass and looked up at the palm tree immediately above her. There were coconuts up there, and the diving knife was still in her hand. With its thick, serrated blade, she was sure she could cut open one of those husks. But there was no way she could climb a coconut tree, not without a good deal of practice.

She sighed, sheathed the knife, and crawled further across the grass and into the bushes. The vegetation was thick, and tore at her tracksuit. Then something went right through the material and into her shoulder. 'Ow!' she snapped, turning round and falling over.

It was a cactus, each large, solid leaf covered in sharp spines. 'Fuck it,' she muttered, massaging her shoulder, which was bleeding. Then she frowned, dim memories of things she had read coming back to her.

She drew the knife, biting her lip as another huge thorn ripped at her flesh, but slashing with the sharp edge of the blade to cut the leaf away from its parent. Already liquid was oozing from the stem. Risking the thorns, Jessica cut the leaf in two, hesitated for a moment, then held the cut edge to her lips. So maybe I'm about to die with horrible stomach pains, she thought. But nothing had ever tasted so good. By the time she had cut and sucked at two more of the huge pods she almost felt replete.

The evening was starting to close in. Although the sun was still obviously up, and she couldn't see the western horizon because of the trees and the high ground inland, she suspected it might be sinking into a bank of cloud. So here I am, she thought, sitting amidst the bushes and gazing past them at the sea and the surf. All alone. But at least not about to die. Yet the idea of being entirely alone frightened her. First thing tomorrow she would have to explore the island and see if she *was* all alone.

And what of Michael? He couldn't have made it. Oh, poor Michael. She reminded herself that he was a kidnapping, raping pervert. Yet he seemed the only man she had ever known. She thought she might say a prayer for him, tomorrow. A prayer to the god of the sea. Michael had loved the sea, had determined to finish his life sailing, and the sea had claimed him at the end. That seemed just.

She was beginning to feel hungry. But that too would have to wait until tomorrow. Then she would have rested, and maybe got her balance back, and be able to see what she could do about those coconuts. Right that moment she just wanted to sleep. The emotional and physical exhaustion of the last few days was resulting in a total collapse of her ability to think. She was only aware that she had survived everything, the very worst the sea could throw at her, from a typhoon to a giant shark...

She thought that might be something to cheer about – tomorrow.

As usual, waking was accompanied by dis-orientation, more complete this morning than ever before because it was still dark. She was lying facing east, and there was just the faintest of glows beyond the surf, which was as huge and loud and ferocious as ever. She reckoned it must be about half past four. Then what had awakened her?

To sleep she had moved back down to the grass so that she would be under no risk of tearing herself on any thorns. As the sun had finally disappeared last night, she had been assailed by a horde of tiny, almost invisible insects, obviously sandflies, which pricked her skin and made her feel she was being attacked by needles. She had slapped and scratched and fallen asleep in the middle of doing so. Now the insects were gone, although her face and hands and feet, the exposed parts of her body, were a mass of itches. Had it been that that had awakened her?

She sat up, and heard a rustling in the bushes behind her. A lizard, she told herself. Or another of those big crabs. But it was too loud, too obviously bulky for a lizard. Or a crab. Unless it was a monster crab!

She felt as if the hair on the nape of her neck was standing on end. She had been quite sure she was alone on the island, had allowed herself to fall asleep without a thought. And now there was some creature, large and no doubt dangerous, only a few feet away.

Jessica reached down to touch the knife, which she had replaced in its sheath strapped to her calf. That made her feel better, but she still had no idea what was threatening her. If it was a big snake ... Did they have big snakes on Pacific atolls? Cautiously she drew the knife, then started to retreat down the beach. There had been no marks on the sand yesterday to suggest that any denizen of the forest ever used it. Besides, if pushed, she could always go back into the sea. She was sure the average snake couldn't swim; things like anacondas were native to South America.

She reached the water's edge, and knelt there, the knife thrust forward, peering into the darkness but seeing nothing, and hearing nothing too – all sound was obliterated by the roar of the surf. She waited, but could discern no movement. Now the sky was definitely lightening, but she remained kneeling until there was an explosion of glowing pink as the sun came above the horizon behind her.

Jessica stood up. In front of her was the

beach, an expanse of golden brown sand, still unmarked save where she had herself scuffed it, and a few other faint scratches clearly made by the crabs. Small crabs. Then there were the coconut trees, and beyond, the bush. She was both hungry and thirsty, and the only place she was going to find any food was in that bush, or at least the trees. But somewhere in there was something alive, and big, and heavy ... but which would not venture on to the sand.

She went into the water and began to wade, to the north of where she had come ashore, keeping kneedeep, where she felt safest, and watching the trees and bushes to her left. They were now rustling in the dawn breeze, but there was no other movement. To her right, the surf continued to pound the reef. Every time she looked at it, she had goose pimples; she found it hard to believe she could have survived that.

When she had waded for several minutes, she turned to look back the way she had come. Now she could no longer make out even the scuffed sand, although she thought she could just see the bright orange of the discarded life-jacket. And beside her the fringe of coconut trees still beckoned. She licked her lips. Hungry as she was, she was still thirstier. Up there, in addition to the possibility of getting her hands on a coconut, would be more of the edible cacti.

Jessica drew a deep breath, looked left and right, summoning her courage to leave the protection of the water ... and saw something as orange as the life-jacket bobbing in the shallows, not a hundred yards away.

Taking great gasps, Jessica splashed through the shallows towards the life-raft. It was floating upside down, but did not seem to have been damaged. The thought of what might be inside it...

She staggered up to it, and collapsed beside it, breathless. She took hold of the outside grab-cord which ran all the way round the exterior of the side panels, even though she realized that the raft wasn't going anywhere. Yet she had no intention of letting go of it.

She got her breath back, rose to her feet, and dragged the raft on to the beach. It seemed to weigh a ton, and by the time she got it half-dry she was again exhausted, and collapsed on the sand, gasping for breath. When she recovered, she determined to turn it over. She knelt, thrust her shoulder under one of the gunwales, and heaved upwards. It didn't budge.

'Fuck you,' she muttered, and inserted her shoulder right under the raft, sliding her body behind it into what seemed like an orange-coloured pit as the sun came full on to the upturned rubber. She looked around her in wonder, because amazingly, everything inside the raft was there, tied exactly as Michael had left it. Even the Armalite was still in place.

Confidence surged into her system. With the rifle in her possession she knew she could handle whatever was in the bush. She was so excited she stood up without thinking, and that completed the operation. The floor of the raft brought her down again with a bump, but she had lifted the gunwales far enough for the breeze to get underneath, and with a little roar the entire craft was lifted off her and hit the sand with an enormous slap. She leapt after it, for fear it was going to get away, but it wasn't moving.

On the other hand, it was still half in the water, and she had no idea how high the tides rose in this part of the world. She got into the water behind it, and, huffing and puffing, pushed it entirely on to the sand. Then she untied the rifle and slung it on her back, took the painter, and went up the beach towards the trees, dragging the raft behind her, to be halted by sheer exhaustion some twenty feet from the grass fringe. Once again she got behind the raft, pushing and heaving, stumbling to her knees and on a couple of occasions falling full length, but gradually making progress, until at last she could extend the painter and tie it round the bole of the nearest coconut tree. That was there for good, she thought with total satisfaction.

She climbed into it and unzipped the survival pack. They had consumed all the food and drink – and the remaining three tins of plum pudding had not survived the capsize. But safe in the pack was a first-aid kit, Michael's binoculars, the spare magazine for the Armalite – and a small hand-held radio in a waterproof container. Jessica stared at it for several seconds in total consternation. Michael had never mentioned it. The bastard! But perhaps the batteries were dead.

She took it out of the container, extended the aerial, and switched it on. It certainly crackled. But obviously it would not have a very long carry. Hastily she switched it off again, lowered the aerial, and restored it to its waterproof pocket. Something, either a ship or a plane, had to come within range of it soon enough.

She sat on the gunwale, pushed hair from her eyes. So here she was, she thought, all alone in the world save for the creature in the bush, but at any rate armed to the teeth. First thing, food!

She stood up, looked up at the cluster of coconuts dangling only a few feet above her head. Each cluster hung by a single stalk. She was such an expert shot that she had no doubt she could hit the stalk with a bullet. But if she were to fire the rifle ... Why not? If there *was* anyone on the island, that would bring them to her. And as for the monster of the night, the sound of the shot would probably scare it off.

She unslung the rifle, ran her hands almost lovingly up and down the barrel, released the safety catch, selected a position where she would stand a better chance of hitting the stalk rather than the coconuts themselves, and took careful aim. The stalk couldn't be more than a quarter of an inch wide, she reckoned. She drew a deep breath, squinted, and squeezed the trigger. There was virtually no recoil, and she lowered the rifle to see what she had accomplished. The coconuts still hung from the stalk, but several had been hit, and were dribbling liquid. While the sounds of the shot reverberated across the lagoon to meld with the noise of the surf. 'Shit!' she commented. She had forgotten that she was both exhausted and that her hands were no more steady than her nerves.

But she was not about to give up now, and fired another shot. This did the trick. The stalk parted, and the fruit came crashing to the sand. Several split open, and she hurled herself at them, lapping at the milk, which tasted like nectar. Then she tore the husks apart with her hands to scoop out the soft jelly with her fingers, cramming it into her mouth. That tasted even better. She sat up and took deep breaths. She didn't know if it was possible to live off coconut, but right now she was happy to try. On the other hand, she couldn't go on shooting them down; she'd run out of bullets in very short order, even with the spare magazine. She simply had to discover how to climb one of these branchless boles.

But that could come later. For the moment she felt replete, and rested, and really able to take on the world. So, priorities. She still had to establish definitely that she was alone on the island – certainly no one had come running to the sound of the shots. The simplest way to do that would be to climb the hill, which was only about a mile away, she estimated. But to get to it she would have to make her way through the jungle, without shoes and with a monster lurking. On the other hand, she reckoned, she would have to do something about that monster anyway, and very soon, or she would never have a full night's sleep. She just hoped there wasn't more than one.

So, the hill it had to be, bare feet and monster and all. She slung the rifle and retreated down the beach with the binoculars, studied the hill for several seconds, looked left and right for a last time, and felt as if someone had kicked her in the stomach. Lying on the sand, a couple of hundred yards away, was a body.

The Ship

Jessica pounded along the beach, feet sinking into the sand, breath coming in huge pants, only stopping when she was twelve feet away from the body. Michael!

She stood still for several seconds while she got her breathing under control, then slowly advanced until she stood over him. He lay on his back, arms and legs flung wide. His eyes were closed and his face was coated with sand. Jessica dropped to her knees beside him. 'Oh, Michael!' she said. 'Oh, dear, dear Michael!'

She leaned closer to kiss him, and his arms went round her. She jerked up, violently. 'I have got to be dead,' he muttered. 'But this can't be hell.'

'Bastard,' she snapped, freeing herself from his arms. 'How long have you been awake?'

'A few seconds.' He tried to lick his lips, and couldn't. 'I have to have something to drink. Have you anything, JJ?'

She stood up and backed a few steps away. The louse had heard what she had said. And when she had said it, supposing he was dead, she had meant it. Now... 'I can get you something,' she said. 'Don't go away.'

She walked slowly back along the beach, thinking. He was alive, and he seemed unhurt. So, it was back to square one. Only she no longer had any handcuffs or any rope to tie him up with. She did have the rifle and the knife, and the revolver had no longer been in his belt. But she would have to sleep sometime. They had to create some kind of meaningful relationship, from which love and lust and hate had to be eliminated. Well, she thought, not entirely. But which had to be strictly controlled. And to which would have to be added mutual trust. Until that could be established, she had to keep possession of the weapons ... and the radio.

She took the radio from the pouch and hid it in the bushes, then selected one of the coconuts and returned to where Michael was sitting up, taking off his life-jacket. 'God, I feel as if I've been through a wringer,' he said.

'Join the club,' she agreed, drawing her knife and sawing at the end of the fruit.

'How'd you know to do that?' he asked.

'I've watched movies.' The end came off, then a piece of the husk, and milk dribbled out. 'Try that.'

He held it to his lips, drank for several seconds. 'Remember it's not actually water,' she pointed out. 'You could get indigestion.'

'Boy, that tastes good. Anything else?'

'Give it back.' She split the husk open with a few blows from the sharp side of the blade. 'You can scoop the flesh out with your fingers.'

He did so, hungrily. 'Well,' he said when he had scraped the shell dry, 'isn't it crazy how things turn out? After all of that, here we are, just the two of us, on an island paradise.'

'There isn't just the two of us,' she said.

'Eh?' He looked left and right, as if expecting Polynesians to pop out of the bush on either side.

'There is something in there,' Jessica said. 'At least one something.' She told him what she had heard in the night.

'We'd better go see what it is,' he said, getting up, and staggering about the beach as she had done when first attempting to walk on dry land.

She watched him fall down several times, cursing. 'You'll get the hang of it,' she said.

'Bitch!' He lay on his back and panted. Then he sat up, and carefully got to his feet again. 'That's better. Let me have the rifle.'

She shook her head. 'No way.'

'Listen,' he said. 'We have to be sensible about this.'

'I entirely agree. We need to have a chat. But let's find out what we're up against, first. Don't worry, I'll cover you. Just walk along the beach, southabout.'

He glared at her, then obeyed. She followed at a safe distance. When he came upon the life-raft he stopped, gazing at it, obviously working out that she had taken whatever she wanted from it. Including the radio. 'Let's go,' she said.

They proceeded along the beach until the scuffed sand and the discarded life-jacket showed where she had spent the night. 'It was just in there,' she said.

Michael gazed at the bush. 'In any event,' Jessica said. 'We need to get up that hill and find out just what we have here. There could be a whole city on the far side of the island.'

'Chance would be a fine thing,' he said. 'You want me to go first?'

'That's the idea.'

'While you hang twenty yards behind. Fat lot of good that'll be in the bush if whatever it is attacks me. At least let me have your knife.'

She hesitated, then knelt and pulled up the tracksuit pants to expose the knife. She drew it and tossed it on to the sand beside him, then straightened again, the rifle held in both hands. 'Now you know this is ridiculous,' he said. 'You aren't going to shoot me and leave yourself all alone.'

'Try me,' she suggested.

Another glare, then he parted the bushes. She listened to him thumping about in there, and slowly followed. 'You keep in sight,' she called. 'If your head disappears from my vision, I am going to take it as a hostile act.'

He pushed on, knife in hand, hacking at various bushes. Jessica found the going less easy, as she had to use the gun to create a passage for herself. But she kept him in sight, and after a few more yards he suddenly stopped. 'Well, what do you know?' he remarked.

'What?'

'Listen.'

She did so, and heard a series of grunts. 'Jesus,' she muttered. It sounded horrendous.

'I've found your monster,' he said. 'Some of them, anyway.'

He didn't sound the least frightened. Jessica pushed through the bushes, moving to the left of him, and found that she was standing on the edge of a small clearing, on the far side of which were several pigs of varying sizes, rooting about in the undergrowth. 'Then there *are* people on the island,' she cried happily.

'I would say definitely not,' Michael said.

'Then how did these pigs get here?'

'It was the practice of the Royal Navy, in the last century, to put a couple of pigs of opposite sexes ashore on these islands, once they were sure there was water. The idea was that the pigs would breed, and that there would be an unending source of fresh meat for any shipwrecked sailors. So, whenever you feel like some roast pork, just let me know.'

'You mean you'd kill one of them?'

'I sure don't mean to eat it on the hoof. No big deal. They're so tame I bet you we could walk right up to them and they wouldn't even run away.' He demonstrated. The pigs merely regarded him with mild curiosity. 'They'll have never seen human beings,' he explained. 'They must be fourth or fifth generation, at the very least. I'd say this island is swarming with them.'

'But to kill one of them ... ugh!'

'You were just contemplating killing me,' he pointed out.

'That's different,' she argued. 'You deserve it. Let's climb that hill and talk about the pigs later.'

He shrugged, and resumed walking. The pigs solemnly inspected Jessica as she followed him across the clearing. 'Anyway,' he said over his shoulder, 'the fact that there are pigs running wild proves three things. One, that there are no other humans on the island, because if there were, the pigs would be penned up. Two, that there are no serious predators on the island, or the pigs would have been eaten. And three, that there's water on the island, somewhere, or the sailors wouldn't have left them.'

★ ★ ★

They walked for about half an hour, once again in thick jungle, Jessica having to pause every so often to pick thorns out of her feet; soon she was limping quite painfully. Her tracksuit top was already sliced in several places, but at least it protected her flesh, although she received several small cuts, which smarted as her sweat dribbled into them. Her hair also kept snagging on various branches and bushes. She was quite relieved that she didn't have a mirror, because she suspected she must look a complete sight. Then Michael stopped and held up his hand. 'Listen!'

'Not more pigs.'

'Water.' He began to hurry, pushing branches and bushes aside, and then checked again. 'Now there's a happy sight.'

Again Jessica veered to the left to keep her distance, with the result that she lost her footing before she realized what was happening, and went sliding down a shallow bank, to come to rest in a large pond of clear water, fed by a stream which tumbled down from the rising ground in front of them; nothing had ever felt so good on her tortured flesh.

'Isn't that something?' Michael slid down the bank beside her.

She had retained hold of the rifle, and this she now brought up, sharply. 'Just keep your distance.'

'Look, all I want to do is drink.' He knelt up to his waist, buried his head in the water, and began lapping at it. 'Boy, that tastes good.'

Cautiously Jessica ducked her own head. 'You don't suppose it's contaminated? Like by those pigs?'

'God save me from nervous women. It doesn't taste contaminated. And if it is, it's still the only water we're likely to find, so we'd better drink it and die happy.'

He was certainly drinking it, and she was realizing how thirsty she was. She tasted it. Pure nectar. She drank, deeply, and only straightened when he did so first. 'Right,' he said. 'I feel like a new man. Let's get up there.'

It took them another hour to reach the summit of the hill. By then it was nearly noon, and the sun was glaring down from a cloudless sky. Jessica thought it would be a bit much if after all they had experienced they were to get sunstroke.

But there was a splendid view from the hilltop, even if there was no sign of any human habitation. Not a trace of smoke, nothing but green jungle, yellow sand, blue water and the booming surf. And not another island in sight.

'I would say we have stumbled upon paradise,' Michael remarked.

'You reckon? How long can we survive here?'

'Forever.'

'You have got to be joking. We've no clothes, except what we're wearing. No shelter...'

'Clothes were out in the Garden of Eden,' he pointed out. 'I don't intend to wear these much longer, except for getting through the bush. Shelter is no problem: I'll build us a hut with palm fronds. We have all the water we can drink. For food we have the pigs and the coconuts, and I'm pretty sure we'll find some other edible fruits or vegetables. There was a fishing line in the survival pack in the life-raft, so I'm presuming it's still there. What more can you ask? I think we should raise a family.'

'Big deal,' she muttered.

But what was the immediate alternative? She had already realized that she couldn't maintain a stand-off for very long; if they remained in opposition he would eventually get her. As with the beginning of the voyage, her best chance was to go along with him and keep him happy. Besides, what he was proposing did sound like paradise. She would have preferred to set up house with someone who wasn't a kidnapper and a rapist, even if she could no longer feel that he was a murderer...

But these drawbacks apart, Michael was an attractive, cultured, well-educated man, while his beard, now a fortnight's growth, made him quite handsome. 'Well,' she said, 'we let bygones be bygones, then?'

'There aren't any bygones for me. Just let's say we're friends and lovers.'

She hesitated a last time. Then she shrugged. 'Friends and lovers,' she agreed. For as long as we are on this island, she reminded herself.

'So let's have the gun,' he said.

Jessica gave him the Armalite, waited to see if she'd made a dreadful mistake. But he took her into his arms and kissed her, very passionately. 'Tell me what you did with the radio,' he whispered into her ear.

'I'll show you. I really want us to be friends, Michael.'

'And lovers,' he reminded her.

He was clearly feeling very deprived. But, while she hated to admit it, even to herself, so was she. The quite traumatic events of the past few days had left her emotions stretched to the limit, her feelings accentuated by the fact that now it was even more the two of them alone, but in circumstances of complete safety, for the first time since they had left Lymington.

They hurried down to the beach, tore off their clothes, and wrapped their arms and legs about each other. Here was yet another new experience for Jessica: making love on a bed of sand – and with her skin a mass of scratches and bites, which seemed to make everything *feel* more intensely. She suspected it was a new experience for him as well.

They rolled and wrestled, panted and stroked, kissed and penetrated, in the wildest passion she had ever known, their emotions continuously accentuated by their physical discomfort, and by the realization that they were alive when they should have been dead. Then they lay on their backs in utter exhaustion.

Jessica was the first to get up, going down to the water to bathe. Michael joined her a few moments later, and again wanted to kiss and couple. In the sea she could wrap her legs round his thighs, and feel him between them, rising again, while the stinging of the salt on her flesh heightened her mood.

'You have a lot of endurance,' she said. 'For ... well...'

'A man my age, who down to a few days ago was impotent?' He grinned and kissed her. 'You have made a new man of me.'

'I suppose it's good to have accomplished something. Do you have any idea what day it is?'

He had lost his watch. 'Not really. Sometime about the middle of February. Hell, it could be St Valentine's Day.' He kissed her some more. 'It sure feels like it.'

'What happens if I get pregnant?' she asked.

'We have a baby.'

'You mean I have a baby. Who's going to do the delivery?'

'I will.'

'Do you know anything about it?'

'Like you with the coconuts, I've seen enough movies.'

'And I wind up dead when you do the wrong thing or can't stop the bleeding.'

He kissed her. 'I'm not going to let anything happen to you, JJ. I love you.'

Did she dare believe that? He certainly loved her body, could not keep his hands off it. Well, she enjoyed his. But there was no way she loved him, or ever could. It was simply that, in the absence of anything else, he was both nice and reassuring to have around. She wondered how many women actually felt that, and no more, about their husbands?

Michael was certainly bubbling with energy. He understood as well as she had that they couldn't keep shooting down the coconuts, and experimented using both their tracksuits tied together to make a large belt, which he put round his waist and then round the tree. 'I've seen this done in the movies as well,' he explained. 'You simply walk up.'

There were several mishaps, and more than once Jessica reckoned he had again been reduced to impotence, but eventually he did get the knack.

'Now for shelter,' he said as they ate and drank the fruits of his success. 'It'll start raining in a couple of months,' he explained. 'We want to have shelter by then.'

But cutting and accumulating palm fronds in sufficient quantity to make a hut was a slow business with just the diving knife, and in any event, they had no means of securing the fronds together; they tried using various vines, but these invariably parted at the least pressure. 'Shit!' Michael commented. 'It always works in the movies.'

For the moment, the absence of shelter was no great problem: sleeping in the open under starry skies was a delightful experience, apart from the sandflies, and they soon came to accept these as a fact of life. They both knew they would eventually need somewhere to take cover when the next storm arrived, and as a result they explored the island thoroughly, and found, to their delight, a cave on the far side of the hill. 'Be careful,' Michael warned when Jessica would have entered the dark aperture immediately. 'We don't know what's in there.'

'What could possibly be in there?'

'Snakes?'

'Do they have snakes on tropical atolls?'

'Haven't a clue,' he confessed.

The first twenty feet remained light from the mouth, and they could see no evidence of any other living creature ever having entered. 'This is certainly far enough for shelter,' Jessica said. 'We can explore the rest later, when we can raise some light.'

This was a problem. Until and unless they could create fire, they couldn't kill any of the pigs, as they would have no means of cooking the flesh. Jessica was actually somewhat relieved at this, although after a couple of days she found herself growing pretty tired of coconuts. They did find some berries with which they very cautiously experimented, and which turned out to be both edible and tasty, but they still did not represent a balanced meal. 'The binocs,' Michael decided.

'Can you get the glass out without destroying them?'

'I don't know. But we don't have anything to look at, and we do have to have fire.'

He made quite a good job of it, although neither of them was confident he would be able to get the glass back in without breaking it. 'Well,' he said, 'we can use it as a monocular.'

Excited at what lay before them, they gathered wood and leaves and piled them on the beach, Michael having scraped out a shallow pit. Then it was a matter of holding the glass at the right angle to the sun. They had a fire in seconds. To their consternation it burned out in seconds more.

'This stuff is too dry and too flimsy,' Michael declared. 'Shit!' Painstakingly they gathered more material, looking now for thickish branches, and determined to sacrifice their carefully accumulated palm fronds. 'When we get this going properly,' Michael announced, 'we'll be able to make a torch and explore that cave.'

They had actually slept in it, at the mouth, for the past two nights, and had been partially relieved of the sandflies. Obviously, if they could get further in, they might be rid of the no-see-ums altogether. 'There is no way we are going to be able to keep a torch alight all the way from here, through the bush, round the hill, and down into the cave,' Jessica pointed out.

'Shit!' he commented again. But he knew she was right. They both got up.

There was equally no way they could carry

all of their recently gathered material to the cave. They had to start from scratch, on the other side of the hill. It took them the rest of the day to accumulate sufficient kindling, and by then the sun was close to the western horizon, which they could now see, as opposed to the eastern, which had been the limit of their vision for so long. 'Ah, well,' Michael said. 'There's always tomorrow. That's the beauty of this place. There's always tomorrow.'

'There usually is in other places as well,' she reminded him.

'Not in the same way. Tomorrow in other places means getting dressed, and getting to work through the rush hour, and coping with problems, other people's as well as your own, and coming home again, through the rush hour, and sitting down to watch something banal on television, or maybe going out to socialize with a group of equally banal people, saying banal things you've heard before anyway.'

'I don't think you really like people.'

'I don't. Never have. I like you. I *love* you. Do you know, JJ, in all our relationship, you have never once said you loved me?'

'I'm a truthful woman,' she told him.

'Believe it or not, one of the things I most like about you is the way you can drive me into a frenzy. You know, you're so beautiful, when I first laid hands on you I felt quite sick at the idea that you were all mine. And ever since then I've been totally frustrated.'

'You could have fooled me.'

'You don't understand. With someone as beautiful as you, sex has to be beautiful too. Well, it is that. But it should be transcendental. It's not just a matter of feeling you against me as I get off, or watching you get off too. It should be possible to do something with you which would be unique, which would send us through some barrier which no one else has even conceived, much less attempted or experienced.'

'I think,' she said carefully, watching the sun disappear, 'that to achieve something like that, the feeling would have to be absolutely mutual.'

'And you could never feel that way about me. Don't you think that's frustrating? God, if you knew what I wanted to do to you...'

'Why don't you tell me?' she asked. 'You obviously want to.'

'Well...' He lay on his back, his hands beneath his head, staring at the darkening sky. 'There are simply things, like sodomizing you. Would you like me to try that?'

In for a penny, in for a pound, she supposed. 'You're welcome to try anything you like. But it wouldn't work. You could never stay hard long enough.'

'Yeah. But it would be fun trying. God, I could do it now.'

Jessica sighed, and surrendered. But as she had known would be the case, it was way beyond him, and the upshot was that she had to go down to the sea to wash off his efforts, which reached as far as her hair.

Predictably, he was depressed and morose. 'And then,' he said, as if they hadn't been interrupted, 'I think about eating you.'

Jessica, just wading up to the beach, checked.

'That would be the ultimate, I suppose,' he said. 'Cooking you on a spit, or something. And then slicing the meat off your ass. Did I ever tell you that you have the most delightful backside I have ever seen?'

'I believe you did,' she said. Perhaps he was mad. Then again, she had undergone a similar feeling of quite obscene mental freedom on the yacht, when she had gained control – and she had put her mental freedom into practice. He was undergoing a similar experience, and as earlier, it was best treated with calm reason. 'If you were to do that,' she said, 'I'd be gone forever.'

'Yeah,' he said. 'I wouldn't want that. I want you forever.' He held her hand as she sat beside him. 'You, JJ. Not just your body. I want your mind, your personality. I want *you*!'

'You can't ever have someone like that, Michael,' she told him. 'Not in the real world. You simply can't own people's minds, their thoughts, their impulses. All you can do is try to share those things. And that's difficult enough.'

'Yeah,' he agreed meaningfully.

She was, as usual, awake before him, and went down to the sea to bathe. She even tried cleaning her teeth on a piece of bark. Wasn't that what the Chinese did? But it wasn't very successful.

When she got back to the cave he had gone, and so had both the rifle and the knife. She brooded on this for a few minutes, but she had to believe they were at last operating together. So she climbed the hill. Even more than on the yacht, to be naked in the open air gave her the most utter feeling of freedom she had ever known. Her feet were by now quite hard enough to cope with the various outcroppings of rock, and there were less thorny bushes up here. Even so she had the odd scratch. But then, it seemed her whole body was a mass of scratches and bumps and sand-fly bites – she was amazed that Michael still found her attractive. As for her hair, that was a tangled mess. Which had to be washed, and thoroughly, even if she didn't have any soap.

She reached the summit, and looked around. There was no sign of Michael; the beach below her remained undisturbed. The lagoon was as peaceful as always. The surf still thundered on the reef, but beyond it the sea was calm, undulating in a long, gentle swell. It was difficult to imagine, or recall, the creatures that lurked out there, beneath that smooth blue carpet. Or that the carpet could itself turn into a violent, destructive monster.

She was just turning away to go down to the stream and the pool when her eye caught something on the horizon. When she looked again, it was gone. She rubbed her eyes, and

293

tried looking again. She was staring north-west, away from the sun rising behind her, and the sky was cloudless, all the way down to the horizon. And there was something there, rising and falling on the swell. Which was why she had lost it for a moment, as now she lost it again. But a moment later it was there again.

It could only be a ship.

Jessica found she was biting her lip. A ship! How far away? At the very limit of her vision. But surely within radio range.

She had given the radio back to Michael, as he had wished, but she knew what he had done with it: he had replaced it in the life-raft pouch. All she had to do was get down there ... and then what? She needed to be quite certain of the answer to that. If she managed to contact the ship, and it came, and she told the crew what had happened, Michael would be arrested – if he wasn't lynched on the spot. Few men would have any sympathy for a man who had kidnapped a woman as his sexual slave, however much they might secretly wish to do something like that themselves.

Did she wish that to happen to Michael? In many ways she felt as if she *were* the wife he so desperately wished her to be. They had shared so much over the past few months. She did not think she could ever be so inti-mate with a man again. Yet the fact remained that he was a criminal, who had probably ruined her life. Certainly he had turned it inside out.

Even if she would not, on reflection, have missed a moment of it, that fact was immutable. He deserved to be punished. But she wanted it done in a civilized manner, with courteous policemen and judges in wigs and whispering barristers, not a lynch mob.

So, say nothing, except that they needed to be rescued. Say nothing until they had been taken back to civilization. And then...

But that was not possible. Her people knew the score, and they were looking for her. Once she again came into contact with civilization her power to make unilateral decisions, regarding either Michael or herself, would be at an end. They would both be in handcuffs then, she to her duties and responsibilities as a police officer, the conventional requirements and behaviour of English society, and Michael would go back to gaol, with all its horrors.

And her mad adventure would be over. She had just reflected that she could never be as intimate with any man again. There were so many things she could never be again. Of course, she would be a nine days' wonder, and some tabloid would probably pay handsomely for her story, but that would complete the separation between her and the rest of humanity. She would cease to be a human being and become an object, of desire to some, of revulsion to others. It would not be possible to be friends with any of them.

The alternative was to stay here with him. For ever and ever. With not a care in the world – save that she was sharing her life with a man most people would regard as a monster.

She closed her eyes, almost wishing that the decision would be made for her by the ship's sudden disappearance, and then opened them again. And in fact it was gone. But a moment later it was back again, rising on the swell. If it wasn't moving, so far as she could see, it had to be a fishing boat. Out of the Marquesas? That could well be. They would speak French, she supposed.

They had to be called. Jessica hurried down the hill, on the eastern side, towards where the life-raft was tied to its tree.

She was halfway down when she heard the shot. It came from almost directly in front of her, and was very loud. She immediately checked. He was there, not a hundred yards away.

She burst through the bushes above the pool, and saw Michael on the far side, dragging a pig by its hooves, leaving a trail of blood. 'Frying tonight,' he called.

'Ugh!'

'Don't you like pork?'

'I do. But I've never seen a pig killed before.'

'That's nature. Kill or be killed. We'll have to hang this chap for a few hours, but he should be ready by tonight.' He frowned. Even though they were separated by some thirty yards, he could see she was agitated. 'What's the matter with you?'

Jessica thought fast. 'I was up on the hill, and I heard the shot. I didn't know what had happened.'

'And you were hoping I'd shot myself.'

'Well, of course I was not.' Desperately she changed the subject. 'Would you have any objection if I washed my hair?'

'I think that would be a very good idea.'

'I meant in the pool.'

'Sure. We'll drink from the stream, and keep the pool for our ablutions. I'll join you. Back in a few minutes.'

He resumed dragging the pig through the bushes. Jessica bit her lip. It would take him at least half an hour to drag the pig to the cave and get back here. Probably more like an hour. But he had said a few minutes. Did that mean he intended to leave the pig somewhere before the cave and come back? It would take her half an hour to gain the life-raft and get back here. That wasn't allowing any time for the call. So, better not to risk it. But if she didn't risk it, and the boat went away again...

It wouldn't. Not out of range, anyway. Michael had said that the radio had a range of about fifty miles, more from the top of the hill. If the fishing boat was within sight now, it surely couldn't get more than fifty miles away by tonight, even if it stopped fishing and left right away. She had to believe that.

She soaked in the pool, which was some eight feet deep in the centre. Fed by a stream emanating from a spring halfway up the hill, its overflow formed another, somewhat indeterminate stream, bubbling down to the beach on the west side of the island. She gave her hair a good rinse, thinking that she might give a year of her life for a bottle of shampoo. But how much of her life did she have to waste? At the present time, she felt, quite a lot.

There was a splash and Michael joined her. 'Tonight we are going to have the best dinner of our lives,' he announced.

'I'm getting hungry at the thought. Michael, how far can a human being see?'

'Depends on their eyesight.'

'I mean, in a straight line, supposing there is nothing in the way.'

'Ah. Well, if the earth were flat, someone with very good eyesight could probably see a long way. But because of the curvature of the earth's surface, when you are standing on that surface at sea level, such as on that beach over there, the furthest anyone can see is just over four miles.'

'That far?' she asked innocently. Four miles! Only four miles, she thought.

'Of course, as you go up, the range increases. Equally, if the object you're looking at is above horizon level, you'd see it at a greater distance, depending on how high it was. I mean, if there was an island out there with a bloody big mountain on it, like this place Hiva Oa you were talking about, you'd see it quite clearly, as long as there was good visibility, even at maybe fifty miles' distance.'

'Oh! Well, how far can we see from the top

298

of the hill, for instance? I mean, something at sea level.'

'That hill must be about a hundred and fifty feet. From the top, we should be able to see ... say thirty miles with the naked eye.'

'Shit!' she remarked without thinking.

'Eh?'

'I mean, what a big difference, in a hundred and fifty feet.'

'Height is the secret. Of course, we have to rely on our eyesight. But with instruments ... For instance, my radar on the yacht, mounted two-thirds of the way up the mizzen, gave me a thirty-mile range. Not even radar can see round corners or over edges. But you mount a powerful radar set in a plane, and you can just about see forever. And of course satellite-mounted cameras can overlook half the earth at one time.'

'Incredible,' she murmured. Thirty miles! If that ship had been thirty miles away this morning, and had decided to pack it in, it could be something like a hundred miles away before she could get to the radio.

He climbed out of the pool, held out his hand for her. 'Let's go cook.'

To her great relief, she didn't have to do anything more than gather some garnishing; she didn't think she'd have been able to butcher a pig. Michael, however, attacked the job with gusto. The resulting chops were a little ragged, but they smelled magnificent when they were being roasted on a home-made spit. 'What we need to do is cook the rest of this fellow right away,' Michael said. 'That'll preserve the meat longer.'

Jessica had never felt quite so replete. It was now nearly dusk, and Michael was building up the fire to get on with his cooking. Maybe the people on the ship would see it? But of course they would not, because they were virtually at sea level, and would therefore not be able to see more than a few miles' distance.

She knew she wasn't going to sleep, so she made herself a torch and did some exploring of the cave. It went a good way into the hill – that much was obvious – and would certainly provide total shelter were they to be caught in another typhoon. And there was no evidence that any living creature had ever been in here before them. But she hadn't gone more than twenty yards before her torch burned out, and she had to feel her way back.

'This is the life.' Michael was thoroughly enjoying himself, even though he was covered in blood. 'I think maybe I should have been a chef. I don't think I ever was a very good bank manager. I always saw the business too much from the other chap's point of view.'

'I don't think you ever saw *this* business from *my* point of view,' she remarked.

'Well, that was different. I mean, the whole concept of what I did was a reversal of personality, of habits, of behaviour. That's what I set out to do.'

'So you won't object if one day I entirely

change personality, habits and behaviour?'

He grinned, and ruffled her hair. 'I would say you already have.'

Well, she thought, that was most definitely that! Any trace of conscience or remorse was gone. He was going to get what was coming to him.

It was necessary to dissemble for the rest of the evening. But she had spent so much time dissembling during the first half of the voyage that that was no hardship. He fell asleep a happy man. For the very last time, she reckoned.

She had to wait until she was sure he was fast asleep. Then she carefully picked up the rifle, and left the cavern. The fire still glowed, and the smell of roasting pork still filled the air. She travelled as fast as she could in the darkness, although, in the full glory of a tropical night, it really wasn't all that dark, even if the moon had not yet risen. My last night of utter freedom, she reminded herself. But she was not going to change her mind now.

She reached the beach on the west side of the island, located the raft easily enough. She knelt and tore open the pouch, took out the radio. Then she set off to the top of the hill. She reckoned she reached it about midnight, and was almost afraid to look to the west. When she did, she gasped. The ship was even closer, a blaze of light which had to be within twenty miles.

Heart pounding, she extended the aerial and switched on the power. As it was intended for use only in emergencies, it only had channel eight, but according to Michael that was the channel all ships listened on anyway. She thumbed the mike. 'Mayday,' she said. 'Mayday, mayday. Do you read? Over.'

She flicked to receive, listened to crackle, and was about to try again when a voice spoke in French.

'Please,' she said. 'Do you speak English?'

Another brief silence. Then, 'Sure I speak English. Where are you calling from?'

'The island. My partner and I are shipwrecked. Please help us.'

'You're on that island? Well, what do you know? How many of you?'

'Two. Just my partner and me.'

'Your partner being a man, right?'

'Right.'

'Okay, babe. We're on our way.'

Jessica found she was weeping with relief and excitement. 'How soon?'

'Well, we have to find a way through that reef.'

'There's a gap on the south side,' she said.

'Right. But we still can't chance our arm till sun-up. Stay tight, babe. We're on our way.'

'There is nothing,' the French naval officer said. 'Our planes have searched every square mile over a fifty-mile radius from the position given to us, and they have found nothing. So, I am sorry to say, either the position was not correct, or the

yacht has gone down.'

Tom looked at Andrea, who was staring at the sparkling waters of Atuona Harbour on Hiva Oa Island. 'Isn't there any other possible explanation?' she asked. 'Supposing the yacht hadn't been dismasted, how far would it have travelled since the signal?'

'Twelve days, at perhaps six knots...' Capitaine de Fregate Perchon shrugged. 'It could have travelled over a thousand miles. But if it had not been dismasted, would not the lady have used the radio over and over again?'

'Not if she had managed to get free for just that one message.'

Perchon looked at Tom.

'I think if JJ had got free to send one message, she would have stayed free.'

'All right,' Andrea said. 'So the yacht was dismasted, and drifting. In which direction would she have drifted, and how far?'

'Oh, she would have come west,' Perchon said. 'That is the direction of the Equatorial Current. It runs quite strongly. In twelve days it could have covered two hundred miles. But my planes took that into consideration, and covered an area two hundred miles due west of the freighter's position, and saw nothing.'

'Is there no way they could have drifted further than that?'

'Not without some additional power.'

Andrea snapped her fingers. 'That's it! The yacht had two engines. Even if she was dismasted in the typhoon, her engines would still have worked.'

303

'But Mademoiselle Hutchins, if the engines were working, in twelve days, why, she should be at anchor out there now.'

'Not if Miller regained control.'

'I'm still sure JJ wouldn't have allowed that to happen,' Tom said. 'He could only have snatched her at all by taking her completely by surprise. She would never allow that to happen a second time. Not JJ.'

'Okay, okay. But what if she managed to use the engines, say, for a day or two, and then the boat sank. That would have taken her outside the two-hundred-mile radius, wouldn't it?'

'Of course. But as we don't know for how long she motored, or when she sank, we have no point of reference.'

'But couldn't they have survived the sinking? The yacht would have had a life-raft, right?'

'It should have done, certainly. But to survive twelve days in a life-raft ... I do not think that is possible.'

'They could have reached land.'

'There is no land west of the given position, not until us here. That is nine hundred miles.'

'Nothing at all?'

'Well, there is one uninhabited atoll...' He led them to the chart table. 'Here. But that is over three hundred miles from the given position.'

'But if they had the use of the engines for part of the time ... Surely it's worth a look. One last look, Commandant.' When Andrea wanted to look appealing, she could look very appealing indeed.

The Captive

Jessica realized that she was panting with excitement. It was done. The nightmare-cum-idyll was ended. Now it was a waste of time trying to foresee the future. She had set her feet on the road back to normality, and she simply had to place one foot in front of the other until it was over.

She remained for several minutes staring out to sea, watching the glow of the ship's lights, reassuring herself that it was really there. Then she went down the hill to the east beach and restored the radio to its pouch. She did not suppose there was anything Michael could do to change the situation now, but it was better he didn't know anything about it until it was too late *to* do anything about it.

Then she made her way through the jungle to the cavern. He did not appear to have moved at all during the couple of hours she had been away, and was still deeply asleep. She lay down beside him, although she knew she wasn't going to sleep any more; she was too excited...

She awoke at first light.

Michael was already up. 'I know it's a bit of

a bore,' he said, 'but do you mind having pork chops again for breakfast? We have to eat all this meat before it goes off.'

'I'd love pork chops for breakfast,' she said.

He rekindled the fire from the embers, and heated the meat. 'Obviously we are going to have to get far more organized,' he said, slicing the head off a coconut for their morning drink. 'I have to work out some way of smoking our meat so it'll last for at least a week. I'm sure it can be done. We also have to set some kind of fish traps so we can vary our diet.'

Jessica drank, then got up; she felt quite sick at being responsible for ending his happy dream. 'I think I'll have a dip before breakfast.' She walked away from the cave, moving slowly and as casually as she could. Michael continued to cook. She pushed her way through the bushes, and reached the top of the beach. From here she looked at nothing but surf; the opening in the reef was to her right. She turned that way, moving down to the water's edge, and walked along the sand, allowing the wavelets to play over her feet. And saw the trawler.

It was not a very attractive-looking ship. It had a steadying sail as well as a small funnel, which was belching smoke as it closed the reef. Even from a distance she could tell that its steel hull was rust-streaked and dented in places, and that its wooden superstructure, which consisted of a wheelhouse with a lower cabin aft, badly needed paint. But it represented civilization – and it was definitely making for the gap in the reef.

She wanted to jump up and down with excitement. And then remembered that she was naked. She turned to hurry back to the cave to dress herself, and found herself staring straight at Michael.

He had obviously followed her footsteps in the sand, and was standing with his hands on his hips, staring at the ship in total consternation. Jessica ran towards him. 'We'd better put some clothes on. They're coming in.'

'But where in the name of God did she come from? And why should she put in here?' he asked, almost plaintively.

'I have no idea,' she panted as she got up to him. 'Maybe they need fresh water.'

'Well, we'd better make ourselves scarce. Then they can fill their tank and go away again.'

'But ... they'll have seen us,' she protested.

'Shit!' he muttered. He knew that even had they not been seen, the crew of the trawler would certainly be able to tell, from the footprints on the sand, that there were people on the island. He glanced at her. 'You happy about this?'

'It had to happen sometime,' she said.

'And just what are you going to tell them?'

'That our yacht was sunk and we were cast away. There's no need to tell them anything more than that.'

'And when they take us back to civilization?'

She gazed into his eyes. 'We can discuss that.'

He hesitated, and she went past him and up the path they had made to the cave, where she pulled on her tracksuit, wishing she had more underclothes than just the knickers, or at least a shirt; the reappearance of civilization was restoring the innate modesty that had once seemed natural.

He joined her, pulled on his clothes. Then he picked up the rifle. 'A ship that size won't have a crew of more than four. Five at the most. We could do the lot, then we'd have a ship again.'

'Are you out of your mind?' she demanded. 'You can't just kill five people.'

His face twisted, but he wasn't a killer. He laid the gun down again. 'You want breakfast?'

'I couldn't eat a thing. I know, we'll go and welcome them and invite them to have breakfast with us. All this meat has to be eaten.' She set off for the beach again, and after a moment he followed her. To her relief she saw that he had left the rifle behind.

They walked along the beach beside each other. This was how they had to present themselves to the fishermen: as a pair.

The trawler was through the passage now, and had dropped anchor in the middle of the lagoon. A dinghy had been launched, and three men were placing an outboard in position. Two more people remained on the ship, looking over the side, and one of them, Jessica saw to her surprise, was a woman; her mousy brown hair wisped in the breeze. Now they saw the couple on the beach, and waved.

Jessica waved back, bracing herself for the coming crisis. But when that arrived, Michael would be outnumbered by three to one. Or four, counting herself!

The outboard chattered into life, and the dinghy approached the shore. 'Remember what we agreed,' Michael muttered.

'I will,' she assured him.

The outboard stopped in the shallows, and the shaft was pulled up to save the propeller from contact with the sand. The boat continued to coast, and two of the men jumped over the side to beach it. Then the third man got out, over the bow, on to the dry sand. He was clearly the skipper, but Jessica didn't much like the look of him any more than his crew; he wore a peaked cap but had not shaved in more than a week, and she doubted he had had a bath or changed his clothes in that time, either – his shirt and pants were as greasy as his lank yellow hair.

The crew also wore short growths of beard; one of them was white-skinned, the other brown, with frizzy hair. They too wore decrepit shirts and jeans. All three were bare-footed.

Michael stepped forward. 'My name is Michael Lomas,' he said. 'This is my wife.'

The trawler skipper nodded. 'She we have spoken with,' he said in English with an

Australian accent, but it was clearly not his mother tongue.

'You what?' Michael turned to Jessica.

She could feel her cheeks burning. 'Well,' she said, 'I saw them out there yesterday. So I called them.'

'That is right,' the skipper said. 'Your wife called us last night. You did not know this?'

'No, I did not know this,' Michael said. 'You unutterable little bitch!'

'Now, wait a minute...' Jessica protested.

The skipper grinned. 'It is not good for husband and wife to quarrel. But perhaps you are not truly husband and wife, eh?'

Jessica instinctively put her right hand over her left, but clearly he had already spotted the absence of a ring, or of any indication there had ever been a ring. 'Is that important?' Michael demanded.

'I do not think so,' the skipper agreed, and held out his hand. 'I am Jacques Manot. That is my ship.'

Michael hesitated, then shook hands. Manot turned to Jessica, and she also allowed her fingers to be clasped. He held them for a few minutes longer than was absolutely necessary. 'You are very beautiful,' he said, 'Mrs Lomas.'

She flushed, and glanced at Michael. But for the moment she was top of his list of least favourite people. 'Would you like breakfast?' she asked. 'We have fresh meat.'

'That would be very nice. You have enough for all of us?'

'Oh, yes,' Jessica said.

Manot spoke to his crew in what could have been French, although Jessica deduced it was some kind of patois, and they relaunched the dinghy, started the outboard, and returned to the trawler. 'Tell me about your yacht,' Manot invited.

'We were dismasted in a storm,' Michael explained.

'And then we were attacked and holed by a whale shark,' Jessica added.

'But this is very bad,' Manot agreed. 'This storm, this was the one a fortnight ago?'

'That would be about right. You knew about it?'

'It was on the weather forecast,' Manot said. 'When last did you give your position?'

'Well...' Michael tried to remember. 'Just before the storm. We lost the use of our radios when we were dismasted.'

Manot raised his eyebrows. 'And since then you have been without trace? But nobody is looking for you in that time?'

'Well, no,' Michael said. 'I gave my position to my base in England. They only expect a call every fortnight or so. They will not yet have begun to worry.'

'Unless they knew of the typhoon, eh?'

'That's true. But they're not very interested in Pacific storms in England. Unless they happen to do a lot of damage. Did this typhoon hit anywhere hard?'

'No, no. This storm ... how do you say?'

'Fizzled,' Jessica suggested.

311

'Yes, that is the word. Fizzled. You were unlucky to be caught by it. And then a whale shark ... pfft. And now, to have disappeared for two weeks. Everyone will think you dead.' He smiled at Jessica as he spoke, and she felt a sudden tightness in her stomach. Oh, my God! she thought.

Michael had not seemed to notice. 'Well,' he said, 'perhaps the first thing you should do is call Hiva Oa and tell them you have found us.'

'Yes,' Manot said. 'That is what we must do. After we have breakfasted, eh?'

The dinghy was back at the beach, and the rest of the crew had disembarked. The woman was taller than Jessica had thought, and strongly built. She was not very old, certainly under thirty, Jessica estimated. Like the men, she wore jeans and a sweatshirt; there was no brassiere, but a lot of breast and nipple outlined. The fifth member of the crew was another half-Polynesian. Jessica's sick feeling began to grow.

'Right,' Michael said. 'Breakfast. We live along here.'

Manot spoke in patois, and his people followed him along the beach. It seemed they did not speak English.

What are we going to do? Jessica thought. She simply had to have a word with Michael. Surely there would be an opportunity when they got back to the cave. And at the cave was the Armalite. Once she had hold of that ... Of course she couldn't go along with just killing

312

these people, but at least they would be in control.

Or was she simply imagining the whole thing?

They walked along the sand, Manot between Michael and herself, the other four following. Jessica had a tremendous urge to look over her shoulder at them, but she felt that would be a mistake.

Manot wanted to know all about the voyage, how long they had been sailing. 'It is very romantic,' he said. 'A man and a woman, sailing alone together. And, well ... you know.'

At that moment someone pinched Jessica's bottom. She gave a little squeal of mingled embarrassment and outrage, and swung round. The Polynesian crew members grinned at her, and Manot, who had also turned, spoke brusquely in the patois. But the sailors did not look in the least abashed. 'It is their way,' Manot explained. 'You must forgive them. It means that they think you are beautiful, too.'

'Well, tell them to keep their hands off my wife,' Michael said aggressively.

'I have told them this,' Manot agreed.

Michael led them up the path to the cave.

'But this is very civilized,' Manot commented. 'And you have only been on the island a few days?'

'We believe in being organized,' Michael said, more proudly than ever.

'And I can see that you are. That roasting

313

pork smells very good.'

'That's our breakfast,' Michael explained. 'I'll have to cook some more.'

They gathered round the still simmering fire and the still roasting meat. No one seemed interested in the cave at this moment. Jessica darted inside, and picked up the rifle. She tucked it under her arm and strolled back out into the sunlight.

All the heads turned towards her. 'What's up?' Michael asked.

'That is a formidable weapon you have there,' Manot commented. 'Do you know how to use it?'

'I practise every day,' Jessica told him.

'And there are still bullets in the magazine?'

'About twenty.' She knew that was stretching it a bit, after the several shots she had expended on bringing down coconuts before Michael had worked out how to climb the trees. But Manot wouldn't know that. How she wished she had thought to take the spare magazine from the dinghy.

'You are a ... what is it they say? An Annie Oakley, eh?'

'I reckon.'

He continued to regard her for several seconds.

'Something on your mind, JJ?' Michael asked.

There was nothing for it. 'I'd like to have a word, Michael.'

He raised his eyebrows and glanced at their guests in an apologetic fashion, as if to indicate, she has these moods.

'You must speak with your wife, if she wishes you to,' Manot said. 'Marie will take over the cooking. She is a good cook.'

He gave orders in French, and Marie nodded. Michael walked to Jessica, and she retreated into the cave. He followed. 'Just what are you playing at?' he demanded. 'Those people could be offended.'

'I hope they are. I don't like the look of them, Michael. I don't like the way that fellow Manot very carefully established that as far as the world is concerned, we are dead. Once you're accepted as dead, if you don't ever turn up again, no one is going to be very surprised, right?'

He scratched his head. 'You really are a nutter. You invited them here.'

'I know, and I'm sorry. I guess I just went wild when I saw that ship, so close.'

'But now you've changed your mind, is that it?'

'All right, yes, I have. As I said, I'm sorry. But for us to go on board that trawler with those people would be to commit suicide.'

'God save me from illogical women,' Michael complained. 'It's the curse of your sex. May I ask you to tell me, even supposing these people are pirates, as you seem to think they are, what possible reason could they have for murdering us? Do you suppose they imagine we came ashore from a sinking yacht with a chest of treasure? We are destitute, darling. We have just the clothes we are wearing. And that rifle you are so carefully protecting. It may be worth a few hundred quid in this part of the world. Whereas if they take us back to civilization, they are going to be the toast of the media. They can sell their story of how they found the castaways. That's what they have their eyes on.'

'Michael,' she said, refusing to lose her temper, 'I hate to be pretentious, but what they have their eye on is *me*.'

'Oh, really? They have a woman.'

'That may be. But I reckon I'm several dozen classes better than her.'

'I can see I've been praising your looks too much. Or are you working on that friendly pinch you got?'

'Friendly, you reckon? Maybe you *have* been telling me too often that I'm good-looking. But the fact is, if you haven't seen the way they have been looking at me you're blind. Okay, we have nothing worth stealing, but they have nothing to gain by taking us back. The story of how they rescued us isn't worth more than five minutes' media time. Whereas, if they *don't* take us back, they can do what they like with us, leave our bodies, and take off, having had a bit of fun, and, as you say, accumulated this rifle. And no one will ever be the wiser.'

'That is absurd,' he insisted. And then added, 'So what do you want to do? Tell them to leave without us?'

'Yes. We'll give them breakfast first.'

'They'll know we're here. If they're as

316

dedicated rapists and murderers as you think, what's to stop them from coming back?'

'They can't approach the island without us knowing it.'

'And when they do come back?'

'We put a shot across their bows. Some other ship is bound to turn up, eventually.'

They stared at each other, and were summoned by a shout from the mouth of the cave. 'Breakfast is ready,' Manot called. 'You wanna eat?'

Michael led the way back into the light. Manot grinned at him. 'You have had a lovers' quarrel, eh? Maybe one wants to go, and one to stay, eh?'

'Maybe,' Michael agreed.

'Actually, we've both decided to stay,' Jessica said. 'I'm sorry to have bothered you. But at least there's all this fresh meat.'

Manot gazed at her for several seconds, then grinned. 'The decision is yours. But my people will be disappointed.'

'I'm sure they will be,' Jessica agreed.

'Let us eat,' Manot said. He signalled his crew, and they sat on the ground on the far side of the fire. Jessica and Michael sat on their side, with Manot between them; Jessica rested the rifle beside herself. Marie passed out the pieces of roasted pork.

'You know what this needs?' Michael said. 'Potatoes and apple sauce.'

'Potatoes and apple sauce,' Manot said. 'Ha ha.' He turned to Jessica. 'That is a beautiful gun, Mrs Lomas. Almost as beautiful as you.

May I look at it?'

'No,' Jessica said. 'I'm sorry, Captain. This gun never leaves my possession.'

'Ah,' Manot said. 'You have enemies on this island?'

'We could have.'

'Ah,' he said again. He wiped his mouth with the back of his hand, then wiped the back of his hand on his already stained shirt. Then, without any warning, he threw both arms round Michael, knocking him to the ground and at the same time drawing his knife from the sheath on his belt and presenting it to Michael's throat.

'You bastard!' Jessica brought up the rifle, but Manot had rolled right over, and was holding Michael in front of him, his knife pressed against Michael's Adam's apple.

'You give up the rifle, or your man dies,' Manot said, and gave one of his grins. 'I do not think you want this.'

Jessica hesitated. Her finger was curled round the trigger. But to shoot would certainly be to hit Michael before she hit Manot. And she realized that the crew had all got up and were standing behind her. She could swing round and blow them all apart, she knew. But that would not help Michael. Then she could probably kill Manot as well, but Michael would also be dead. She just could not contemplate that. 'If I give you the gun, will you let him go?' she asked.

'Of course.'

'And you will not harm us?'

318

'Why should we harm you? We came here to help you, at your request, Mrs Lomas. It is you who is threatening to harm *us*.'

Jessica bit her lip. But there was no alternative now. She held out the gun. Manot released Michael, who was gasping for breath, and stood up, replacing the knife in its sheath. Then he took the gun. 'This is sensible of you.' He ran his hand up and down the barrel. 'It is a very beautiful gun. A beautiful gun, a beautiful island, a beautiful woman, and they are all mine. Am I not a fortunate man?'

'You said you would not harm us,' Jessica said, her stomach a tight knot.

'Of course.'

One of the crew gave a shout, and Manot turned. Michael had been left lying on the ground. Now he suddenly reacted with great speed, rolling over, away from Manot, and reaching his feet in a bound, to go running into the forest. Jessica stared after him, open-mouthed: she had not expected to be deserted.

The sailors were whooping and making ready to chase behind Michael, and Manot levelled the rifle and fired a single shot after the fleeing man. It was impossible to say whether Michael was hit or not; he had disappeared into the bushes. Manot gave instructions, and two of the sailors set off behind him. 'Your man is crazy, eh?' Manot asked.

Jessica bit her lip. It had simply never

occurred to her that Michael was a coward; he had not appeared so at sea. When she thought of how he had gone over the side of the yacht in an attempt to fix the rudder, knowing that that monster shark was within a few yards of them...

'Now, you see, it is all changed,' Manot explained. 'But it does not matter whether he is alive or dead. Take off your clothes and let us look at you.'

'No!' Jessica folded her arms. 'You said you would not harm us.'

'I am not going to harm you, *cherie*. I am going to have sex with you.'

'And I say no. I do not wish it.'

'But you have no choice. You are not going to pretend that you are a virgin, after sailing alone with a man?'

'What has that got to do with it?' Jessica snapped. 'Who I have sex with is my own business and my own choice.'

'But now I am making it *my* business,' Manot said.

Jessica heard movement behind her, and tried to turn, but before she could do so her arms were gripped by the remaining male crew member. She tried to free herself, but he was far too strong for her. 'I do not mind if you wish to fight me,' Manot said, coming to stand in front of her. 'But if you do, then you may be hurt. It is better not to fight.'

Jessica kicked at him, but he caught her ankle, leaving her even more helpless, as she was afraid to move her other leg in case she fell down; that would be the end. But it was going to happen anyway.

Manot was right against her now. He jerked his head, and the woman Marie came round to hold the ankle. Somehow that was even more humiliating than the idea of rape. Jessica pulled on the foot, but like the men, Marie was too strong for her.

Manot put his hands on her hips, gathering the tracksuit top and slowly lifting it to her shoulders to expose her breasts. 'Very beautiful,' he said, stroking them, and then pulling the nipples.

Jessica choked back a scream of shame and despair; she didn't want to give them that much satisfaction.

Manot said something in French, and the man lifted her arms above her head so that he could take the top right off. She panted with outrage, and again tugged futilely on her captive leg. Manot continued to play with her breasts, and then, to her disgust, lowered his head to suck the nipples.

Why can't I faint? she thought. But she had never fainted in her life. And besides, she was too angry. All manner of things were rushing through her mind, dominated by the desire to have this man at the end of a gun. But she had no idea if that was ever going to happen!

Manot grinned at her. 'I am going to kiss your mouth,' he told her. 'Do not bite me, or when I am finished with you I will have my men cut these off. They will like to do that.' Jessica started panting again as he placed his

321

lips on hers, forcing them open so violently she tasted blood where his teeth had sliced her flesh. His breath was surprisingly clean, and he tasted of roast pork. She supposed she did too.

The two men came back through the bushes, speaking at the same time. Manot released Jessica's mouth. 'Your man seems to have got away. But no matter. We can find him later. It's you we want. And you we have, darling.'

But he was no fool. He gave instructions, and two of the men left, reluctantly. Clearly it had occurred to him that Michael might attempt to gain possession of the trawler, and leave. It would be just like the bastard to abandon her, Jessica thought.

She again tried to free herself. But she knew she was not going to succeed as she was laid on her back, and held immobile while Manot took off her tracksuit bottom and the knickers. 'You grow more beautiful with every bit of you I see,' he told her.

Jessica stopped fighting. She had survived by not fighting Michael, and in time the tables had turned. She had no idea how these tables could ever be turned, but she knew she had to survive, for as long as possible. She had become a great survivor.

Lie back and let it happen, she had told herself on the boat, and it had worked. Because Michael was essentially a gentle man. Manot was not. Neither were any of his companions. As Jessica lay with her eyes shut, panting and suffering, she supposed she should be lucky the woman Marie didn't want to have a go as well. Maybe she did, and had. After the first time they felt the same.

'You are a mess,' Manot told her. 'Go into the sea and bathe.'

For a few seconds Jessica couldn't move. She felt totally exhausted, even if she had done nothing more than lie on her back, except when they had wanted her on her front. She felt bruised and battered, but more mentally and internally than physically and externally. She was again glad she didn't have a mirror, or any means of seeing herself.

Manot kicked her in the thigh. 'Didn't you hear me, Mrs Lomas? Go and wash your skin.'

Jessica pushed herself to her knees and then reached her feet. She staggered, and almost fell, and someone caught her arm. It was the woman Marie giving her what was presumably intended to be a friendly smile. Now she realized that she was actually in pain, mainly from her lips, which were cut in several places where they had forced their mouths against hers. She followed Marie down the path to the beach; they were not even going to leave her alone long enough to drown herself!

The sun was drooping towards the western horizon: she had been in the hands of those men for some four hours! The water had never felt so good, despite the salt stinging her various cuts. Marie came in with her, not bothering to take off any clothes, but standing up to her waist in the water. She smiled and talked a lot, but Jessica had no idea what she was saying. 'Don't you speak any English?' she asked.

'Sheet,' the woman said. 'Fuck. Bugger eet.'

'I don't see any conversational openings,' Jessica said.

She bathed herself, slowly and carefully. She had to wash them away. And besides, bathing served another purpose – it kept her away from the cave. She debated attacking Marie, but decided against it: Marie was both bigger and stronger. And even if she managed to lay her out, what was she going to do then? She had nowhere to go. No doubt Michael was somewhere in the bush, lurking. But she had no desire ever to see Michael again.

Manot appeared on the edge of the forest. 'What are you two trying to do?' he shouted. 'Drown yourselves?'

So it was back to the cave, and an afternoon of being handled as if she were a lump of plasticine. While she was in the water the crew had changed places, the one who had originally raped her going back to the ship, and the two who had missed out returning to the cave; now they wanted their turn. Yet she kept herself as calm as possible. Survival! But for what? And for how long?

'What is going to happen to me?' she asked Manot when the men were finally tired, if not of her, at least of sex.

'There's a question. Me, I'd just as soon turn you loose when we're ready to leave.' He grinned. 'Then we'd know you'd be here, waiting for us, whenever we come back.'

'Yes,' she said, almost too eagerly.

'Oh, we'd take your radio,' he said. 'We wouldn't want you calling up any passing ship.'

'Of course not.'

He ruffled her hair. 'You're a spunky woman, Mrs Lomas. You know, you never did tell us your name.'

'Jessica,' she said.

'I like that. Jessica. Sounds like a queen.'

'So, when were you planning to leave?' she asked.

'You'd like that, eh? I bet you would. Trouble is, the lads feel we should kill you. They say that if by any chance another ship did come along, and you managed to signal it, you'd be able to identify us. Certainly you'd be able to identify the ship.'

Her stomach was tying itself in knots again. 'You can always change the name of your ship.'

'And all have a bit of plastic surgery, eh? You know something, I don't believe you would be able to find us and identify us. The police around here have more important things to do.'

'Well, then...'

'Trouble is, the lads *want* to kill you. They want to do it, nice and slow. They're butchers at heart, you know. They spend all their time butchering fish. So they get to wondering what it would be like to butcher something else. Can't blame them, really. And when it comes to a real looker like yourself, well, you can see their point of view.'

'No, I can't,' she snapped. 'And you're going to let them do that? You're the captain, aren't you?'

'Sure. But I run a democratic ship.'

And she had supposed she was in danger of her life with Michael! But, having survived so much, she was not going to give up now. 'Wouldn't you like to have me all for yourself? For always?' she asked. 'You could take me with you when you leave the island. I'd stay with you, always.'

'You expect me to believe that? The moment we got back to civilization you'd go to the police.'

'I couldn't if we were married. And anyway, you haven't committed any crime.' She doubted this man would know anything about the intricacies of the law.

'Come again? How're we going to get married before we get back to Hiva Oa?'

'You're the captain of your ship. You can marry us any time you want.'

He stroked his stubble. 'And suppose you want a divorce. Afterwards?'

'It wouldn't make any difference,' she said. 'Listen, does this island belong to anyone?'

'Not so far as I know. Who'd want it?'

'Then that's it. If no one owns it, no one has jurisdiction over it, so you can't commit a

326

crime on it. Committing a crime means breaking a law. You can't break a law if there aren't any laws to break. Laws have to be made by governments. Therefore it follows, no government, no law. Believe me, I know what I'm talking about. I'm a law student.' Which was not altogether a lie, and she could tell he was interested.

'That would be something,' he remarked. And then sighed. 'The guys would never go for it. And don't remind me, I'm the captain. Let's sleep on it.'

She did not suppose she was going to do any better than that at the moment. But she felt she had made progress. When the rest of the crew wanted to play with her before falling asleep, Manot looked at them with smouldering eyes. And he had the Armalite. She noted that he went to sleep with it crooked in his arm against his body.

The crew didn't seem concerned about this; they accepted that he probably valued the rifle more than the woman. Soon they were all asleep, save for Jessica. They hadn't even bothered to tie her up. Why should they, as she had made no attempt to escape them, and as they presumed they could easily find her tomorrow if she chose to run away? But if she could run away with the rifle...

They were sleeping in the cave, and Manot was closest to her. But the rifle was so caught up against his body she knew she would never get it away from him without waking him up. She wasn't even sure she could leave the cave

327

without waking *somebody* up, and that would probably mean a beating. If she could just be patient, he might roll over and away from the gun. It seemed her best bet.

She lay in the darkness. She ached in every bone and every muscle, and it was a mental ache, too. She felt utterly vicious. If she *could* get that rifle she would happily kill them all. And once she had thought she had hated Michael...

She raised her head to look at the cave entrance. And there he was.

The Avenger

For a moment Jessica couldn't move, she was so surprised. But it was undoubtedly Michael, and he looked a capable, dashing figure. The pirates had not had the time to search him before he had made his escape, and they had been unaware that the diving knife had still been strapped to his calf beneath his tracksuit. This he had now drawn, and looked as if he was prepared to use, should anyone get in his way.

He beckoned her, and again. Slowly she stood up. All around her, the sailors, even Marie, were snoring. She cast a last look at the gun, then slowly stepped over them and reached the cave entrance. 'Come on,' he whispered.

'My clothes,' she whispered back.

'Stuff your clothes. Let's get out of here.'

Jessica hesitated a last time, then followed him into the trees.

'I didn't really abandon you this morning,' he said.

'You don't think so?'

'If I had stayed, they would have killed me. And that wouldn't have helped anybody.'

'Do you realize they all had a go at me? Jesus, I feel as if I've been turned inside out.'

'You invited them here,' he reminded her. 'I've just saved your life.'

'I could've escaped by myself,' she said sulkily. 'I was just waiting to see if I could get that rifle.' She didn't want him to know how relieved she was to see him, or how delighted she was that he had been working to a plan, and not just running away to save his skin.

He led her to the stream and they drank, then she went into the fresh water of the pool to bathe. Not that she supposed she would ever be able to wash those bastards out of her system. The anger still bubbled.

'Now let's get further into the bush and wait for them to clear off,' Michael said.

'You mean you're just going to let them get away?'

'Do you have a better idea? There are five of them, and two of us. And they have the rifle. Which you virtually gave to them, by letting them know we had it.'

She couldn't dispute that. 'Couldn't we capture their boat and leave *them* here?'

'There are two of them on board,' he pointed out. 'I had that idea too, but I abandoned it. Firstly because it would have meant abandoning you, and I wasn't prepared to do that. And secondly because I felt the odds were too long. We can't use their dinghy because the sound of the outboard would wake everybody up. We can't use the life-raft because the oars are gone. So we'd have to swim out, and if one of them happened to be on deck we'd be sitting ducks.'

She could not help but wonder which of the two was the more compelling reason. But she supposed he was right, however much it went against the grain to let these raping scum get away with it, not to mention the rifle and their radio.

They had a coconut breakfast, sitting in as deep forest as they had been able to find: a grove of high ferns. The pigs had very sensibly made themselves scarce.

Naked, Jessica was even more a mass of cuts and bruises. However had Eve managed in the Garden of Eden? Or maybe the thorns hadn't appeared until after the Fall? 'How will we know when they've left?' she asked.

'We'll hear the engines, both the outboard and the one on the ship.'

She lay back with her hands beneath her head. He lay beside her, on his elbow. 'JJ...'

'Don't touch me, Michael. The next man

330

who touches me, without my invitation, is going to die. I swear it. Even if I have to go with him.'

He gazed at her for a few seconds, then sat up. 'Shit,' he muttered.

She sat up as well, and listened to someone shouting. He was using the patois, as was the man answering him. But neither was very far away. 'Jesus!' she whispered. 'They're not leaving. They're looking for us.'

'And they've found the raft,' he said. 'That means the spare magazine.'

'What do we do?' she asked.

'Keep absolutely still. There's no way they can track us through here.'

She hoped he was right, but she didn't feel the least confident. There were five of the pirates, supposing the two from the ship had come ashore, and they seemed to be advancing slowly and carefully over a wide area, constantly calling to keep in touch with each other. Michael was coming to the same conclusion. 'Maybe we'll have to move after all,' he muttered. 'Keep in front of them.'

'If they're all ashore,' she said, 'couldn't we try for the ship? That's what Captain Blood did in the movie.'

He raised his eyebrows. 'Don't tell me you're an Errol Flynn fan? Bit ancient for you, isn't he?'

'I am not an Errol Flynn fan,' she said. 'But my grandmother is. Every time I go to stay with her, we watch *Captain Blood, The Sea Hawk, Robin Hood* and *The Charge of the Light*

Brigade back to back, day in and day out.' As she spoke her eyes filled with tears. She had never expected to cry again in her life, but she had no idea whether or not she would ever see Grandma again. Or even if the old lady was alive or dead: she was eighty, after all.

Michael ruffled her hair. 'We'll make it. But getting out to the ship will be tricky in day-light, and while they have the Armalite. We have to lie low until dark, and hope that this time they all remain ashore.'

'That's not on,' she said. 'Firstly because it's another ten hours to darkness, and because they're never going to be so daft as to leave the ship unguarded. And meanwhile, they're getting closer.' Certainly the shouting was coming from all around them.

'Okay,' he decided. 'You sit tight. They seem to be pretty widely separated. I'm going to wriggle off and see if I can find out which of them has the gun. If we can get that back...'

'It'll be Manot. But Michael...'

'Don't worry. If they hear me, they'll follow me, and leave you alone.'

'Yes, but if they catch you, they'll kill you. It's me they want. Shouldn't I just surrender, and leave you free?'

'No way. Have you any idea what they'd do to you if they decided to make you tell them what I was up to?' She bit her lip, and he squeezed her hand. 'Besides, this is man's work.'

'Michael!' She hung on to his hand as he would have released her. 'I don't want you to

332

get killed.'

'I feel the same way.' He grinned at her. 'How about sending me to gaol?'

'Oh ... No, I'm not going to send you to gaol, Michael. Not now.'

'Then I've got a good reason for making a success of this. Don't move until I call you.' He slithered away into the bushes, the diving knife in his hand. Michael Lomas, bank manager turned jungle fighter! With a small diversion into abduction and rape on the side. But she had, really, forgiven him for that. However abominably he had behaved, he had too much guts to spend the next ten years in a prison cell.

She waited, her muscles tensed, listening to the shouting. As they continued to use the patois, she couldn't tell what they were saying, but she rather felt the voices were moving away from the fern grove. Then she heard more urgent shouts. Jesus, she thought, they've spotted Michael. Or heard him.

Remaining still, doing nothing, was no longer a practical possibility; besides, it was not in either her nature or her training – she had always led from the front. She had to know what was happening, had to help him, if she could. She heard a shot, and her heart seemed to be trying to escape through her mouth. Cautiously she parted the ferns, lying on her stomach, and began to wriggle towards the sound, quite careless of the earth and roots over which she was pushing her naked body, or of the leaves and branches that were scratching at her back.

There were as yet no shouts of triumph. Someone, almost certainly Manot, had seen something and fired. But he wasn't sure what he had hit, or if he had hit anything at all. She continued to wriggle forward, and was surprised when she heard movement very close. She froze herself against the ground. It was Manot, and he was shouting something in the patois. Jessica didn't dare breathe. But he was very close, and he was alone, and carrying the Armalite...

She couldn't do anything without a weapon; there was too much at stake to risk him hearing her if she tried to get close enough for a karate chop. All he had to do was turn, and he could blow her into several pieces. But there, inches from her hand, was a large stone. Tentatively she touched it, and it moved. It was at least as big as a football. Did she dare? But wasn't it fate that had put her here, and the stone there, and Manot *there*?

He was shouting again, giving directions. Very slowly and carefully Jessica rose to her knees. Then she picked up the stone. It was heavier than she had supposed, and she gasped at the weight. She was only going to have the opportunity to use it once. And if she missed...

With continuing caution, driving her strength down to her thighs, she stood up, the stone clutched to her breast. And there, not four feet away, was Manot, grasping the Armalite in both hands; the spare magazine

334

was thrust through his belt.

There was no one else in sight; they were all looking for Michael, or Michael's body. Jessica drew a very deep breath, lifted the stone above her head, and stepped forward. As she did so, she brushed against a bush, and the rustle alerted Manot. He turned sharply, bringing up the gun, but Jessica was already bringing down the stone, and it landed on his face. He gave a strangled gasp of mingled pain and dismay, and fell backwards. As he did so, Jessica snatched the gun from his suddenly flaccid hands. Then she watched him crash through the bushes to lie on his back. For a moment she stood above him, panting. Then, holding the gun muzzle against his chest, she knelt beside him and pulled the spare magazine from his belt.

He looked a dreadful sight, his face a mass of blood, his nose obviously broken, as were several of his teeth, while his lips were cut to ribbons. But he was still alive, and as he felt the movement of the magazine against his stomach he endeavoured to sit up, arms flailing. Instinctively, Jessica squeezed the trigger. The sound of the shot took her by surprise. So did its effect; she had used this weapon often enough in deadly earnest, but always in self-defence and never at a range of two feet. Manot's chest seemed to explode into mingled flesh and bone and blood, some of it splashing over her. She gave a little shriek of horror and disgust, and reared backwards, falling over to sit down. But she still clutched the rifle. And Manot was again lying on his back, undoubtedly dead.

Shouts, one at least coming closer. She looked down at the gun in her hands. They, and the gun, were trembling. There were still four of them left. They had all raped her, except for the woman. Not one of them deserved to live, save for the woman – perhaps. Jesus, she thought, what am I thinking?

But what was the alternative, even if she didn't believe they should all die? This was the real world, not the over-civilized world of England, where criminals had open season on the rest of the population, certain that no matter what crime they committed they were not going to be executed, and no matter how long the sentences they were given, the odds were that they would be out again in ten years.

This was reality. The jungle. Kill or be killed. She had felt that way on the yacht, after the typhoon. She was Cleopatra and Catherine, Semiramis and Zenobia. Zenobia, who had fought and killed with the ferocity of a tigress to preserve both her chastity and her kingdom, was a perfect role model in these circumstances.

Jessica stood up, the Armalite thrust forward. And saw that her task was made easy for her. Running towards her through the bushes was one of the Polynesian crew members, the man who had first assaulted her with that pinch ... and he had a shotgun. Jessica levelled the Armalite and squeezed the trigger. The sailor's torso exploded even more dramatically than had Manot's, and he fell over backwards, arms flung wide.

Jessica ran to him, and picked up the shotgun. Now she was in complete command, but she was also on a killing high, the adrenaline pumping through her arteries. She checked the shotgun. It was of the pump action variety, and had not been fired; there had to be several cartridges in the magazine. She looked left and right, then backed against a tree. 'Michael!' she shouted. 'Where are you? Are you hurt?'

There was no reply from Michael, but she heard movement in the bushes some distance to her right. She stepped away from her tree, went towards the rustle. 'Michael?' she asked. 'Is that you?'

For reply, another of the crew emerged, running at her. Jessica dropped the shotgun and squeezed the trigger of the Armalite. Even as she fired she heard movement behind her, and swung round, but before she could level the gun again she was struck a shoulder charge that sent her tumbling into a bush. The man did not have a knife, or she supposed she would be dead, but having thrown her aside, he leapt on to the shotgun and brought it up – and then hesitated, unable to bring himself to kill a naked woman.

Jessica had no such compunction: he was fully dressed, and she reckoned he would soon get over his hesitation. Again she squeezed the trigger – and heard only a click.

337

Now it was her turn to throw herself to one side, reaching for the spare magazine. The shotgun exploded, and she again expected to be killed by a hail of pellets. But it had been loaded with solid shot rather than buckshot, and the single two-inch-long lead slug had smashed through the bushes above her head.

The man swung the gun, pumping a cartridge into the chamber as he did so, but Jessica had already slammed the spare magazine into place, and she fired before he did, a three-second burst which utterly destroyed him. Then she was on her knees scrabbling forward to regain the shotgun, looking for the fourth man. But he had taken to his heels into the bush.

The noise of the shots continued to reverberate through the trees for several seconds. I have killed three men, she thought. Three men! Three raping bastards!

She was panting too hard to hear any movement, and again stood against a tree, a gun in each hand, the butt resting on her hips, waiting for both her heart and her breathing to settle down. She could hear nothing but the rustle of the breeze through the trees. 'Michael!' she shouted. 'Call me. We're in control. I have both guns, and three of them are dead.'

Still there was no response. So she'd just have to find him. From the proximity of the men who had attacked her, she didn't think he could be that far off. All she had to do was make sure she wasn't jumped by either the remaining man or Marie.

It wasn't difficult to deduce where her attackers had come from, by the trail of broken branches and disturbed bushes. Jessica crept cautiously forward; both guns had slings, and she slung the shotgun on her back, retaining the Armalite as her principal weapon. Still she heard not a sound. She was nearly at the east beach, and could see the trawler through the trees, riding gently to its anchor, when she heard a groan. Instantly she dropped to her knees, but turned aside to follow the sound, and a moment later saw Michael.

He was lying on his back, and his shirt was bloody. But he had groaned. He was alive! She dashed forward, knelt beside him, laying down the Armalite. 'Michael!'

He opened his eyes. 'You are the sweetest thing a man could see,' he muttered.

'Where are you hit?'

'Somewhere in the back.'

'Is it bad?'

'I don't think it's very good.'

'Well, listen, I'm going to turn you over.' Biting her lip, she pushed him on to his face, gasped in horror at the huge wound in his back, quite visible through the torn tracksuit top; it was oozing blood, while the amount of it already on the sand was frightening. She had to plug the blood loss before she could do anything else. But to try to take off the top might make matters worse. She tugged at the pants.

'You do the sweetest things,' he muttered, turning on his side to help her. She tugged on the pants, got them off, crammed them inside the top and against the wound, her hands now covered in blood. 'Bastards,' Michael muttered. 'You must stop them JJ.'

He was looking along the beach. Jessica turned her head, saw the remaining male crew member and Marie running across the sand to the dinghy. She picked up the Armalite and fired a single shot over their heads. They stopped, almost at the dinghy, and turned to face her. 'Back up,' she shouted.

Slowly they retreated up the sand. 'Stop there,' she commanded when they had nearly reached the tree line. 'Lie down, on your faces.'

Marie protested, and Jessica fired another single shot into the sand at her feet. Hastily Marie lay down, gesturing her companion to do the same. 'Just don't move,' Jessica shouted.

Then she could turn her attention back to Michael. 'Listen,' she said, 'I need to get to the life-raft, and pick up the first-aid kit.'

'You reckon it's worth it?' he asked.

'Yes, I do. But we have to keep them covered. Which would you rather have, the rifle or the shotgun?'

'The rifle,' he said. 'Can you handle the shotgun?'

'Sure.'

'You can handle anything, JJ.' He clutched her hand. 'You'll hurry back?'

'Ten minutes, most.'

Still he held her hand. 'What do you mean to do?'

'After I've fixed you up? I thought we'd take the trawler and get out of here. I reckon I can handle her, too.'

'Of course you can,' he said. 'And it'll have at least one radio; you can see the aerials. What about them?'

'We'll leave them here. If we could survive, so can they. At least until we send the police for them.'

'You meant what you said? No charges against me?'

She kissed him. 'No charges. We'll have to concoct some kind of story. But we'll have a couple of days to think of one. Now I have to hurry; you're losing too much blood.'

'Listen,' he said. 'JJ, I love you. I loved you from the moment I laid eyes on you. Would it have been different if I could have proved my innocence?'

She grinned at him. 'Maybe. But ... I guess I sort of love you too, you old bastard.' She freed her hand and stood up. 'Don't go away.'

She looked along the beach to where Marie and the sailor still lay on the sand. 'You are covered,' she shouted, and tried desperately to remember her schoolgirl French: languages had not been her strong point. *'Vous êtes couvrir,'* she called, hoping they would understand her despite her inability to decline the verb.

She backed along the sand for several feet,

keeping them covered herself with the shot-gun. When she reached the curve in the beach she turned and ran as fast as she could, reaching the raft a few seconds later. She tore the first-aid box from the pouch, ran back ... and saw them on their feet, slowly advancing towards where they must have determined Michael lay. 'Bastards!' she shouted, pumped the shotgun, and fired over their heads. Immediately they dropped to the sand again.

Jessica dashed into the bushes and knelt beside Michael. But Michael was dead.

Jessica remained kneeling beside him for several seconds before raising her head. Marie and the sailor had also raised their heads, obviously trying to decide what to do next. Jessica slung the shotgun, picked up the Armalite, stood up, and stepped from the bushes on to the sand. 'Come here,' she called, and waved her arm in a beckoning gesture.

They looked at each other, then stood up and slowly came towards her. 'Bury him,' she commanded. She pointed at Michael's body, then scuffed the sand with her toe.

Marie protested, and made a shovelling movement with her arms while shaking her head. Then she pointed at the trawler, to indicate that there was a spade on board.

'Forget it,' Jessica said. 'Use your hands.' She opened and shut one of her own.

Muttering at each other, they knelt on the sand and began to dig.

Jessica squatted and watched them, keeping the rifle pointing at them. Where she was making them dig was well above the high water mark, and if she made them go down deep enough there was every chance that Michael would not be disturbed by the sea or the wind. But no matter how deep she put him he would no doubt be found by the crabs. There was a horrible thought. But then, the whole past twenty-four hours had been a nightmare.

All because she had summoned these murdering thugs to their aid. Or to put it another way, all because she had been determined to end her situation. A situation she had actually been enjoying, if she dared admit it. She blinked back her tears as she watched the pit deepening. Marie and her companion kept talking to each other, and throwing glances in her direction. If they saw the slightest chance of getting at her...

She almost wished they would attack her, because then she could shoot the bastards. She wasn't at all sure she wasn't going to do that anyway. The adrenaline was still flowing, and she was still a long way from salvation. As for Michael, well, this was perhaps the ending he had always anticipated, even wanted. He had to have known there was no way they could return to civilization together without too many questions being asked, without the truth being forced into the open, without his being gaoled as a sex-monster, with all the horrors that would entail. No matter what she might do, or say.

The trench was about two feet deep, and Marie and the man were streaming sweat; their fingernails were caked with blood. Now they looked up and asked a question. 'Deeper,' Jessica commanded.

They muttered, but resumed scraping at the sand. After another back-breaking hour the man got into the pit and began shovelling sand up in handfuls. Marie looked at Jessica, touched her lips and then her stomach. 'When you are finished,' Jessica told her.

It was well into the afternoon when at last she reckoned the pit was deep enough. 'Okay,' she said. 'Put him in.'

Staggering with exhaustion, they lowered Michael's body into the grave. 'Now cover him up again,' Jessica said. 'And get on with it.'

It was still broad daylight, but she had to be outside the reef before it was dark; they would be certain to try something during the night if she was still here. They covered Michael up, then Jessica made them back up and lie down while she stamped the sand flat. She supposed she should say a prayer, but she wasn't sure that was what Michael would have wanted.

She reckoned it was about five o'clock. It was going to be a near thing; dusk invariably passed in a whisker this close to the Equator. That meant there was no time to return to the cave and find her tracksuit. But surely there would be something belonging to the woman Marie on board the trawler.

She pointed the rifle at the man, and made a jerking movement. He looked at Marie, who shrugged, then he got up. Jessica gestured him to walk along the beach to the dinghy. Again he hesitated, then went in front of her. When they had covered about fifty yards, Jessica turned round. Marie was on her feet, staring after them, but when she saw Jessica looking at her, she dropped to her knees again.

By the time they reached the dinghy, she was out of sight. But even if she was coming through the bush, Jessica didn't reckon there was much she could do to help her friend. He was now standing by the boat, waiting for her.

'Back up,' Jessica said, moving the gun to and fro. He retreated, and Jessica climbed in and sat herself in the bow. 'Okay,' she said. 'Push us off.'

He put his shoulder to the gunwale and heaved. It took him some time, but at last the dinghy was floating. He panted, face crimson. 'Get in.' She gestured at the transom.

He climbed in, sat beside the outboard. 'Get it going,' Jessica said. 'And take me out to the ship.'

He put down the shaft, used an oar to push them into deeper water, and then pulled the ignition cord. The engine chattered into life, and the dinghy moved out to the trawler while the sailor stared at Jessica. She stared back, the rifle always levelled. The sailor cut the engine, and they coasted into the side.

There were high bulwarks, but a door opened beside the wheelhouse. Jessica climbed up, and turned to level the gun as she reached the deck. The man continued to stare at her, obviously all manner of aggressive thoughts roaming through his mind. Jessica sighted, and fired three shots. One missed, the other two slammed into the engine. The man gave a shriek of alarm and fell on his face in the bottom of the boat while shattered metal cascaded around him.

The dinghy drifted away from the trawler's side. 'Use your oars,' Jessica recommended as the man's head emerged above the gunwale. Marie stood on the beach, watching them.

Slowly the man seated himself amidships and got out the oars. Jessica went into the wheelhouse, looked over the controls. There was only one engine, but as it had a heat start she reckoned it was diesel; she was delighted with how familiar everything was. Biting her lip in apprehension she turned the switch halfway, waited, and then turned it the whole way. The engine spluttered into life, giving off a cloud of black smoke from the funnel. Jessica sighed with relief, and looked over the rest of the controls. They were very like those on the yacht. She was sure she could cope with them, but that had to wait until she was outside the reef.

She found the switch for the anchor winch, and pressed it. Slowly the anchor came up to seat itself on the bow. As it did so, there was a faint bump on the hull. Jessica grabbed the rifle and went outside. The sailor had brought the dinghy back alongside, and as she emerged, so did his head, over the side of the ship. Jessica reversed the Armalite and hit him in the face. He fell back with a shriek, and Jessica peered over the side. He was lying in the bottom of the boat, stunned. She levelled the gun again, taking care to aim away from him, and fired three more shots into the floor of the dinghy. The plastic shattered and fell apart, and, dragged down by the weight of the outboard mounting, the boat sank like Michael's proverbial holed bucket. The sailor came to and began to swim, desperately. 'You brought it on yourself,' Jessica said to him, gave Marie a wave, and went inside.

The trawler had started to drift, and she hastily grasped the huge wheel. With only one engine it was much harder to manoeuvre than with two, but she got the hang of it after turning round twice, and then lined it up for the gap in the reef, surprised at how calm she felt, how confident of success.

To either side the surf remained enormous, great white crested waves crashing on to the reef and sending spray hundreds of feet into the air. Immediately in front of her was the blue water of the passage, but this too was surging to and fro, and she had no idea how deep it was or how wide.

But the trawler had got in. Jessica turned the ship once more, looking at the beach as she did so. Marie still stood on the water's edge, waving her arms and no doubt cursing. The sailor was swimming laboriously towards her. Jessica concentrated, lining the trawler up with the very centre of the opening, and then pushed the throttle forward and gripped the wheel in both hands as tightly as she could. The trawler gathered speed, slowly at first, and then surged into the gap. Jessica was surrounded by roaring noise, but she refused to turn her head, and stared straight in front of her at the heaving but unbroken water of the passage. The trawler was fighting her now, being thrown to and fro by the undertow, but she fought back, muscles aching, sweat streaming out of her hair...

And suddenly she was through, back into the huge swell, but moving up and down steadily and easily. And gradually the swell was diminishing as she left the land. When it had entirely settled, she reduced speed, then went on deck to look back at the island.

The beach was hidden behind the swell and the surf, as it had been when they had first seen it, but she could see the hill. Their island, she thought. She wondered if she would ever go back.

Suddenly the tears came, thick and fast. They were at least partly the result of her emotional and physical exhaustion. But she was crying for Michael as well. Yet even as she was crying, she was finding out how the automatic pilot worked, and locating the GPS. Then she dried her tears, set a course for Hiva Oa – it was a few days away but there were ample supplies of fuel, water and food on board, not to mention a refrigerated hold full of fish – and then began to work the radio.

Half an hour later an aircraft swooped low overhead.

'Do you want to talk about it?' Tom asked, sitting beside her on the flight to London. They were alone together, for the first time since Jessica's rescue; the island was several weeks in the past.

'Haven't you been watching TV?' Jessica asked. 'Or reading the tabloids?'

'Yes, but I don't always believe what I see. Not even the offer of a six-figure sum for your story.'

'That is actually true,' Jessica said.

'About how you were kidnapped, raped, tortured, made to crew for that monster, were shipwrecked, and shot your way out of a confrontation with pirates.'

'What did you expect me to do?' Jessica asked. 'Although I sometimes wonder if it wasn't a dream.'

The edges had become blurred over the past weeks. Had she known exactly what would be involved she sometimes wondered if she would not have done better to shoot both Marie and the sailor and live on the island by herself. The excitement aroused by her arrival in Hiva Oa, escorted by a French destroyer, and then in Sydney by her reappearance from the dead, even Commander Adams flying out to welcome her, the media, excited all over again when Marie and her companion had been arrested and brought to Hiva Oa for confrontation and trial – they had betrayed themselves in their efforts to accuse her of mass murder by trying to deny that Michael had ever existed, whereas she had been able to direct the police to his grave ... had it all really happened?

But the decisions that still lay ahead, what she was going to do with her life, with the hundreds of crank offers of marriage that she had received, these were real enough. Questions to which she had no answer, at that moment.

Because hadn't she, at the end of it all, betrayed Michael by inviting those pirates on to the island?

'Well?' Tom asked.

'Well what?'

'Two things, JJ. First, you don't have all of those experiences, and come back the same person you were six months ago.'

'I don't think I am the same person,' Jessica said. How could I be? she wondered. I have survived rape and intended murder and a good deal of sudden death. All of those save rape had happened to her before, but somehow this experience had been different, because it had been outside the line of duty: it had not happened to Detective-Sergeant Jessica Jones, but to plain Ms Jessica Jones. For the first time, and she hoped the last, her private and professional lives had become intermingled. But that was not something she could ever hope that anyone, even Tom, would be able to understand. 'And the other?'

'Well,' Tom said, 'you spent four months alone with that man. I mean, he couldn't have been raping you and beating you *all* the time.'

'No, he didn't,' Jessica said. 'And yes, we formed a relationship. He asked me to marry him, time and again. I even said yes, once. But things were fairly fraught at the time.'

'Supposing he had survived, and you got back to civilization together, would you have shopped him?'

Jessica stared out of the window at the fleecy clouds below her. How remote was the yacht and the island, the sun and the sea, the horror ... and the excitement, the sense of power she had known when she had taken over the yacht, the feeling of sexual satisfaction when she had raped Michael. Things she would never know again. Never dare know again.

But would always yearn after?

She turned to face him. 'Do you know,' she said, 'I simply have no idea.'

He sighed at his inability to get through to her. 'So,' he said brightly. 'What's the first thing you want to do when we get back to England?'

'Reopen a thirteen-year-old murder case,' she said. 'And then buy a boat. A sailing yacht.'

'We don't know how to sail.'

'I do,' she said.

351